The Scammer's Trail

The Scammer's Trail

SMARAK SWAIN

BLOOMSBURY
NEW DELHI • LONDON • OXFORD • NEW YORK • SYDNEY

BLOOMSBURY INDIA
Bloomsbury Publishing India Pvt. Ltd
Second Floor, LSC Building No. 4, DDA Complex, Pocket C – 6 & 7,
Vasant Kunj, New Delhi, 110070

BLOOMSBURY, BLOOMSBURY INDIA and the Diana logo
are trademarks of Bloomsbury Publishing Plc

First published in India 2025

ISBN: PB: 978-93-61318-03-0; eBook: 978-93-61310-08-9
2 4 6 8 10 9 7 5 3 1

Typeset in Minion Pro by Manipal Technologies Limited
Printed and bound in India by Thomson Press India Ltd

MIX
Paper | Supporting responsible forestry
FSC® C010615

To find out more about our authors and books visit www.bloomsbury.com and sign up for our newsletters

For sale in the Indian subcontinent only

The Scammer's Trail

Prologue

Bharat Institute of Medical Sciences (BIMS) at Sri Aurobindo Marg in New Delhi is India's premier medical university and hospital. The BIMS building, a majestic red-brick behemoth, lords over the Delhi traffic like a stern but slightly dishevelled aunt. Its sprawling lawns offer weary souls a moment's respite from the honking cacophony of the busy ring road. Inside, the air hums with a unique din of its own—the rhythmic beeping of machines, the hurried whispers of doctors, and the occasional outburst of a particularly vocal patient. The air is sterile and calm, echoing with the hushed footsteps of doctors and nurses on their rounds. Patients and their families wait patiently in waiting rooms, hope glimmering in their eyes. The aroma of antiseptic hangs heavy, mingled with the faint scent of medications.

The basement of the administrative block, which houses the IT support team of BIMS, is the last place one expects to find any action. But it was not so one fine morning in the sweltering summer of April. The patient management system of BIMS had been inaccessible since morning, forcing all staff to revert to the paper-based records system of an earlier era. Digitalized medical records of patients were not accessible, thus leading to much confusion and disruption. Doctors were frantically calling up the basement of the administrative block to complain about the difficulty they were facing. But the IT support team was just stonewalling them without telling them when the system would be operational again.

If this was a system failure, the response in the basement of the administrative block was surely disproportionate.

The institute's director was sitting there in his office, perplexed, sweat dripping from his brow. People from the government, who appeared important, were rushing in constantly, flashing their identity cards at the reception. Many of them were from a little-known organization called CERT-IN, or Indian Computer Emergency Response Team. Uniformed policemen from Delhi's cyber cell had also burrowed into the office.

The first reporter to get wind of what was happening was Shiv Prakash Tiwari of New Bharat, a Hindi news channel. Tiwari oversaw the medicine and healthcare beat at the daily and generally worked on post-COVID stories. He had meticulously cultivated contacts inside BIMS, which included the receptionist in the administrative block. The receptionist told him that something was happening between the government's sleuths and the IT guys while the entire server of BIMS was down.

At the time, Tiwari was loafing around Nirman Bhavan, which houses the Ministry of Health and Family Welfare. Upon getting this intel, he called ministry officials he had befriended over time, asking them if there was some crisis with the 'server' being down in BIMS. Most officials were tight-lipped and evasive, which proved that something was wrong. Something more serious than a server failure. He called up a few doctors in BIMS, but they seemed clueless about what was happening, except that the server was not functional, and it was becoming difficult for them to work. He knew that there was a scoop here and persistently bombarded ministry officials with his theories.

Finally, when he called up a section officer and asked about the hack in BIMS, the officer presumed that he already knew and spilled the beans. BIMS's internal server had been hacked. While the database remained inside the server (BIMS had not migrated to a cloud server), it was locked. And the hackers had set an auto-deletion program which would delete the entire data if anyone tried to breach the lock to access the database. The hacker group had already contacted BIMS and was demanding a ransom of 1,000 bitcoins within a day, which on this day translated to 115 crore rupees.

The seriousness of the event was not lost on Tiwari. Many important Indian personalities, including ministers in the Government of India, were customers of BIMS, and BIMS had patient records of all these VIPs. If a hacker group had accessed these specific records, it was not good news. BIMS conducts a large amount of proprietary research for the government, and records of years of research were in that server. If the database was deleted or infected, it could mean financial losses to the tune of thousands of crores. But Tiwari's problem was that he could not find anyone who could go on the record to say this. He took the scoop to his editor, who wanted a second-party verification and some evidence of the scoop. Tiwari was stonewalled by everyone he approached. He was also mired in the fear of someone else breaking the news. So, he and his editor decided to run the story as 'Breaking News: Is BIMS under a Ransomware Attack?' The story covered 'speculation' about a possible hacking attack compromising years of research and private patient data. Within minutes it got wide coverage, innumerable retweets and Facebook forwards and galvanized many other reporters into action. News vans and satellite trucks lined up outside BIMS office and across the road outside Safdarjung Hospital. They waited for long hours but did not get any further news from the basement of the administrative building. After some time, they pulled out in search of other news. The BIMS servers became operational after a day, and things went back to normal in the hospital. The director sent an internal email to the doctors and nursing staff informing them about the technical glitch which had brought down the system and congratulated the IT support team for its dexterous troubleshooting. He ended by remarking that not all heroes in BIMS came in scrubs; some toiled away from the limelight to make heroes out of the men in scrubs.

1 The Ransomware Task Force

North Block, draped in a cloak of red sandstone, flanks the presidential palace to its left on Raisina Hill. Built by the British as a monument to their power, its neoclassical facade now houses 'native' Indian bureaucrats, the so-called *babus*. Its grand, colonial arches mislead an onlooker with a sense of grandeur. In reality, the building is dilapidated and in ruins. It now contains many times the number of officials it was meant for. Due to a shortage of space, many common areas have been encroached upon by temporary structures with cubicles. It is the headquarters of the home and finance ministries of India, although the government plans to shift these offices to a new building and convert North Block into a museum.

For a newcomer, the offices inside are a maze. An officer newly posted to North Block takes at least a fortnight to get a sense of the place and may still lose their way after working here for years. On the first and second floors of this building is an area colloquially called 'Pakistan'. Legend has it that when India was partitioned, Mohammad Ali Jinnah insisted on partitioning many things, including offices used by the British Indian government for administration. He and other officers of the breakaway country Pakistan were allotted a few rooms in North Block, which was the nerve centre of the country's bureaucracy then as it is now, for officiating over Partition formalities. But Indian bureaucrats hated him so much for the Partition that they built a wall, cutting off access to the area under Jinnah's control from the rest of North Block. While Jinnah and his minions left long ago, the Partition walls remain, and so there is only one access route to this area called 'Pakistan'. Tucked away here is a conference room dedicated to the Multi Agency Centre (MAC), the nodal body for exchange of intelligence inputs between the many agencies protecting this country. As if not confident of the security cordon of North Block, the conference room has its dedicated guards who check the identity of everyone going into the room for a meeting. These meetings are considered to be top secret, so much so that jammers are placed inside, and no unauthorized person is allowed to take in or bring out any digital equipment from the conference room.

A meeting of RCORD was convened in this conference room in early May of 2023 under the chairmanship of Rajshri Mehta, a retired policeman and now senior advisor to the home ministry. RCORD stands for RTF Coordination Committee, a lousy bureaucratic acronym containing another acronym: RTF, or the Ransomware Task Force. Every agency involved in investigations of the BIMS ransomware attack had sent representatives for the RCORD meeting. In his seventies, Mehta did not have much patience for introductions. He jumped on a senior functionary from the home ministry and asked him why there was still not a face to the criminals who had hacked into the BIMS server.

The official tried to explain in a roundabout way how most hackers were Chinese and affiliated to China's People's Liberation Army, how it was difficult to trace hackers operating behind layers and onion peels (Mehta made a face on hearing the kitchenware term), how most hackers did not get caught, etc. Mehta cut him short and addressed everyone in the room sternly: 'We have no option but to find out who is involved in this attack and what they are up to. It is a matter of national importance. CERT-IN has already found in its forensic analysis that sensitive medical records of many VIPs were accessed by the hacker group when they lay siege to BIMS server. We have paid them off, and they have complied. But we do not know them, and we do not have any leverage against them. What if they now try to sell the data in the black market to Pakistan? Or worse, China? Maybe we can still do nothing if they decide to sell the data. But we should know who they are.'

After a pause, he continued, 'CERT-IN was trying to backtrace the bots which had infected the BIMS server. Any luck there?'

A senior functionary from CERT-IN looked at his notes and reported that he had had no success; that the bots were controlled through the TOR browser, and it was almost impossible to trace the command centre. He then tried to explain that TOR referred to The Onion Router which encrypts online traffic in multiple layers, like the peels of an onion. He continued explaining the encryption technology of the TOR browser. Mehta lost interest and asked him to stop.

'This is a lousy attempt at saying that we cannot do anything. BIMS maintains a backup of its database in a separate server. This backup server is behind an air gap. It means that the backup server did not have a linkage with the internet. The backup was accessed, and its data was deleted. That is not possible without having a person on the ground to physically connect the backup server with the internet. We have not even managed to find out who this person on the ground was.'

The home ministry official meekly said that Enforcement Directorate (ED) had had an important breakthrough. Mehta asked ED to explain what it had found.

ED was represented on the table by Arun Kamat, special director. A man in his late forties, his hair had greyed prematurely. He explained in a Goan accent, 'Sir, the Financial Intelligence Unit [FIU] had been instructed to maintain a close surveillance on the ransom paid to the hackers. The hackers had asked us to deposit the thousand bitcoins to a specific wallet address. From this wallet, the bitcoins have been moved through multiple other wallets. It is easy to see the movement, since everything is on a public blockchain. However, the layering can become really complex by using a tool called a mixer. Within days of the attack, the ransom was distributed among thousands of wallets. We have lost track of quite a few wallets to which the ransom was distributed due to the mixers, but we still have track of most of them.

'Now the funny thing about bitcoins is that you can move them around wallets without your identity being known. But if you want to encash them, you have to open an account with a cryptocurrency exchange. Only on a crypto exchange can you exchange bitcoins for fiat currency. The hackers have opened an account with an Indian crypto exchange called KuberX. They transferred just 0.15 bitcoins from a private wallet to the exchange and encashed 3.5 lakh rupees from a KuberX ATM. The FIU has instructed crypto exchanges operating in India to keep the KYC records of all persons having an account with them. KuberX had KYC records of the account which was used to encash part of the ransom. The account is registered to one N. Gandhi Kumar, a doctor. We received a suspicious transaction report from the FIU and immediately started profiling N. Gandhi Kumar. We found out that he is a paediatrician. He has done both his MBBS and MD from BIMS! Many of his classmates are working in BIMS, and he frequently visits BIMS. He evidently is well acquainted with the place.

'But the most conclusive information we found was from Internet Protocol analytics. The IP address used by the hacker to open the account with KuberX was a computer to which only he has access. The command to the private wallet to transfer our bitcoins to KuberX was also given from this IP. So, we think this is our man.'

Kamat stood up and pointed a remote in his hand towards a screen at a distance, and a face showed up. The accused in the photograph had the look of a man weighed down by the world's troubles. He must have been in his forties. He had a thick, well-groomed moustache and sported a pair of oversized, rectangular glasses. He had a round face and a warm brown skin tone. His hair was meticulously parted and combed to the side—thick, black and perfectly arranged. He looked hassled and worried, his forehead was slightly furrowed, and there was a nervous intensity in his overall look.

Mehta's eyes lit up. The septuagenarian could not keep up with the pace of evolution of internet technology. While he pretended to understand what cybercrime was, he really had no clue. His strength was good old-fashioned policing from the old days, when there was a criminal and the equation was personal to both the investigator and the criminal. That's why it was important for him to put a face to the criminal mastermind. He looked intently at the screen, as if trying to make eye contact with the criminal. He belonged to a breed of investigators that has immense confidence in intuitive policing. He secretly believed, like many other seasoned policemen, that he could identify a criminal when he saw one.

But from his looks, Gandhi Kumar appeared like someone hit severely by midlife exhaustion. Something did not seem right. Then Mehta recalled how Leonardo da Vinci's Mona

Lisa portrait looked different from different angles. He had heard much about it and had got a chance to see it for himself in the Louvre when he was in France for a meeting with Interpol officials. The woman in the painting looked like a welcoming slut from one angle and a coy virgin from another. Mehta changed his position and looked at Gandhi Kumar from a new perspective. Now he looked sinister, and Mehta was sure he had identified a hardened criminal.

'N. Gandhi Kumar. Who are you?' Mehta said to the picture on the screen with dramatic effect. 'Bearing the name of Gandhiji, the father of the nation, and stealing Gandhi from the nation.'

Technically, the hackers had stolen bitcoins and not 'Gandhi' (meaning rupee notes with an image of Mahatma Gandhi on them), but no one in the room dared to factually correct Mehta.

'And have we got men on him?'

'Yes. This man lives in Hauz Khas, within walking distance from BIMS,' Kamat said conspiratorially. 'He is behaving exactly the way we would expect a criminal to behave after committing the biggest heist of the year. He is going about his daily routine too punctually and trying too hard not to raise suspicion. Home-hospital-home-clinic-home. That's his routine. He is married and has two kids, a boy and a girl. The wife is a homemaker and does most of the heavy lifting on the home front, including seeing off the kids to school and picking them up. The wife may also be involved in this. We are still analysing his phone records, but we don't think we will get anything. These techie types use encrypted messaging to communicate with their associates.'

'Good. What do you propose we do now?'

'Sir, time is of the essence here. Already we have lost track of much of the ransom we paid. If we do not act immediately, it may be too late to recover the ransom and the evidence. We need to raid the fellow, search his house and office. I am sure his laptop and computer have the digital evidence we need to trace the ransom and nail this criminal,' Kamat said.

Simrandeep Singh of the Indian Cybercrime Coordination Centre (I4C) waved his hand, indicating that he wanted to speak. A specialist in economic security, Simrandeep was a turbaned Sikh. Around the same age as Arun Kamat, Simrandeep was built like a mountain bear, broad-shouldered and thick-limbed. His turban was a crisp white beacon in contrast to the dark waves of his beard. He had a reputation for keen observations and sharp insight. Mehta allowed him to speak.

'Sir, the FIU had disseminated its suspicious transaction report to us also. We understand that the report was also disseminated to the CBI [Central Bureau of Investigation], IB [Intelligence Bureau], the income tax department, DRI [Directorate of Revenue Intelligence] and Delhi Police as well. The FIU has done a fantastic job, so has the compliance team of this company, KuberX. Naturally, we have also done our profiling. Our objective results are the same as Arun's, but our understanding of the matter is different. This Gandhi Kumar guy has been in Delhi for years. He is a paediatrician and not a hacker. It needs a different area of expertise to be a child doctor, and a very different set of experiences to be a hacker. There is no indication that he has the technical acumen to hack into the BIMS server—BIMS relied on multi-layer security protocols. Nor does he match the profile of a hacker. He is a middle-aged family man without any criminal record or any indication of possible involvement in a heist. Moreover, his family is active in community events in Hauz Khas Enclave, and his neighbours have not found anything suspicious about him. He is definitely not our man. I think we should call him in for questioning and seek his cooperation to trace the real culprits.'

'If he is not involved, why do the KYC records show him as the owner of the account with KuberX? The KYC must have been verified when he opened the account with the exchange. And his computer has been used to move the money around. Don't you think that's conclusive?' Mehta asked.

'Sir, we are seeing many cases of mule accounts, and Arun will agree with me here. Even with Aadhaar authentication, we find many cases of stolen KYCs. A stolen KYC is used by cybercriminals to open multiple mule accounts. These accounts are then used as conduits to move money. Maybe it's a mule account. That's why we need to call in Gandhi Kumar for questioning,' Simrandeep said.

'I will not argue with Simrandeep here. When he speaks, each syllable carries the weight of careful thought, delivered with a calmness that could silence a storm. My only point is that we are speculating. He is speculating as much as I am. And time is running out. If we bring in Gandhi Kumar for questioning, he may be alerted. He may destroy electronic evidence, and we cannot afford that. We need to take custody of the digital evidence, and the surprise element is paramount here. That's why we need to conduct a search operation on Gandhi's residence, office and clinic. We have already conducted our recce and are ready with our operational plan of action. We just need your go-ahead,' Kamat said.

Simrandeep replied, 'There is another angle that we have to consider here. Many types of cyber-enabled frauds all over the world are being perpetuated from India. Delhi and its satellite cities are among the hotspots from where cybercriminals defraud victims in other countries. In recent years, we have busted many criminal call centres that were defrauding citizens of the US, France, Canada, Australia and many other countries. In fact, the US government has sent a dedicated FBI officer to their embassy in Delhi to liaise with state authorities and the CBI in busting these call centres.

'Now, Interpol has informed us about a group most probably working from India that has conducted ransomware attacks in many European countries. This group, which they identify by the given name Null Cyphers, typically injects a bot into the laptop of an unsuspecting victim. Not only does it clandestinely steal the victim's data, it also switches on the laptop's webcam and records a victim in the act of watching pornographic content. Then the victims are blackmailed for the data as well as compromising videos taken through the webcam. The group takes ransom only in bitcoins. Two weeks ago, I was in Interpol headquarters in Lyon, when they showed me how some of the wallets used by the BIMS hacker group to move the ransom were earlier used by the Null Cyphers group. It means that the BIMS hack was done by this group. They have already included the BIMS ransomware attack in their file for the Null Cyphers group. I had disseminated an intelligence report to all agencies and to the RTF secretariat immediately on coming back to India.

'This is important information. We now know that whoever attacked the BIMS server has been operating in an organized way for at least the last two years. And they are quite sophisticated in their operations. To identify vulnerable targets, they need to scan through systems and look for loopholes. It takes days, even months of rummaging on the internet to be able to identify loopholes in a system.

I am visualizing an organized group with specialists in handling bots, handling security flaws, moving money around and supervising the work. But I cannot see how a paediatrician contributes to the criminal group's work.'

'You cannot see because you don't know. We do not know. Just a few days back, someone told me about the case of a fifteen-year-old hacker who choked many government websites just for fun. All this is new, and we don't understand the terrain well. It does not mean that we sit and do nothing,' Mehta said. Then he stood up and walked around to the screen. He looked intently at Gandhi Kumar's photograph on the screen, as if trying to stare him down. It was already becoming personal between him and this cybercriminal. With a resolve in his tone, he said, 'Arun, you get this bastard. We will then use the entire government machinery to take out the others.'

2 The Unrelenting Predictability of Monotony

N. Gandhi Kumar, MD, MBBS, woke up one Friday morning with the same feeling of gloom he had been experiencing for a few weeks now. He knew that this day was no different from any other workday in his life, with the same predictable routine that he had been religiously following the last many years. He had no clue how unpredictable his world was about to become.

Dr Gandhi Kumar did not always harbour this feeling of gloom. Rather, he lived a contented and happy life, always looking forward to the small things that gave him and his family joy. As a sought-after paediatrician in South Delhi, he had his scheduler full of appointments. He took delight in meeting his little patients, and in diagnosing the minor ailments their parents got worked up about. More often than not, it was an anxious parent who needed medication rather than the patient; but the parents paid the fees and decided how good the doctor was, so he would prescribe some probiotics and vitamins for the patients. Sure, the vaccinations he administered to the babies and children were blandly routine, but he loved the easy money they brought along.

The feeling of gloom had set in after he met a creative director from Mumbai at a party he attended a few weeks back. The party was hosted by a lobbyist in his bungalow in Defence Colony. Any outsider who had stayed in Delhi for as long as Gandhi Kumar had would know how important it was to network with lobbyists. They wielded immense power, some of which could brush onto you if you were in their network. That was why Gandhi Kumar, who was not otherwise a party person, was there. And he did not mind meeting some interesting people, like this creative director.

The creative director was looking for a story; not just any story, but the next big thing that he could adapt into a web series. There was a huge demand for a good story, he educated the few guests assembled around him, and he was looking for a real story he could adapt. Gandhi Kumar got interested and started peddling his experiences as a story. How his work was so challenging, how it was a sensitive business to supervise the growth and development of small kids, the typical birth complications some of his patients had faced, blah blah blah.

'Cut the crap! I will never develop a story about you. Do you know why?' said the creative director, rather rudely.

'Why so?' asked Gandhi, almost in a whisper, after being taken aback by the tone of his voice.

'Because we make stories about extraordinary things. We don't make stories about routine things. You won't find a story about a monotonous life, unless it's an art film. Even the art films that capture the mundaneness of a life of routine highlight some emotion or some tension leading up to a climax. Now, let's see you. You are a successful paediatrician, so you are also wealthy. To make money, you keep working in your hospital. You religiously sit in your clinic to make that extra money. You go on vacations with your family, during which your wife nags you and your children ignore you. You pester your children and dodge your wife, and your vacation ends. Am I right?'

Gandhi Kumar nodded, quite involuntarily. He shrugged, because he did not know what to say. The creative director was so correct it seemed he could see through Gandhi Kumar. The idea did not immediately weigh him down, largely due to the couple of drinks he had had. But Gandhi Kumar woke up the next day feeling gloomy. He realized how predictable his life was. The idea had taken root in his mind and kept spiralling into a hurricane. Gandhi Kumar took great pride in his struggles and his success. Hailing from a small town near Madurai down south, he had been a good student all through his formative years. He cleared a difficult medical entrance examination to get into BIMS, India's foremost medical college. And then there was no stopping him. He slogged to complete his MBBS and MD, got employed in a good hospital and ran a clinic on the side. For the first time, Gandhi Kumar started seeing these achievements with contempt.

Although his mother had selected a girl for him, he had had quite the romance during the courtship period.

His wife, Sumathy, behaved in a passive-aggressive way with him—or so he felt—but did bestow him with affection and indulgence from time to time. After that evening's conversation with the creative director, his wife appeared unbearable to him. She was always fretting about Anjali's (their younger child) bad grades at school, and how she suspected Senthil (their older one) was keeping bad company. Her fretful behaviour hadn't bothered him earlier, but now it got on his nerves.

Gandhi Kumar spoke about this with his sister, the only person he thought understood him, and she suggested he take a vacation with friends. She knew well that Gandhi Kumar did not have any steady friends and was not in touch with people he had known in school and college. So, she suggested he take a trek with an adventure club group. She even suggested that he visit Bengaluru, where she lived, so she could help him out of his midlife crisis. Gandhi Kumar liked the idea of a long break—of three or four months of an unhurried vacation—but did not have the heart to broach this subject with his wife. Sumathy would flare up and remind him of how he had not been doing enough for his children and that he had to do his share of parenting before running away on a vacation.

It was not that there was no thrill at all in his life. Gandhi Kumar could count two distinct sources. First was the money he made in his clinic. He charged 900 rupees per consultation and kept a 20 per cent margin on all vaccination costs. He also got some good cuts for referrals. All in all, the take-home pay was good. And all of it was in black. He never disclosed the clinic's income in his tax returns, and this money piled up in cash bundles in an attic in his house. Over the years, he had managed to purchase a swanky builder floor in the posh Hauz Khas Enclave of South Delhi (for which you could pay up to

70 per cent in cash), the basement office which housed his clinic, a large plot in a posh locality in Madurai (his wife still did not like Delhi, and looked forward to going back to Tamil Nadu someday), and a luxurious duplex in Gurgaon, which he rented out. His lifestyle was still low-key, largely due to his wife's insistence on not letting go of the habit of prudence their middle-class background had built in them, and also because they did not feel the social pressure of ostentatious display like the local Punjabi and Jat communities, being immigrants in Delhi.

So, the cash bundles kept piling up, without them knowing how to spend it all. Sumathy would take out the bundles once every week, dust them, keep count in a pocket diary she maintained, and tuck them back safely in a cardboard box in the attic. Collaborating with people to buy real estate and to explore other means to use the cash was something exciting he did. The fear of being raided by the income tax department added some more excitement to the venture.

The second source of thrill in his life was Ananya Dang, the most beautiful thing to have ever happened to N. Gandhi Kumar. Ananya had first approached him in response to an ad he had placed for employing nursing staff in his clinic two years ago. She had no formal nursing degree nor any experience. But she seemed to be the most desperate of the interviewees. Ananya was tall and beautiful. She had sharp features, a Roman nose and brown eyes. She was blindingly fair, a feature his mother placed an irrationally high premium on. In moments when his mother and wife would fight, his mother would lament to herself for choosing such a 'dark' girl for her little prince, who definitely deserved better. Gandhi Kumar had learnt over the years not to support or contradict either of the combatants but personally found it unfair of his mother to raise the fairness issue.

During the interview, Gandhi Kumar asked Ananya if she had any training in child-rearing, although he had already half-decided to hire her. Even if she proved to be a disappointment, she would be a pleasant face to be around. She would gel well with the swanky decor built during a recent renovation. It would be good for business in a city where posh looks mattered. Ananya gave a disarming smile in response to Gandhi's question and said that what kids as patients wanted was love and affection, and she had lots of it.

Gandhi Kumar finally hired two candidates, a seasoned nurse who fit the bill, and Ananya. Within days, he found that this was a good investment after all. Toddlers liked her, because she was doting and playful with all of them. Parents observed how easy it was to administer injections to them after a playful interaction with Ananya. Fathers, the ones who usually paid the fees, liked to come back to the clinic, Ananya being easy on the eye, and this improved customer retention. Ananya was hard-working and eager to please. She took over Gandhi's scheduler and kept meticulous records of clients, medical representatives, business partners and appointments. There was a marked increase in profitability within three months of her joining the clinic, and Gandhi Kumar did not mind giving her a generous raise.

On the day he gave her the raise, Ananya fluttered around his cabin looking for a chance to thank him. After he was finished with his consultations, she went inside the cabin and profusely thanked Gandhi Kumar. She sat on a stool across from the examination table (the same stool on which little kids apprehensively sat as the paediatrician poked a stethoscope into their chests) and told him how much she needed that raise. Up till now, Gandhi Kumar had desisted from asking anything about her personal life; he had not even done an employee due diligence and was content with the good character certificate from the local police that she presented. But here she was, being so grateful to him. Apparently, she had left her abusive husband. Now she was staying alone, with a daughter to care for. And she had no support system, being the only child of parents who were deceased. Originally from Faridabad, she had moved to Delhi to stay far from her husband, who turned up every now and then to create problems for her. She needed the money to maintain a decent household and pay for her daughter's school. She had been working double shifts to ensure a good quality of life for her daughter; in the clinic during the daytime and in a bar in Nehru Place as a steward late into the night.

Ananya got emotional, her eyes full of tears, and explained to Gandhi Kumar how he was God's avatar for her. Gandhi Kumar did not know what to say, so he got up, walked over to her and offered his handkerchief to wipe her eyes. But up close, he could not bear to see this beautiful creature of nature in such a vulnerable state. He had to do something to comfort her; after all, he had now been elevated to the status of God. He went down on one knee and rubbed her shoulder.

'I did not know you had to put yourself through all this. Leave the bar as of today. I will provide for you and your child,' Gandhi Kumar said. He was not sure what he meant when he said he would 'provide for', but after having said this, he wondered if it meant he had promised to adopt her as a devotee or protégé or mistress. His words brought a smile to Ananya's face, which emboldened the otherwise chicken-hearted Gandhi Kumar. He wiped her eyes and cheeks with the handkerchief and planted a kiss (or was it a peck?) on her cheek. Ananya went forward and hugged him.

Gandhi Kumar dislodged himself from her and stood up. He was not sure what they were doing. Ananya also stood up and whispered 'sorry'. She turned to leave the room, but Gandhi Kumar instinctively grabbed her hand and pulled her to him. He was not over with her. They looked into each other's eyes for a while. At 5 feet 8 inches, Ananya was 2 inches taller than Gandhi Kumar (his wife was just an inch taller than him). She bent her head and gave Gandhi Kumar the smooch of a lifetime. The excitement of making out with an employee, nay a devotee, in the clinic when there were other staff just outside the cabin got to Gandhi Kumar. He grabbed her savagely and started eating through her salwar. He could feel a rush of blood through his boner as he felt her breasts.

This first act of intimacy started a series of secret love sessions between the doctor and the (unqualified) nurse, sometimes inside the clinic, sometimes in a guest house or hotel room, at times in public washrooms, and once in his hospital chamber. Ananya was skilful and always eager to please. She truly considered Gandhi Kumar her saviour and God, as could be seen from the various ways she tried to please him. The feeling when she put her mouth around Junior Gandhi Kumar for the first time and licked it with love was celestial. To a bard, it would appear that the world was a theatre, Gandhi Kumar's cabin her stage, and his Junior the mike she sang her masterpiece into. Gandhi Kumar's pleasantly hypnotized countenance, as he spread his legs apart around her, would make the bard confuse him for a prop.

Fuck all the creative directors from Bollywood. If they couldn't make a series on Gandhi Kumar's experiences, it was their loss.

But then, all good things come to an end. And Gandhi Kumar's adventures almost destroyed his family. Ananya's nosy husband found out about the affair. Apparently, he had been freelancing for security companies and knew a thing or two about spycams. He managed to capture Gandhi Kumar and Mrs Dang live in action, primarily to blackmail his wife to withdraw the domestic violence cases she had lodged and surrender custody of the daughter. But after going to such trouble, when he showed the videos to Ananya, she just shrugged and asked if he wondered why she never fucked him this passionately.

This piqued Sunil Dang, the husband. He had been unable to get a decent job in spite of a good engineering degree because of the domestic violence case against him. He had spent a considerable amount to snoop on his estranged wife, but the espionage did not seem to get the desired results. Dang drowned in cheap country liquor that night. Sometime in the morning the next day, while seething in the middle of a hangover, he realized that he could use the footage against 'the bastard doctor who is fucking my bitch'.

A little bit of research helped him profile Dr N. Gandhi Kumar. He even got to know that N stood for Nataraja, his father's name. These south Indians have no surname, definitely not a name as manly as Dang, he had then concluded. He went to meet Gandhi Kumar at the hospital; he knew Ananya would not allow him to meet the doctor in the clinic. He borrowed a child from somewhere and queued up to meet the paediatrician. When his turn came, he confronted the doctor with the videos. Gandhi Kumar was left speechless.

Now, this was something unpredictable and exciting. But Gandhi Kumar had not seen it that way then. This would kill his marriage. He had wondered what would happen to him when his wife threw him out. Of course, there was Ananya, who would not leave his side and stay loyal. But she represented only a vacation, while Sumathy, Anjali and Senthil were home. Home was what he had built by toiling over the years. It was not made only of brick and mortar; it represented the prestige and reputation he had built over the years. Home connected him to the community in Delhi as well as back home. Gandhi Kumar was not ready for the disruption.

Fortunately, Ananya cooperated fully with him. They had a series of negotiations with Dang. The problem was that there was no guarantee Dang would not use the videos against him even if Gandhi Kumar accepted his demands. So, he roped in an advocate and a local strongman as witnesses to the negotiations. Gandhi Kumar agreed to give 20 lakh rupees for Dang to keep quiet. In addition, Ananya agreed to withdraw the cases she had filed in court. She also agreed to visitations between Dang and their daughter. Dang signed a non-disclosure agreement, committing to kill all copies of the videos he had. He also agreed to an informal blood contract with the strongman, meaning that he would face consequences if the videos were to surface somewhere. Gandhi Kumar paid another 20 lakh rupees to the local strongman and 50 lakh rupees to the advocate, and the episode was finally over.

Having come so close to destroying his family, Gandhi Kumar did not want to take any chances. His wife had already grown suspicious. He had been tense all through the period when negotiations were going on with Dang. When the deal was done, he had to take out money from the attic, about which Sumathy asked many questions. He made up a story about a new instrument he had to purchase for his clinic, but she was still suspicious.

Gandhi Kumar decided to sever all ties with Ananya. He purchased a property in Greater Noida for Ananya and relocated her there. He got Ananya's daughter admitted in a school there and managed to get Ananya employed at a clinic run by an old friend from college. Greater Noida was not too close, and yet not too far. Ananya was just beyond reach, but he could reach her when he wanted. Or so he thought. As it turned out, Ananya drifted away from him gradually, and they had not been in touch for months now.

As Gandhi Kumar got out of bed and started preparing for the day, he wondered why his life was not dramatic enough. What would induce the creative director from Mumbai to make a web series about him? Little did he know that from this Friday morning, his life was not going to be the same anymore. The mundane, predictable life he lived was about to be disrupted beyond repair.

The calling bell buzzed while Gandhi Kumar was ruminating over the unrelenting predictability of his monotonous life. He washed his face and went to the drawing room. He opened the door to find a short man in a formal dress standing on the other side of the grill door.

'Yes?' Gandhi Kumar asked.

'Courier,' the man said nonchalantly. Gandhi Kumar would later replay this moment in his mind again and again and wonder why it did not occur to him that a courier boy would not come in formal office attire to his house.

Gandhi Kumar opened the grill door to collect the package. The short man barged into the house and exclaimed, 'Enforcement Directorate! This is a raid.' Almost immediately, a few people in civil dress and three in police uniform rushed up from the stairs and entered his house, pushing him rudely aside in the process.

3 Operation Root-Out

Operation Root-Out began at 6 a.m., Friday. Planned by the Special Cell of ED, the operation had mobilized five teams. Three teams in Delhi to raid the subject's residence, hospital and clinic, one team to raid the subject's ancestral house in Kariapatti in Tamil Nadu (the nearest airport was 30 kilometres away in Madurai), and one team for his in-laws' house in Chennai. The strike time was 8 a.m. A team from ED's Chennai office was already in Madurai to cover the Kariapatti operations. Arun Kamat was in charge of the control room in ED's Delhi zonal office.

Sitting in the control room, Kamat was supervising the movements of all teams. It was important to strike all premises at the same time so that no one got tipped off. In the very first raid of his career, some twenty-five years back, he was leading a team that was to raid a hawala operator connected to the main subject of that raid. He reached the premises ten minutes after the strike time. The hawala operator had been warned about the raid in the ten-minute lag time and had burnt all his accounts. Kamat's supervisor had been visibly upset. He had tried to explain that he could not strike on time as the hawala operator lived in a crowded neighbourhood without clear door numbers, but his supervisor did not relent and had him blacklisted from search operations for a year. This was unbearable for Kamat, a person who could not tolerate failure.

These days, it was much easier to synchronize strikes thanks to Google Maps and WhatsApp groups. In this particular case, the most important location was the subject's residence. His private clinic would be empty at 8 a.m., and the hospital he worked in would be just opening for the OPD.

The team heading towards the subject's residence was led by Ashwin Jain, a seasoned officer. It included officers from the CBI and the income tax department, and also digital forensic specialists. The officers successfully managed entry into the house at the strike time and took control of all entry and exit points. They identified the subject, Dr N. Gandhi Kumar, his wife and his two children, and herded them to the drawing room. Gandhi Kumar was visibly shocked, which is usually the case with subjects when raids begin. Ashwin comforted the shaken couple and asked them to relax. Following due process, he explained that it was a search and seizure operation under the Prevention of Money Laundering Act. He explained the search procedure and served a warrant on Gandhi Kumar. Gandhi Kumar looked smaller than he was. His shivering hands signed on the acknowledgement that he had read the warrant.

He did not look like the cybercrime mastermind Ashwin and his boss Kamat were after. Ashwin had his doubts during surveillance, but now he was getting a clear feeling of a misstrike. He communicated this observation to Kamat when Kamat called. Kamat was not pleased and asked him to thoroughly rummage through the residence. Kamat then called the team at Gandhi Kumar's hospital office and took a status update from them. They had secured the room and were interviewing the office manager. The key evidence in the hospital was his desktop, from which commands were given for moving the bitcoins paid by the Indian government as ransom. But a detailed forensic analysis of the computer would take hours. Kamat had to wait.

Impatient and fidgety, Kamat was getting both bored and nervous sitting in the control room. A person of average height, with a large belly, Kamat's face was stern, with deep-set eyes. His hair was cropped short, practical and no-nonsense, mirroring his approach to his work. He sat on a large executive chair and leaned back, brooding. This case had the potential of catapulting him to the zenith of his career. The ED director was due to retire in six months, and special directors had a better chance of getting his post than any outsider. But for Kamat to overtake the other special directors in this race, he needed visibility. This was the case that could give him visibility. No government liked to be held to ransom, and everyone in the establishment was seething with rage about paying for protecting the BIMS server. The home minister, the national security advisor, even the prime minister would know who had cracked the BIMS ransomware case. He would become a natural choice for the post of director of enforcement.

An excruciatingly slow hour passed after the strike, and there was still no result. Ashwin Jain sent Gandhi Kumar's preliminary statement by WhatsApp. Preliminary statements are taken before the rummaging of premises and usually do not contain anything of importance. Gandhi Kumar had mentioned that he did not immediately remember details of all his assets, and he needed to consult his chartered accountant. He declared that his house contained approximately 200 grams of jewellery and 50,000 rupees; there was nothing extraordinary about it. The first good news came after another hour. The forensic team in the hospital had established beyond doubt that Gandhi Kumar's office computer was used to transfer some of the bitcoins between private wallets. This same computer was used to open an account with the KuberX cryptocurrency exchange. The raid team seized the computer and prepared a chain of custody which they said was solid. They could defend it in court. Kamat phoned Ashwin for updates. They were still rummaging and had not found anything.

The forensic expert phoned back in another fifteen minutes. He had got down to making a record of the computer's hash value and detailed documentation. This is necessary to validate digital evidence in court. He had found something peculiar. The telnet port of Gandhi Kumar's office desktop was open. Telnet ports are kept closed by default, as they are especially susceptible to a security breach.

'What does this mean for the case?' Kamat barked into his mobile. The forensic expert said that he could not be sure if there was actually a security breach, but he would need support from a cybersecurity expert to analyse the system logs and find out. And there was no malware on the desktop. An antivirus software was installed and had been running security checks.

'Then what is the problem?' Kamat asked, this time his voice louder and more irritable. The forensic expert said that in theory it was relatively easier to access the computer remotely if there was an open telnet port, but he could not say if this compromised the quality of evidence; a different kind of expert who could analyse system logs would be able to confirm this.

'Why do you have to worry about a different kind of expert? You are an expert in retrieving data and recording evidence. You do your job and make a good forensic report that we can defend in court,' Kamat said and hung up. He then phoned Ashwin for an update at Gandhi Kumar's residence. He was still rummaging.

Kamat got a call from the team at the clinic after another fifteen minutes. They had not found anything, but had picked up some important gossip. The nurse, a woman in her late fifties, said upon prodding that her boss was having an affair with a young nurse he had hired more than a year back. She was a 'waste girl with loose morals', had worked in some bar in Nehru Place and had no qualifications to work as a nurse. Gandhi Kumar was screwing her at the clinic, and he thought no one knew, but in fact everyone did. She had stopped coming to the clinic abruptly one day. According to another staff member, she had moved to Greater Noida. This was good news, leverage that Kamat could use. He got the woman's phone number and used it to trace her location. A backup team in the control room was quickly dispatched to Greater Noida to apprehend her. Kamat made another call to Ashwin.

Ashwin was methodical and meticulous. None of his search documentation had ever been struck down in court on procedural grounds. His rummaging was detailed and he covered every inch of the premises he was sent to. But he was not a go-getter. He would not use the third degree to extract information from a subject, nor treat them to intense interrogation techniques. His conduct during raids was always by the book, aimed at collecting evidence. But this search was too valuable for Kamat to leave to Ashwin. He regretted his decision to send Ashwin to the subject's residence.

At long last, Ashwin phoned and informed Kamat that he had found cash. Three crores of rupees and change neatly bundled and tucked away in an attic. The subject had declared only petty cash during the preliminary statement, so there was a clear reason to conclude that this money was unaccounted for.

'Did you ask him about the source of this cash?' Kamat asked enthusiastically.

'Yes, sir, I did. He is saying this is his income from his clinic. He has not shown any income in his tax returns,' Ashwin said.

'Bullshit! This is money from cybercrime. Some of it must be from the 23 crore ransom he got from the government,' Kamat proclaimed.

'It looks like he is telling the truth. You should see this guy. He has already pissed in his pants. I took his wife to a separate room and interrogated her. She is also claiming that it's income from the clinic. She is nervous. These are the kind of people who get frightened by small things. I don't think either has the nerve to participate in an elaborate racket.'

'My foot. He is a criminal. Financial crime is fundamentally different from street crime. Those committing financial crimes are swindlers; they are good at maintaining a facade. I have seen many such people.'

'Sir, I phoned the team at the clinic; they have found the customer ledgers. This guy makes 3 crore at his clinic in a single year.'

'Who told you to contact the clinic? Control and supervision is my job. Let me take reporting from the team at the clinic. You handle your premise,' Kamat said irritably. He asked if the forensic expert had found any incriminating evidence from the laptops and mobile phones at the residence. Ashwin replied in the negative, which further irritated Kamat. He disconnected and lit a cigarette. He realized that he was almost there; his case was almost ready to be solved. He just needed a confession. A confession given to the police had no evidentiary value in court, although it was also proof of guilt for investigators. That confession had to be affirmed in front of a judge for it to be useful as evidence. On the other hand, a confession given to an ED officer was admissible in court. The subject must be under significant duress at the moment, and getting a confession during the raid would be easy. But it wasn't something Ashwin could deliver; Kamat had to do it himself.

4 A Brutal Interrogation

Kamat called for his car and instructed the driver to take him to Gandhi Kumar's residence. By now, the backup team had reached Greater Noida and apprehended Ananya Dang, the nurse with whom the subject had had an affair. They found many compromising photographs on her phone. These were sent to Kamat's phone. He browsed them gleefully as he went towards Gandhi Kumar's residence. Gandhi Kumar, the ordinary-looking 'simpleton', as Ashwin considered him, was a gamer. Kamat even showed his driver some selfies in which Ananya and Gandhi Kumar were posing in the nude. Now there was nothing to stop him.

Kamat phoned Shiv Prakash Tiwari, the journalist who had scored the scoop on the BIMS ransomware story, and asked him if he wanted to be the first to know who was behind the ransomware attack. Tiwari was interested, of course. But Kamat wanted the news to be released in a narrative of his choice. The BIMS ransomware attack was a delicate matter, and the intelligence community would not be happy with the investigation details being leaked out in the media. So Kamat gave it a twist. He would give a statement to the media that the subject was the kingpin of the notorious Null Cyphers hacker group being pursued by Interpol. Tiwari, who had scooped the BIMS ransomware story, would add in his reporting that his 'sources' in Interpol believed that this same group was also involved in the BIMS ransomware case. Kamat asked Tiwari to reach

Hauz Khas in an hour with his cameraman to cover him cracking the case live.

Kamat took half an hour to reach Gandhi Kumar's residence from the control room. He realized that it was 5 p.m., and it would get dark soon. His plan was to parade Gandhi Kumar in daylight under live coverage of the media. For this to happen, he needed to be quick. When he entered Gandhi Kumar's house, the search party came together to receive him. Junior staff stood to attention, in deference. Kamat walked with a slow gait, intently gazing around the drawing room as if surveying a crime scene. Gandhi Kumar's living room was well lit and expansive, painted in soft, soothing hues, the walls adorned with a serene shade of pastel blue, complementing the natural light that streamed in through the large windows, draped with flower-embroidered curtains. A plush, oversized couch with creamy white throw pillows sat at one corner of the room. There was a wooden coffee table between the sofa and a large TV fastened to the opposite wall. Above the sofa there was a large, framed photograph of the family, capturing a moment of laughter and joy. Around it, smaller frames held pictures of the children receiving prizes at school. The floor was covered with a large, soft rug in a shade of crystal blue, grounding the room and adding depth to the overall colour scheme. Books, artfully arranged on a rack, and a vase of withered flowers were placed in one corner.

Kamat's sight fell on Gandhi Kumar, who looked pathetic and frightened. He had been dressed in pyjamas and a banian when the raid started, and he did not get around to changing into anything more appropriate. True to what Ashwin had reported, he had peed in his pyjamas. His wife was standing beside him in a cotton sari, pouting, as if she had been wronged in some way and Kamat owed her an explanation. She was an ordinary-looking middle-aged woman, and Kamat could not help contrast her looks with the attractive Ananya Dang. Gandhi Kumar pleadingly looked at Kamat with folded hands. His children sat meekly on the sofa, indignantly looking at the pathetic situation their father was in.

'Sirr, sirr,' Gandhi Kumar murmured, then gulped and told Kamat, 'I have made a mistake, sir. I will pay my taxes. Please help me. This raid has been going on since morning. My neighbours are whispering about what is happening. I will fully cooperate. Please end this.'

'Mister Gandhi Kumar! It is not going to end for you so easily. It has just started. You have to buckle up, cough out the names of your accomplices and surrender the whole amount of the ransom you collected. After that we may think about ending this,' Kamat said in a slow and intense voice.

'Sir, Ashwin sir has been asking us about a hacker attack in BIMS. I don't even know about it! I heard about such an attack just today, from your officers. I have nothing to hide there, sir. I am clean. I can take a lie detector test if you want.'

Kamat asked a uniformed staff member if there was a room in which he could talk with Gandhi Kumar alone. He was shown to the children's bedroom. Ashwin looked at Kamat apprehensively while the staff member roughly pushed Gandhi Kumar into that room. Kamat entered the room after the uniformed staff and Gandhi Kumar and closed it from inside. He then turned towards Gandhi Kumar and slapped him hard in the face.

'I have lost my patience with you. Just confess your involvement in the BIMS ransomware case. Or the consequences are going to be bad for you.'

'Sir,' Gandhi Kumar said with folded hands and moist eyes, 'I am telling the truth, sir. I have no idea about any hacking. I cannot even operate my laptop properly. I think there has been some mistake.'

Kamat grabbed him by the hair and slapped him hard. Then he kicked at Gandhi Kumar's left knee, making him fall down. Grasping him by his right ear, Kamat pulled Gandhi Kumar up. As the weight of his body fell on his little ear, Gandhi Kumar felt a searing pain and cried out loud. He tried to stand up to reduce the pain, upon which Kamat started punching him ruthlessly. He could be a wild bear if he so wanted.

Ashwin could hear Gandhi Kumar's desperate cries from the other side of the door, and so could Gandhi Kumar's wife and children. His wife pleaded with Ashwin to help. Ashwin himself was uncomfortable; it was just stupid to resort to the third degree in front of *pancha*s (the two independent witnesses required when conducting any law-enforcement raid). But he knew his boss well; he would mind if Ashwin intervened. So he just stood outside the door. After some time, when the cries from the other side of the door did not subside, and Ashwin did not seem to do anything about it, Sumathy banged on the door and shouted, 'Do not dare touch my husband or I will not spare you.' Then she started hurling abuses in Tamil at the door. After half a minute or so, she broke down and leaned on the door, crying.

Inside the room, Gandhi Kumar could not take the pain anymore and said that he was ready to confess anything. Kamat asked him about his associates, but he had no names. He said he would take any name Kamat wanted him to take. Kamat pushed him down and kicked at his guts. Then he again asked Gandhi Kumar about his associates. But he kept mum. Kamat assessed that he kept acting dumb and was not ready to give up names. His wife was distracting Kamat by banging on the door and crying out loud. He especially flared up when the wife shouted from the other side of the door that she knew her husband and he would not do anything wrong. Redirecting his anger at Gandhi Kumar's wife, he opened the door and let her in.

'So you know your husband?' Kamat asked.

'Yes. He is not a criminal. Why are you behaving like this? You can ask questions in a civilized way, no? We keep telling you: you are mistaken, we do not know any computer hacker. And still you beat us,' she said. On seeing Gandhi Kumar lying on the ground, his face bloody, she rushed over to him and hugged him. Gandhi Kumar's children apprehensively peeked into the room from behind Ashwin. They were also crying.

'Sir, can I speak with you for a minute?' Ashwin asked Kamat, indicating for him to come out of the room. But Kamat was not done.

'You think you know your husband? How well do you know your husband?' Kamat shouted at Sumathy.

'I know him better than I know myself. He is an honourable man, and has done so much for the community and his patients. This is not how you should treat him,' Sumathy said, and continued, 'We also know the law. What you did is illegal. We will file complaints with your superiors.'

Kamat laughed hysterically and took out his phone. Pulling up the photos of Ananya and Gandhi Kumar, he showed them to Sumathy.

'See, see how honourable your husband is. See closely … see this one … see this photo, how honourably he eats the bosom of this lady,' he said, swiping photographs on his mobile screen. Sumathy saw them in utter shock.

'That's Ananya,' she whispered, more to herself.

'Yes, Ananya Dang. A nurse for your husband to bang!' Kamat said, and became pleased with himself on realizing that he had said something witty. Then he turned and went out of the room, signalling Ashwin to follow him.

In the sitting room, he instructed Ashwin to start concluding the search and seizure proceedings. He said they would have to arrest the subject because he was evasive and did not explain the real source of the cash—the incriminating evidence—at his residence. They already had a foolproof case against the subject, due to the evidence collected by the computer forensics team at the office. He told Ashwin to complete the paperwork while he took Gandhi Kumar into custody.

'You will personally take him into custody?' Ashwin asked incredulously. 'I think an enforcement officer or a few sepoys can be put on the job.'

'No, I will take him to the station. I need to interrogate him before producing him before a magistrate. You complete the paperwork and close the proceedings here. Give me two sepoys to assist,' Kamat said.

5 Public Disgrace

Kamat came out of the building exuding a palpable sense of authority and satisfaction. He was wearing his sunglasses even though the sun was setting, and he walked with a stylish gait, each step measured and deliberate. Gandhi Kumar came out after him with two uniformed policemen, his hands cuffed behind his back. He was bent forward, infirm, and was finding it hard to match Kamat's speed, but the policemen nevertheless pushed him on. His foot caught a stone lying on the road, due to which he lost his balance and stumbled forward. But the policemen's grip on his arms was so firm that they could steady him. A news van of the New Bharat Channel was parked in one corner of the road, and two cameramen were closely recording the scene. Kamat's car was parked at a distance from the building in which Gandhi Kumar's house was located, so as to ensure that he managed to do his pageant walk. A police jeep was parked behind it. This was a residential area of Hauz Khas; Gandhi Kumar's neighbours were standing on verandahs and balconies looking at the parade with a degree of concern and curiosity. As Kamat reached his car, Tiwari approached him with a mike and asked if the raid was connected with the Null Cyphers ransomware attacks. Kamat pretended to be irritated and tried to shoo him away. Tiwari insistently asked if Dr Gandhi Kumar, paediatrician, was the kingpin of an organized cybercrime group. Kamat said into the microphone, 'We are still investigating. Please let ED do its job.'

Kamat wanted to move on, but Tiwari stood stubbornly and blocked his way. 'What has your investigation revealed till now?' Tiwari asked.

'Well, this cybercrime is part of a large, organized effort to make money by blackmailing victims. This group typically hacks into digital systems of victims to scrape material that could be used to blackmail the victim. Sextortion is a modus operandi frequently seen in their actions. Money was extorted from victims in bitcoins. There are victims all over the world, and this was orchestrated from Delhi. The investigation is in progress, and we are still looking for accomplices and co-conspirators. We are also trying to trace the bitcoins extorted from victims. I personally thank Interpol for its important inputs that have helped us zero in on the perpetrator.'

As Kamat tried to move past Tiwari, he pleaded for an answer to one last question: 'Is this case related to the BIMS ransomware case?'

Kamat feigned a look of concern and evasiveness and said, 'I am not aware of any such case. Thank you, that's all.' With this, he sat in his car. Gandhi Kumar was packed into the back of the jeep, but not before the cameramen could take a zoomed-in video of his face, which expressed a mixture of disbelief, fear and resignation.

6 Racing Against Allegations

Gamini N. first heard about the raid past lunchtime, almost five hours after it started. She was eating with her colleagues when she got a call from a neighbour of her parents in Kariapatti. She immediately phoned her brother, Gandhi Kumar, but her call was not answered. She made multiple calls to her parents, brother, sister-in-law, but no one answered. She worried and phoned cousins in town. Before long, she got to know that it was an ED raid on Gandhi Kumar, in which his parents and parents-in-law were also covered. Gamini's immediate instinct was to book the next available flight to Madurai. As team lead at a mid-sized software development firm, she was between projects, and it was not a problem at the time to take an unannounced leave from her office. She intimated her boss and sent an email to human resources (HR) asking for an initial leave of two days after the coming weekend, then rushed off to the airport in an Uber. Ruma, her friend and roommate, was at home at this time. She packed Gamini's suitcase with enough clothes for three days and set off on the airport road in another Uber. The two met at Hebbal junction and Ruma handed over the suitcase to Gamini. They hugged and Ruma asked if she should come along. Gamini promised to let her know if things were really bad.

The raid team in Kariapatti wound up by 4 p.m., sooner than the other teams. Gamini's father phoned thereafter and informed her that the raid was uneventful; there was nothing to find, and the raid team did not discover anything at their house. But the team was convinced that Gandhi Kumar was engaged in cybercrime and probed multiple times about his associates. And they were extremely rude and bossy. They had taken control of all phones and taken backups of phone data using instruments they had brought with them. They did not allow the aged couple to communicate with anyone outside their home while the raid proceedings were underway.

Father and daughter chatted about how absurd the allegation sounded. Gamini wondered why ED, the premier money-laundering investigation agency of the country, would land up at Gandhi Kumar's doors to probe cybercrime. Her brother knew zilch about hacking, and Gamini knew this. She was a cybersecurity expert. Forget hacking, he needed Gamini's help to reset the access password of his Netflix account once when he could not recall the old password.

Gamini had initially booked a flight to Madurai. Before reaching the airport, she cancelled it and booked the next available flight to Delhi. She got a phone call from Senthil, her nephew, just when the flight was about to take off. The ED search action had ended, but they had arrested Gandhi Kumar. Senthil was in tears, so Gamini could not extract much information from him. All she could do was console the boy and promise him that everything would be all right. One piece of information she could glean from Senthil was that her brother was suspected to be the mastermind of the BIMS ransomware case. Gamini phoned Ruma and informed her about the development; and asked her to find a suitable advocate in Delhi to take up her brother's case.

Gamini fidgeted and worried after the flight took off. A Law Enforcement Agency raid was one thing (although it violated privacy and brought ignominy), and being arrested for a ransomware attack was another. Although the BIMS ransomware case got subdued coverage in the media, it was discussed in great detail within the cybersecurity community. Chat groups and web forums on cybersecurity were abuzz with analyses of the attack. Trails of messages on these forums bore witness to speculations about the hacker group which could have executed it. A few cyberpunks, going by aliases in these forums, had claimed that they could trace the wallet to which the Indian government paid the ransom—thus proving the authenticity of the news. Bitcoin payments are recorded on a blockchain and can be analysed by anyone on the internet. You only need to know what you are looking for. These cyberpunks had analysed the volume data of bitcoin transactions in the period of the BIMS server outage and had zeroed in on a bulk payment to a private wallet worth about 23 crore rupees. Going by the modus operandi and the pattern in which bitcoins were moved through layers of private wallets, they had concluded that this was the work of a sophisticated group.

The national money-laundering investigative agency would not normally do a roving enquiry in such an important case. But it was absolutely ridiculous for Gamini to even think that her anna—her brother—could have been involved with a hackers' group. He was the good sibling in the family, always sincere and with a strong moral compass. Often too conscientious, Gamini sighed and thought. A person who had been like this since childhood could not possibly be unmasked as a fraudster.

7 Strength in the Storm

By the time Gamini landed in Delhi, Gandhi Kumar was all over the news. A leading news channel ran the ticker: 'South Delhi paediatrician is kingpin of sextortion ring'. Another channel flashed: 'Hacking child's play for Delhi paediatrician'. Gamini's heart sank on seeing such coverage. She worried about how her parents would react on seeing this news. Or how Sumathy and the kids must be feeling. On the phone, she managed to connect with a Delhi-based criminal lawyer through a friend of Ruma. She wanted to go and meet him immediately, but understood the moral support Sumathy and the kids would be needing at this delicate moment. So she took a cab to her anna's house in Hauz Khas.

On the way, she managed to reach out to a few people who could be of help. Most of these were advocates with experience in fighting money-laundering cases, or former employees of ED. She managed to connect with a computer forensics expert at ED's cyber lab. But he did not appear eager to discuss the case and made an excuse to disconnect the call. Most of the people she talked with gave a grim picture of the situation. They said that it did not matter if Gandhi Kumar was guilty or innocent; his being arrested in an important case was bad news. One former employee of ED explained that the criminal justice system in India was difficult to navigate, and court processes could take years to conclude. And the process under the money-laundering law took longer, since the burden of proof was on the accused.

That is, the accused was deemed to be guilty by the judge until they proved their innocence. And bail conditions under the money laundering law were more stringent than under criminal law. The veteran concluded by saying that the process was the punishment; and anyone the investigating officers considered guilty was punished by the process. An advocate she phoned referred to a recent statistic that showed a handful of convictions in money laundering, a single acquittal, and thousands of cases pending in trial. If the money-laundering agency made a case, it was reason to worry even for the most virtuous of people.

As the seriousness of the event dawned on her, Gamini felt stuffy and claustrophobic. She reached for the window control, pressing it gently. The glass began to slide down smoothly, letting into the cab a gentle gust of cool air. Now almost thirty-four years old, Gamini looked at least half a decade younger, largely due to her disciplined workout routine and strict dietary choices. Her skin had a warm, dusky hue that glowed due to her frequent yoga and breathing exercises. She closed her eyes for a moment, tilting her head slightly towards the opening, allowing the refreshing breeze to caress her face and play with strands of her hair. She murmured to herself, 'I am strong.' She often did this in times of crisis.

8 Nightfall in Hauz Khas

It was past 10 p.m. by the time Gamini reached her brother's house to find an inconsolable Sumathy. To Gamini's surprise, she was swearing at Gandhi Kumar and crying loudly. Anjali was in shock, and Senthil did not know what to do. Finding Sumathy completely destroyed, Gamini took charge of family affairs. She ordered food and collected the documents left by the raid team. She consoled Anjali and coaxed her to eat. She did all this while arranging for a lawyer and arguing with Sumathy about Gandhi Kumar's guilt. She agreed with Sumathy that it was bad of Gandhi Kumar to have had an affair with his nurse. But while Sumathy was convinced about Gandhi Kumar's involvement in cybercrime, Gamini was convinced of his innocence. She expressed her displeasure at Sumathy for believing even for a moment that Gandhi Kumar could have been involved in a ransomware scam.

'Are these guys from ED and the police idiots? Why would they arrest him without a reason?' Sumathy had asked.

'Because they keep making mistakes. The internet is full of such stories. This is not unique to India. It happens everywhere. Law enforcement makes mistakes. But how can you mistake anna for a criminal after living with him for years?' Gamini had said.

'Like I mistook him for being faithful. You should have seen the pictures of Gandhi and the bitch ... the pretentious bastard kept professing love to me while screwing his nurse. And I am such a fool, I never even thought he could do such a thing.'

Gamini just shrugged and evaded the issue of Gandhi Kumar's infidelity. Sumathy's eyes, usually full of life, were clouded with feelings of hurt. Her tears flowed freely, adding to the deluge that had soaked her blouse. Probably the right thing to do was to empathize with her, give her a hug and console her. But Gamini felt she did not have the time for this. She had to supervise pressing legal matters. ED was required to produce anna to a magistrate within twenty-four hours of the arrest. This was her chance to get him out on bail. If they failed in securing bail, he would be in custody for weeks. None of the lawyers she spoke with were upbeat about the prospects of securing bail immediately. She hired the advocate who appeared the most optimistic. Then she convinced the family to go to bed. Senthil went to his room, while Gamini and Anjali made a bed in the guest room. Although she forced Sumathy to her bed, she knew that Sumathy would not get much sleep that night.

Gamini switched off the light in the guest room and tried to sleep. Both she and Anjali were finding it difficult to sleep. Anjali narrated the events of the day again (Senthil had told her all that had happened in greater detail when Gamini had arrived) and shivered when recalling how the investigators had manhandled and beaten her father. Beating up anyone was definitely not legal, and the investigators had done it to a father most insensitively in front of his children. They had wounded a family for life: brazenly invaded the personal life of a person, made him appear small in front of his kids, strained his marriage, and lent him ignominy by parading him in misery in front of the neighbourhood and media. Gamini was furious, and vowed not to let this cruelty go unpunished.

9 Digital Forensics

Gamini woke up at 5 a.m. daily and punctually did yoga for an hour and light jogging for half an hour. She woke up at the same time in Delhi, but did not have the heart to follow her routine. She took a shower, got dressed and collected the documents on the raid proceedings. The lawyer had asked her to bring them to his office at 8 a.m. The kids were sleeping, while Sumathy was sitting absent-mindedly in her bedroom. Her eyes were moist and dreary, and it did not seem like she had slept for even a minute. Gamini went over to the bed and tried to hug her, but Sumathy shooed her away. Gamini sat at arm's length and murmured that everything would go back to normal.

'Nothing will be normal again. Our neighbours, our friends, the children's school, nothing will be the same again. They even went to my parents' home. How are they involved in what Gandhi does? Everyone is talking about us. It is all over the news, all over the country. Now there is no place for us to hide.'

Gamini did not know what to say, so she decided it was best to leave Sumathy alone. She went to the living room and started reading the documents left behind by the raid team. The main document was a carbon copy of a form titled 'Panchnama', which was the record of proceedings by the *pancha*s. The *pancha*s had made a declaration at the bottom of the form that they were witness to the proceedings, and what was mentioned in the *panchnama* was a true representation of all that had happened during the raid. One of the points in the *panchnama* read: 'We further certify that no untoward incident occurred during the search proceedings and the search was conducted smoothly.' Gamini wondered if violently beating a person was not an untoward incident. She made a note to profile the *pancha* witnesses.

The *panchnama* had annexures that contained reports on valuables found and seized, documents seized, the forensic expert's report on digital evidence seized, and copies of statements taken. Gamini studied the forensic expert's report closely. The report merely stated that a cloning process had been followed to make a digital copy of the mobile phones of all family members, and Gandhi Kumar's laptop. Gamini surmised that the investigators would take time to process the digital evidence to detect any incriminating evidence. She coerced Senthil to wake up and help her locate Gandhi Kumar's mobile phone. She browsed through the mobile phone while Senthil got Gandhi Kumar's laptop. Both had no password locks, as was typical of Gandhi Kumar. Messages, documents and chats on the mobile phone did not indicate any information that could incriminate Gandhi Kumar for sextortion or ransomware. There was not a single mention of Bitcoin or cryptocurrencies.

Gamini took out her laptop, which had tools for recovering archived and deleted chats. The forensic experts had used similar software. She patiently analysed the archived and deleted chats and was relieved when she didn't find anything incriminating. Using just the tools in her laptop and a few connectors, she could retrieve gigabytes of data that Gandhi Kumar had deleted and assumed ceased to exist. Digital content can be retrieved years after it is deleted, but most people do not know this. Among the deleted data, Gamini found intimate communication between Gandhi Kumar and Ananya Dang, and also a few photographs. She noted that Gandhi Kumar looked happy in her company. Around the time he turned forty, Gandhi Kumar had become grumpy and depressed. The affair was probably his way of finding something exciting and feeling lively. This, however, did not alleviate his sin of adultery. She was disappointed, but this was not the time to break heads over an extramarital affair.

Having put aside the phone, she rummaged through Gandhi Kumar's laptop. It had hundreds of gigabytes of case histories of his patients, and a few scientific papers. Nothing incriminating. Not even the basic tools used by hackers were installed in the laptop. This itself corroborated her theory that Gandhi Kumar had no connection with the cybercriminals. But she was not sure if lack of evidence in electronic devices could be proof of innocence. She had to speak with the lawyer.

Senthil offered to accompany her to the lawyer's chamber. Gamini knew that her sixteen-year-old nephew was resilient and had nerves disproportionate to his young age. It was not wise to let the kids go to school on a day when their father was in the headlines, and Senthil would just increase her mother's burdens if he stayed at home. So Gamini agreed to take him along. They booked an Uber and first went to Gandhi Kumar's clinic. On the way, Gamini asked Senthil how he was after all that had happened. Senthil pursed his lips but did not say anything. His eyes were moist. Gamini brought him closer and gave him a tight hug.

Senthil looked taller every time she met him; she often speculated that he would grow to be the tallest in their family. Both her parents were of short height, and Gamini and her brother had inherited that. But Sumathy came from a family of tall people; she was taller than Gandhi Kumar by an inch. Senthil already looked almost as tall as Gamini. He had a lean, agile build, and a dark complexion. His dark hair was thick and unruly. Gamini could see a light dusting of soft, fine hair above his upper lip, precursor to a full moustache, reminding her that Senthil had started the transition from boyhood to manhood.

A staff member was waiting to hand her an envelope containing the *panchnama* drawn by the raid team at the clinic. After collecting the envelope, they went to Gandhi Kumar's hospital to collect the *panchnama* drawn for the raid at the hospital. Although Gamini had previously coordinated with the staff in the hospital, she was made to wait for a long time. The clerk on duty was instructed by the hospital management's legal team to give a photocopy to Gamini and retain the true copy. He took time to untie the *panchnama* and its annexures and photocopy the documents.

Gamini and Senthil reached the office of Raman Chopra, the lawyer she had hired to represent her brother, almost an hour late. His office was located in the basement of a residential building of four floors in Defence Colony. It had a low ceiling and no access to natural lighting but still looked spacious and bright. This was largely because there was excess artificial lighting and everything was painted in white. An associate took their introductions and herded them to Chopra's chamber. A chubby man with a pot belly and grey hair, he appeared busy multitasking, with case records of multiple cases cluttering his work table. He was poring over another case file when Gamini entered his chamber. He did not mind the delay, and informed Gamini that Gandhi Kumar was in custody inside ED's office on APJ Abdul Kalam Road. He had established contact with Gandhi Kumar and had taken a briefing from him over the phone. He intended to meet him sometime in the day before the hearing.

'What are the chances of getting bail?' Gamini asked.

'Getting bail immediately after an arrest is rare. Difficult when the charges are this serious,' Chopra explained. 'What I am looking at is containing the immediate damage. I will make a case for judicial custody instead of police custody. I will also plead for custody for just a week, so that we get a chance to fight for bail at the end of the week. Then we take the week's time to build our case.'

'What's the difference between judicial and police custody?'

'Judicial custody means he will be lodged at Tihar Jail. Police custody means he will be kept in ED's jail till the next bail hearing. Police custody can turn nasty; the investigators who have arrested him can resort to torture to get leads. There are no checks, so the third degree cannot be ruled out. Judicial custody is safer. Although there will be hardened criminals in Tihar who may ill-treat him, criminals are much better behaved and more predictable than Law Enforcement Agencies (LEAs). I have good contacts in the jail. I will try and ensure that he is put in a cell with a well-mannered inmate.'

'But why is it difficult to get bail today? My brother is innocent. This arrest is most absurd. Either someone has a vendetta against him or the detectives on this case are mistaken. Why would the court find it difficult to give bail?'

Chopra indicated that he wanted to talk with Gamini in private. Picking up his cue, the associate asked Senthil to come with him. Senthil obeyed, and they left the room.

'I spoke with my contacts in ED. They have got some hard evidence, which gives them reason to believe that Gandhi Kumar was involved in multiple acts of sextortion in Western countries, as well as in the BIMS ransomware attack. The Special Court has to decide on a prima facie basis whether to grant bail or not. ED will plead that he may destroy evidence if he is released on bail. How do I beat this argument? I am working on my arguments, and I hope the judge will be convinced. But it is important for us to be realistic here,' Chopra said.

'Let's take a step back. What is this hard evidence?'

'An account with a cryptocurrency exchange where KYC records contain his name and identity documents. The exchange had verified the email address using a one-time password, and the email address belongs to Gandhi Kumar. This account was used to sell a fraction of bitcoins for money. The money was later withdrawn in cash from an ATM operated by the exchange. Then, during the search yesterday, they retrieved digital evidence that his computer was used to move some of the bitcoins extorted from the Indian government across wallets on the blockchain. I do not understand this fully, and do not expect you to understand too. But staff from ED's computer forensics team are vouching for it.'

'I actually understand this quite a bit, having worked in the cybersecurity field for some time. My point is that my brother is innocent, so there has to be an explanation for all this. Before coming here, I analysed anna's phone and laptop. I scraped out all deleted content, system logs, archived files, and I did not find a single bit of evidence to suggest he could be involved in a large-scale cyber fraud racket. He has zilch knowledge of technology, and even if he did, executing this level of hack and fraud requires an organized group. How is he interacting with the team?'

'I don't know.' Chopra shrugged. 'But today, if we raise this, the prosecution counsel will say Gandhi Kumar may be using a second phone which he has hidden away somewhere. If he is released on bail, he will destroy the evidence on the second phone. So there is all the more reason for keeping him in ED custody for further questioning.'

'Which computer do they say my brother used to move bitcoins across wallets?'

'The one at his hospital. He had a dedicated chamber, and the attendants have given a statement that only he used the computer. The details would be in the *panchnama* documents.'

'I want to check the computer. But I doubt the hospital will allow me to. They did not appear cooperative when I went there to pick up the *panchnama* documents in the morning. Their legal team will take days to decide on giving me access. What else can we do to get bail?'

'Demolishing their "reasons to believe" is the best bet. But they have two prima facie strong reasons: KYC documents with the cryptocurrency exchange, and evidence from Gandhi Kumar's computer. Otherwise, we can argue that he is unwell and needs medical supervision. He will still not be granted bail, but can get admitted to a hospital under police supervision. For this argument, we will need a chronic condition in his medical history to satisfy the judge.'

Gamini shook her head and said, 'There is no chronic medical condition I know of.'

'And ED's "reasons to believe" cannot be demolished today. Today the court will go into the issue on a prima facie basis only. I will try to make other arguments, such as Gandhi Kumar's stature in the community as a paediatrician, he being a low flight risk, and his zero history of deviant behaviour. But you also need to understand the context here. This search action was conducted by Arun Kamat, the special director for Delhi zone.

'He is a devious fellow ... he usually conducts searches on Fridays and arrests the accused by the end of the day. Do you know why? Because he has to produce the accused in court within twenty-four hours, and the court is on leave on Saturday and Sunday. So the bail hearing happens in a judge's residence. The judge is generally in a hurry, and in no mood to listen. Kamat has a favourite prosecution counsel, Sohail Hossain. Hossain confuses the judge by bombarding a lot of details about the case unrelated to the issue at hand and creates a sense of alarm.'

Chopra had pulled out the documents Gamini had carried and was looking into them while talking with her. He exclaimed after a while, 'It's good news that there was no confession during the search.'

'They beat up anna to take his confession. But as it appears from the statement, they did not manage to get a confession. But what if they have threatened anna and taken a confession in ED jail?'

'That is highly unlikely. Confession under duress was becoming a routine for the police. So in 2020 the Supreme Court ruled in a seminal case that confessional statements have to be recorded under CCTV. A confession during a raid action—a search and seizure action—does not have to be under CCTV. But confessions in custody have to be under CCTV. But tell me more about the raid team beating Gandhi Kumar.'

'Well, I was not there. And my sister-in-law is not in a good condition to narrate what happened. What I learnt from my nephew and niece is that the raid team was cordial and professional. But a senior officer came towards the evening and took anna into a room. He locked himself and anna inside. Then he beat anna badly. The kids could hear anna scream and moan in pain. Later when he opened the door, the kids could see anna all bloodied.'

'This is important information. The judge understands his weighty responsibility of discharging justice. With this information I can easily avoid police custody. If the judge is moved, he may also grant bail with conditions. Later in the week, I will ask for the deposition of the *pancha*s too. Bring your sister-in-law for the hearing.'

Gamini knew she could not coax Sumathy to the hearing. She was still not ready for this.

'Why do you need her there? Does she have to depose?'

'No, she has to just sit there. I will show her to the judge and build my narrative of a vindictive ED violating basic human rights. The judge may like to question her about what had happened.'

'Then maybe I can bring my nephew there. Anna's wife is not in a good condition. I doubt she could face a courtroom, even if it's in a judge's residence.'

Chopra thought for a while and said, 'I can manage with that. That's even better. I will build a narrative that the wife is traumatized. The son is witness to the brutality meted on the father.'

'And I will see if I can lay my hands on the desktop in my brother's hospital chamber.'

10 Digital Evidence

Gamini went back to the hospital with Senthil in tow. She tried to talk her way into Gandhi Kumar's chamber, but the staff was extra-sensitive about letting anyone in. They behaved as if his chamber was a crime scene. They had placed two sets of locks on the room, and a white paper reading 'No Entry' in bold on the door. It was a Saturday and the usual hospital staff were on holiday. The staff members managing the in-patient department and emergency care were not very helpful. Through a colleague of Gandhi Kumar, she managed to contact a senior doctor who was Gandhi Kumar's supervisor. The doctor expressed his sympathies and concern, but was non-committal about giving access to Gandhi Kumar's room. He asked many questions, apologized for asking so many questions, but said it was necessary due to the law-enforcement angle. He evidently did not understand what the case was, or why it was important to access Gandhi Kumar's desktop. After Gamini explained over the phone for some twenty minutes, he arrived at the bizarre conclusion that Gandhi Kumar was recording nude videos of foreigners and keeping them on his office desktop.

Gamini worried that she was giving fodder for office gossip, but as she saw it, there was no other way. She again narrated the case, explained that the allegations were about misuse of new technologies on which most people were not clear, but it was important to analyse Gandhi Kumar's desktop to prove his innocence. She repeatedly stressed that Gandhi Kumar was innocent but was mistakenly arrested because ED lacked experience with the new technologies. The senior doctor said he would talk with his superiors and get back.

While Gamini waited for the senior doctor's phone call, she went to the cafeteria and looked for some food. She was not hungry but it was going to be a long day, and she had to take care of Senthil. The cafeteria had a limited menu of fried food which Gamini abhorred. But Senthil liked fried food. He had two samosas and a plate of chilli pakora, while Gamini gulped down a Diet Coke.

When the senior doctor phoned back, he said that upon hearing about the raid, representatives of the legal department had approached the raid team with an offer to cooperate. Because the computer was an important piece of evidence, the raid team had locked it in a cabinet inside the room and placed a prohibitory order over it. It prohibited anyone from accessing the cabinet, and any violators would be prosecuted. That was why the management decided to lock Gandhi Kumar's room, and now it was not possible to access the computer.

This was a dead end on which Gamini had wasted too much time. She went back to the advocate's chamber with Senthil. Chopra was dictating notes to an associate while another associate was studying the bundle of documents

Gamini had brought in the morning. Before Gamini could say anything, Chopra said, 'No use looking for the computer in Gandhi's office. It has been put under PO.'

'PO as in prohibitory order,' Gamini said. 'But how do you know this?'

'It's mentioned in the *panchnama*.'

'You could have told this to me. I wasted so much time chasing hospital staff.'

'I found out just now. We are doing a thorough review of the *panchnama* documents. But let me give you a piece of advice. I know how anxious you are. You feel you should do something to be helpful, but the best help you can be is to support your family members in this difficult time, and take rest. It's going to be a long-drawn legal battle, and you need to save your energy. Take some rest before the evening's hearing.'

'Have we found out when the bail hearing is?'

'Yes. It's at 6 p.m. in the residence of Justice Sushil Kumar in Civil Lines. My staff will give you all the details. Be there by 6.30 p.m. sharp.'

'6.15 p.m.?'

'You can come earlier, but since the time given is 6 p.m., we can expect the hearing to commence at 6.30 p.m. or 6.45 p.m. There is good news. Sushil Kumar is balanced and has scathingly criticized law enforcement in the past for shoddy investigations.'

'So, there is hope of getting bail today?'

'I would still not be very hopeful if I were you. The way the Prevention of Money Laundering Act works is an accused is guilty unless proven innocent. This metric is used at the time of trial. And this principle also weighs upon the court at the time of granting bail. That's why the court takes time to give bail in cases under this Act.'

'What can I do?'

'As I said, the best way you can help ...'

Gamini cut short the advocate and said, 'Can I go through the *panchnama* of anna's office premises?'

Chopra smiled indulgently and said, 'It is yours. I will ask an associate to make a copy for you.'

11 The Scammers

Nestled within the bustling heart of Delhi city lies Shadi Khampur, a village that retains its distinct character amidst the urban sprawl. As one ventures deeper into the village, the streets become narrow, high and uneven buildings lean towards each other, joined together in a canopy of hanging wires and telephone lines. The buildings, which display a patchwork of old brick and faded paint, are interspersed with a few ancient havelis that distinguish themselves with their intricately carved doors, grand entrances and expansive courtyards. It is said that the village has been in continuous habitation since the seventeenth century, and the havelis remind a visitor of times when it would have looked spacious and scenic. There are lanes in which there is not enough space for two persons to walk side by side, and yet a scooter or a cycle rickshaw can be found inching its way through, lousily manoeuvring around pedestrians.

A lane that goes through the village is locally called 'border' because it goes further into the Ranjit Nagar area where it divides the area into a Muslim-majority settlement (literally called the 'XYZ Block', probably to keep it nameless) and another with mixed settlement. A branch out from this lane snakes through the interiors of

Khampur. An old building of three floors on this branch-lane has a board over the entrance that reads 'Intelligent Coaching Centre'. This building has remained closed for months. No one has been seen going in or coming out of the building in the past many weeks. A decision had been taken by the partners running the coaching institute—or whatever it was in the garb of a coaching institute—to keep the building abandoned until further notice. But the front door is unlocked on this day, and a light glows from a room on the second floor.

A large man of 6 feet and 2 inches height, weighing more than 100 kilograms mostly in muscle mass, and wearing a thick golden necklace, stood at the window of the room. Dressed in a white kurta and pyjama, he had short hair and a thick beard, which had greyed at places, and brownish eyes which were intently watching the road below. About half an hour after he entered the building, a lean man of average height walked past. He was dressed formally, a sky-blue shirt tucked into charcoal-grey, straight-leg trousers with matching charcoal-black shoes. He went ahead for about 200 metres, looking intently at the buildings on either side of the lane, then came back on the same path and went into the building. He closed the door from the inside and went up. On the second floor, the two men met like old friends and hugged. The big man bear-hugged so tightly that the other one felt uncomfortable in his embrace and moved back. Then the big man slapped him on the shoulder and said in a Lucknowi dialect of Hindi, 'How have you been, Master?'

'As you can see … have not gained any weight even after turning into a couch potato,' said Master. 'How about you?'

'We are doing good, Master. Doing good. We are pumping two sisters, you know. It is an incredible experience for us. We can see how similar, and yet how dissimilar the two beautiful girls from the same house are. They are our neighbour's daughters, one twenty-one and the other eighteen. The elder of the two is getting married next month … to one of our boys, the wedding fixed by us. Just a few days back, she caught us pumping the younger sister at our house. We thought for a moment we are gone. But she was incredibly mature. The younger one was a bit inconsolable for a while, but she is also broad-minded. She has understood that our heart is big enough to accommodate both.'

'I have always envied you for how simple you make things. Let me guess. You will rehabilitate the younger one too with one of your boys.'

'Are you mocking us, Master? We don't know why it feels as if you are mocking us.'

'Not at all. I am appreciating your talents, as I always do. What else is happening other than pumping young girls?'

'Well, we have been promised a ticket for the upcoming elections. Social work is keeping us busy.'

'Good to hear that you are not missing our other work!'

'We miss that work. Politics is a hobby, that is the profession. Listen, Master, there is so much money to be made. We need to get the team together again and restart the work.'

'It is still too risky. This is why I wanted to meet you. Did you see the news?'

The big man shrugged and said, 'What news?'

'The police have caught someone for the BIMS project.'

'Who? One of our team?' the big man asked, his facial expression turning from jovial to tense.

'No, no idea who he is. He is a doctor, and they are calling him the mastermind of the BIMS case. When I saw his photo in the news yesterday, he looked like a frightened middle-aged man to me. But the more I see his photo, the more he looks like the mastermind.'

The big man's expression turned from tense to jovial. He laughed out loud and said, 'You are the mastermind, Master. Master and Mind! We are sure you had a hand in this. So now what? The police are off our trail?'

'No, I do not know anything about this doctor. It has come out of the blue. And this is not good news. It means the police are hot on our heels. Even if they make mistakes, they are on to us. We do not know what the police are up to, and why they have arrested this doctor. But we need to find out.'

'Oh, you worry too much, Master.'

'I worry for all of us. See, they are getting close. The New Bharat channel claims the BIMS server was hijacked by the same group that has been involved in phishing and sextortion across Europe and America: Null Cyphers.'

The big man's expression turned from jovial to tense. 'How did the police find out?'

'My first guess was that they matched IP addresses. But that's not possible. We were particularly careful not to leave any trace of our digital activity. We used many routers, proxy sites and bots. The BIMS attack was launched from a compromised laptop in Frankfurt, and most of the attacks in Europe were launched from computers in Nigeria which we were controlling through intelligent devices in Canada. It would take them years to trace back through the chain of command to reach us.'

'Then?'

'Someone is following the money. Interpol has been chasing Null Cyphers for the last two years. We were careful in using new wallets for moving the bitcoins we received from the BIMS work. But you know, so many wallets are needed in a peel chain that we must have used a few of the older wallets which were used to wash bitcoins we got from the phishing cases. That's the only explanation.'

'You know well that we do not understand much of these technology-fechnology terms. What is this peel chain?'

'I had explained this to you earlier too, Sandhu,' Master said and frowned. 'It's a technique to launder large-value cryptocurrencies. Unlike bank accounts, cryptocurrency wallets are publicly visible. When we received the ransom from the Indian government, the transaction was publicly recorded on the Bitcoin blockchain. You can see the transaction even today, because it is immutable. Let's say we approach a cryptocurrency exchange to convert the bitcoins into cash. Since the movement of the bitcoins is visible to all on the internet, law enforcement would get to know and freeze the money before the cryptocurrency exchange could pay us. To avoid this, we engaged in forming peel chains. In this, we move the bitcoins through layers of wallets. In every layer, we peel off a small value and move it through another bunch of wallets. As law-enforcement authorities move through layers, they will find every succeeding layer more time-consuming to trace than the preceding layer.'

'You explain so nicely. That's why you are our Master,' Sandhu said and grinned.

'Now think of how intricate a chain of transactions we have conducted. And yet, if they can link our attacks in Europe and America with the BIMS attack, it means they are utilizing a lot of resources in tracking us. This is bad news. We need to lay low and stop any further movement of bitcoins.'

'No,' Sandhu objected in a loud, agitated voice. 'We have been sitting on what … hundred crores of dough … and you said the value is increasing with the rise in Bitcoin's value… but all of that is lying on this blakchain flakchain. What use is it if it is not in our hands? We need hard cash; we have an election to run. We are losing patience, Master. You have to get us our share.'

'I am afraid you have to wait a bit longer. It's too risky.'

'This is just not fair. Master, you have invested your brains into this venture, but we have invested our money. All the computers, gadgets in this building cost us money. Running this call centre costs us money. We paid for all your experts all this while, and we are yet to break even. We are only told there are crores on blakchain and flakchain.'

'I know, Sandhu, but we are partners. We swim or sink together. You think I do not want to encash my part of the profits?'

Sandhu shook his head in dismay.

'And has Fatichar converted any bitcoins into cash? We sent him abroad a month back. What is he doing, wasting our money?'

'It is absolute suicide to convert the bitcoins into cash in India. That's why we had to send him abroad to convert the bitcoins into dollars. There are countries in which cryptocurrency exchanges are opaque. There is scant regulation and the exchanges hand you cash for bitcoins, no questions asked, no KYC taken. But Interpol has eyes even there. These exchanges could report suspicious transactions to the authorities. So Fatichar is experimenting with withdrawing small amounts which would not attract suspicion. It takes time. He is now in Seychelles and has established a rapport with a manager at an exchange. He trusts that the manager will not report him if he makes a large withdrawal. But after yesterday's news, I want to tread more cautiously.'

'You do not understand, Master. We have an election to run. The election will not wait for matters to settle. If Fatichar trusts this manager, let him withdraw something. At least a couple of crores! You know how much running an election costs.'

After reflecting over Sandhu's suggestion for a while, Master answered: 'Okay, I will ask Fatichar to go ahead and do one transaction … withdraw some 2 crore. You do what you do best: shadow this doctor's family to find out what he knows; get intel from ED about what they know.'

'As if you have not already got into his computer!' Sandhu said in a teasing tone.

A smile came on Master's face. 'It is not that easy. But don't worry, I will provide you "air support" while you conduct your enquiries.'

They walked together to the room's entrance. Master said, 'You leave now, and I will go out half an hour after you. We will meet again in five days, but somewhere else next time. We have to shut this call centre for good.'

12 The Trojan

Gamini reached her brother's home and checked on Anjali. The cook had turned up earlier and prepared a basic lunch of curd rice and beans, which Anjali had consumed. Sumathy was sleeping; as Anjali informed, she had not eaten anything since the raid the previous day. Gamini served some curd rice to Senthil and got some for herself.

Gamini spent time poring over the *panchnama* drawn in the hospital premises, but could not make much headway. She found the legal language arcane and difficult to follow.

She could appreciate the computer forensic report, but it was also couched in a lot of legalese. Because of her strong belief in her brother's innocence, she felt there would be a mention of a hack or security breach into the computer. But she did not find anything. On the other hand, the forensic report unequivocally mentioned that no virus or trojan was detected; the computer was uninfected; and the chances of a hack since the last formatting were close to nil. Gamini's heart sank. The forensic experts knew what they were writing, and she did not doubt their competence.

The report contained an analysis of the computer's internet browsing history and reference to a digital record of it taken during the raid and stored in a sealed hard disk. The hard disk had an index number, and Gamini guessed it had been taken by the raid team as evidence. The report also included a chapter on Internet Protocol (IP) analytics, which a separate forensic expert had certified. The expert had found Word files on the computer containing public keys of a few of the wallets used to transfer extorted bitcoins in the BIMS case. The internet history showed that the computer was used frequently to access the KuberX crypto exchange. A software wallet client was installed on the computer, which was used to access the wallet used to transfer those bitcoins to KuberX. The forensic expert concluded that a clear money trail could be formed on perusal of data on the computer's hard disk. Gamini's heart sank further. She wondered if her brother had actually got involved with some hackers.

The report was voluminous, and Gamini had almost given up on reading it when her eyes caught an observation made as a footnote deep inside the verbose report that the computer's telnet status was 'turned on'. There was no further comment, no conclusion on this. This was surprising and exciting news for Gamini. Her hands trembled in anticipation as she flipped back to read the computer's specifications. It had an Intel i5 processor with 8 GB RAM and 500 GB Solid State storage.

Telnet is a facility that allows one computer to remotely access another computer on the same network. Gamini recalled how she used to explain telnet to new recruits during training: a thief has to break into a house with closed doors to steal; but they do not have to break into a house with open doors—they can just walk in. If the telnet of a computer is turned on, it means anyone on the network can use the computer remotely. Only if the telnet is turned off, a hacker has to send a virus or other malware to infect and control the computer. In older computers (of the 1990s), the telnet was 'turned on' by default. This increased their vulnerability; they could be used remotely as a front for committing cybercrime. And they were. So newer computers come with default settings of the telnet 'turned off'.

Gandhi Kumar's desktop specifications showed that it was a newer computer. It must have had the default settings of the telnet 'turned off'. A saboteur had intentionally turned on the telnet. Physical access to the computer was needed for less than a minute to turn the telnet on. The hospital was a public place, and many patients, nurses and staff frequented Gandhi Kumar's room. Just about anyone could have sneaked in for a minute and changed the telnet settings. Gandhi Kumar would definitely not have turned on the telnet, unless he had reason to specifically give remote access to someone. Gamini doubted Gandhi Kumar even understood what the telnet was.

This important information was buried in a footnote midway through the report. This fact vitiated the statement of hospital staff that only Gandhi Kumar had access to the computer. Everyone on the hospital network had access to the computer. And since the hospital's network was connected to the wider internet, everyone on the internet had access to the computer!

Another interesting angle, Gamini contemplated, was that anyone who had access to Gandhi Kumar's computer had access to his email application. She went to KuberX's website on her laptop and tried to open an account. To open an account, the website asked her to:

Fill in a form

Upload identity and address proof

Confirm the OTP sent to both the phone number and email address.

Gamini let out a whistle. There was no requirement to provide identity proof physically at a local branch. There was no requirement for a video KYC in which a manager interviewed the applicant over a video call. Opening an account on KuberX needed one to upload just a scanned identity card and verify the OTP sent to email. If a trespasser had accessed Gandhi Kumar's computer, he would have access to Gandhi Kumar's email as well as any identity card scan he had saved in his computer.

Gamini quickly phoned Chopra and tried to explain what she had found. Chopra asked her to reach the judge's residence sooner so she could explain her findings in a clearer way to him. She disconnected the phone and went to check on Sumathy, who had woken up and was wallowing in bed. Gamini took curd rice on a plate and sat by her. She coaxed Sumathy to eat a few spoonfuls.

While Sumathy was eating, Gamini said: 'I will get anna out on bail today. I have got clear evidence that whoever committed the cybercrime fooled the law-enforcement authorities. And anna is innocent.'

Sumathy looked listlessly at Gamini and kept chewing her food slowly. Gamini went on: 'It was wrong of anna to cheat on you. He has to answer for what he has done once he is back.'

Sumathy looked on without reacting. Gamini waited on her patiently while she ate. Senthil peeked into his parents' bedroom after a while and indicated to Gamini that it was already 5 p.m. Gamini rose and went out with him. Packing her notes and laptop in a backpack, she followed Senthil out. They took an Uber to the judge's house.

13 The Judge's Chamber

The judge's residential quarter was a one-storey bungalow in the middle of a large plot in Civil Lines. It was painted white and looked stately and imposing from the road. A guard stood at the entrance and showed Gamini the way to the residential office, which was situated in an outhouse. It was a spacious room with a long study table, a big chair with intricate embroidery on its top-back on one side of the table, and many plastic chairs placed on the other side in three rows. The walls were decked with cabinets that contained thick tomes on various bare acts, commentaries and case laws.

Chopra asked Senthil to sit on one of the plastic chairs and took Gamini to the side. Here, Gamini explained to him the importance of the remark on the telnet. Chopra had many questions, but seemed to easily pick up the arguments made by Gamini. He took brief notes and asked Gamini how they could know without doubt if someone else had accessed the computer.

'The system logs would show if anyone else has accessed the computer,' Gamini said. 'There are forensic tools that would have to be used to analyse the logs.'

'And we do not know what the system logs say because the computer forensic experts did not care to investigate this issue of an open telnet. Right? This makes sense. Now, if there is someone else who is doing this, what is their motivation to implicate Gandhi Kumar?' Chopra said.

'That someone else does not want to implicate anna. They are trying to hide themselves. They are using layers of stooges to prevent LEAs from catching them. And LEAs are falling into their trap.'

'Okay. In money-laundering jargon, we call such people "mules". Their KYC is stolen to open mule accounts, which are then used as vehicles for laundering criminal proceeds. But usually mules are inconsequential people. Using an established doctor as a mule is not usual. Anyway, that is for the prosecution to find out. This working theory rhymes for me. Now, there is this other issue of the cash found in Gandhi Kumar's residence. His statement says it's his income from the clinic, which he has not disclosed to the income tax department. If he had another advocate, that advocate would have recommended him to retract his earlier statement and say that the statement was given under duress. Since Gandhi Kumar was beaten during the search, the story adds up. But I recommend consistently admitting that it was his income from the clinic on which he has not paid taxes.

'There are many reasons why I am suggesting this: first, it seems to be true that the money was income earned at the clinic. One member of the raid team I could chat with said that a ledger seized from the clinic corroborates his statement. Second, even though it implicates Gandhi

Kumar in a tax evasion case, making an excuse would look bad. You will have to make a story about the source of the cash found, and you will be justifying a false money trail by creating false documents and false witnesses. The trial judge will feel that we are hiding something … remember that he is presumed to be guilty under the money-laundering law unless found innocent. Third, the tax department would anyway not accept any argument you make. When the findings of the raid are shared with them, they will swoop in and impose tax and penalty on this money. The good thing is that tax evasion is a civil offence. Tax and penalties have to be paid but can be litigated once this case is closed. The tax department may launch a prosecution too, but there are ways to quash it on procedural grounds.'

'Sounds fair to me.'

'Good. Let your brother also know this. He will be here any minute now.'

Shortly afterwards, the public prosecutor, Sohail Hossain, arrived with Ashwin Jain and two other ED officers in tow. Hossain was fair, stout and had the airs of a know-it-all person. He greeted Chopra and whispered something to him. Chopra smiled and replied in whispers, which elicited a smirk from him. A turbaned officer also arrived and sat in a corner chair in the third row. Ashwin Jain walked up to him and greeted him. Pointing at him, Chopra told Gamini, 'This is Simrandeep Singh. He is an old hand in the Narcotics Control Bureau … has a reputation for being a straightforward and sharp investigator. He is now the CEO of I4C. He is senior in rank to Arun Kamat and has access to both the finance minister and the home minister. His attending the bail hearing means that the case is important for the government.'

Gandhi Kumar was led into the judge's res-office in handcuffs by two uniformed policemen. He looked tired. His face was swollen under his left eye, and he also had a lesion on the lower lip. As soon as he came in, Gamini and Senthil rushed to him. Gamini asked him in Tamil if he was okay. Gandhi Kumar pursed his lips and grimaced. Gamini hugged him and patted his back. Gandhi Kumar murmured that she should not have brought Senthil for the bail hearing. It was too embarrassing for him to stand in handcuffs in front of his minor son, but this had not occurred to Gamini.

Before Gamini could say anything, Chopra butted in and introduced himself. He had spoken with Gandhi Kumar over the phone in the morning, but this was the first time they were meeting. He studied Gandhi Kumar's face keenly and was satisfied with the bruises on his face.

'Chopraji, I am innocent. I have no idea what all this is about,' Gandhi Kumar said. 'I had not declared my clinic fees. They found the money in my house, but they are saying I got it by sextortion. By God, I don't even know what that is.'

'Do not worry, everything will be all right. For now, I need you to confirm that the raid team beat you during the raid action yesterday. Did they?'

'Only Arun Kamat did. He is the top boss.'

'I know him. Now my second question: Did they beat you after they arrested you? Or threaten you?'

'They did not beat me, but they questioned me in the morning today. There was some threat of dire consequences. One of them suggested that I could get a commuted sentence if I turn approver and expose the gang involved in the cybercrimes they are investigating. But I do not know anything about this gang. I said this, but they did not believe me,' Gandhi Kumar told the advocate.

14 The Burden of Proof

The judge came into the room from the other side. Everyone stood up, and those standing around the room quickly found chairs. The judge was in his early fifties. He was a plump man with a thick nose and a receding hairline. His dark complexion and Bihari accent would help someone associate him with one of the tribal communities of Jharkhand. He sat down and greeted Hossain and Chopra. Both remained standing, while others were instructed by a clerk assisting the judge to sit down.

'It is just one case I am hearing today, right?' the judge asked the clerk. The clerk nodded and passed on a document to the judge to look at.

'Yes, Mr Hossain, please tell me.'

'Your honour, this is a sensitive case being pursued by ED, the CBI, the cybercrime cell of Delhi Police and Interpol. We have made a major breakthrough and arrested a key member of the gang. ED seeks fifteen days of custody under Section 167 of CrPC for questioning the accused,' Hossain said.

'Interpol?' the judge asked and looked at Gandhi Kumar.

'Yes, your honour. This case involves an organized crime group that is largely based in India but has committed fraud across eighteen jurisdictions, including the US, Canada, Austria, Australia and France,' Hossain said.

'Yes, defence. What do you have to say about this?' the judge asked Chopra.

Chopra said, 'My lord, my client has been wronged and humiliated in the worst possible way without any fault of his. My client is not part of any organized criminal group, nor does the prosecution have any evidence to prove this.

They are desperate to pin the blame of a series of extortions on someone, and they have found a convenient scapegoat in my client. There is no case for remand, so I plead you to grant bail,' Chopra said.

'We have hard evidence, your honour,' Hossain said. 'This group typically approaches a victim through social media and Telegram and encourages them to install a gaming application on their mobile phone. The gaming application—'

The judge cut him short and asked, 'Do we have to get into the facts now? Can you explain what ED's allegations against the accused are?'

'We can conclude the case based on the prosecution's conclusions, your honour. It is in the paper book shared with you and the defence,' Hossain said.

'I beg to differ, my lord. This is a complex case and involves mistaken identity. I plead with your good self to hear the facts of the case briefly,' Chopra said. The judge impatiently shook his head and indicated to Hossain to continue.

'Your honour, this case involves multiple instances of sextortion, and one serious theft of privileged and private data. A hacker gang by the name of Null Cyphers has developed mobile applications that can be used to collect confidential data from mobile phones. This gang approaches victims through social media and Telegram groups and encourages them to install gaming apps with an enticement to make huge profits by playing free games. Once the victim installs the app, the app collects photographs, videos and chat messages, as well as phone contacts, from the mobile phone and sends them to Null Cyphers. The gang then scours the data for compromising photos, videos and chats. They use this information to blackmail the victim and extort money from them.

'When a victim cannot pay the amount demanded by the group, they leak the compromising data on the internet and also forward it to the victim's contacts. If the victim is married but mobile messages hint at adultery, they leak the information to the victim's spouse as well. All of their victims are located in Western countries. Interpol has reported that at least one victim has committed suicide due to shame after Null Cyphers released their nude photographs on the internet. They receive payment in bitcoins, due to which it is difficult to freeze these funds. Recently, the group seized sensitive data in a government-run healthcare facility in India.

'If your honour turns to exhibit 2, this is a report by ED's analyst on the movement of bitcoins received from such cyber-enabled fraud. The analyst has painfully retraced how funds have moved in bitcoins across wallets. The analyst has found that a small fraction of the bitcoins were sold at KuberX, a cryptocurrency exchange, and the consideration for the same was withdrawn in cash. Exhibit 4, your honour, is the statement of the chief compliance officer of KuberX. It corroborates the analyst's version.'

The judge flipped through the paper book with furrowed brows and a puzzled look and asked, 'Has KuberX corroborated that the fraction of a bitcoin sold on its platform is the proceeds of the crime you allege?'

'No, your honour. It does not have to corroborate that part. All transactions in Bitcoin happen on a blockchain. Null Cyphers provides the victim with a wallet address and instructs the victim to send money in bitcoins to that wallet. Once the money is deposited in that wallet, Null Cyphers moves the money across layers of private wallets. All these wallets, all the transactions are recorded and cannot be manipulated. The records are publicly accessible on the internet. So they do not need any corroboration. KuberX only corroborates the exchange between cryptocurrency and cash. KuberX also confirms that the accused has an account in KuberX, which was used to effect the exchange.

'Now, if we move to exhibit 7, this is a copy of the *panchnama* drawn during search and seizure proceedings at the accused's office. Annexure 3 to the *panchnama* is a forensic report of the accused's office desktop. It lays out multiple pieces of evidence to link the accused to the movement of stolen funds in bitcoins across wallets. Annexures 5, 6 and 7 of the same *panchnama* are statements under oath of office staff, who state that only Gandhi Kumar accesses and uses the desktop.

'Your honour, the evidence is clear and incriminating. This is an important case having cross-border ramifications and national security implications. It is important to bust the entire criminal network, for which we need custody.'

'Seems quite technical,' the judge quipped.

'Over and above this, we have managed to find part of the proceeds of the crime at his residence during the search and seizure operation yesterday, totalling 3 crore rupees. He has admitted in a statement under oath that this money is unaccounted.

'Your honour, this is a sophisticated gang of criminals and hackers. Those who write codes to develop apps to steal data to extort people can destroy evidence in seconds. If released, the accused can destroy crucial evidence which my client is still investigating. I rest my case.'

'Okay, defence? The evidence does not look good for you,' the judge said, looking at Chopra.

'My lord, I agree with ED's counsel that this is a serious and complex case involving transnational criminal syndicates,'

Chopra started. Then, with a frown, he continued, 'There may also be a national security angle … owing to which I am seriously concerned about the incompetent and casual way in which ED has built its case. ED has no case, and instead of going after the perpetrators, they have victimized a responsible member of our community.

'My lord, my client Dr N. Gandhi Kumar is a paediatrician based in New Delhi. He is also involved in philanthropic activities. He and his spouse are actively involved in social activities in the Hauz Khas area where they reside with their children. He has no history of any criminal activity and rather has a strong and impeccable record of community service. Having said that, he is a busy man; he works in a hospital and also runs a clinic from which he makes substantial profits. His high ratings on the Practo app are proof of his professional excellence. He makes good money from his profession but is grounded and maintains a very middle-class lifestyle.

'My lord, ED barged into his house yesterday morning and started a search and seizure operation without following proper procedure. They were required to arrange two independent *pancha*s to witness the proceedings. But they had brought *pancha*s with them. The *pancha*s were part of the raid team that mounted the search and seizure operation! One of them is an employee in a bank being investigated by ED for money laundering. The other *pancha* is a stenographer in the finance ministry. These are definitely not at arm's length from ED. They are not independent.'

Justice Sushil Kumar shook his head disapprovingly and told Chopra, 'Chopraji, let us not go into procedural infirmities at this stage. You will get your chance to present these to the judge during trial.'

'Definitely, my lord,' Chopra said, and continued, 'I want to briefly address the so-called "evidence" of the learned prosecution counsel briefly. My lord, please refer back to exhibit 7, annexure 3 which is the forensic report of my client's office desktop. Please refer to footnote 8 in this report. This footnote clearly mentions that the computer's telnet was turned on. This is a material fact that has been overlooked by ED because of their lack of competence. My lord, the telnet is a facility that allows anyone to remotely connect with a computer. If the telnet of a computer is on, anyone can use the computer remotely. Everyone knows this. I asked my nephew, who is in class nine, and he too knows this. ED did not care to make any further investigation into this matter. Now, my lord, ED's case is built on the presumption that only Gandhi Kumar had access to the desktop. They are displaying statements of Gandhi Kumar's office staff as evidence. My lord, everyone on the internet had access to the desktop. Their counsel had access to the desktop, I had access to the desktop, even your lordship had access to the desktop.'

Hossain threw a furtive look at Ashwin Jain, who was sitting behind him. Jain shrugged and took out his phone, seemingly to google 'telnet'. The judge sifted through the paper book furtively. Gamini was eagerly studying their body language when the person sitting to her left asked, 'What is this tele-net? Is it telephone over the net?'

Gamini was too involved in the proceedings to be mindful of who was sitting by her side. Senthil was sitting to her right, but she had not paid any attention to the man sitting to her left. She glanced at him momentarily to find a large, muscular man wearing a thick, golden necklace, with short hair and a thick beard, which had greyed at places, and brownish eyes.

'It's telnet … a feature in a computer that allows someone from another computer to remotely access it,' Gamini whispered while closely studying the judge's body language. She wondered if this man was an interested party from the prosecution side, because she and her nephew were the only ones from the defence side in the room.

'So you spell it as T-E-L-N-E-T. Has this angle been investigated?' the judge asked Hossain.

'Your honour, it has been just a day. We are actively making enquiries, but these are highly technical things. It takes time,' Hossain replied.

'But Mr Chopra says even his nephew knows about it. I frankly do not know what it is. The forensic report indeed says that the computer's telnet was turned on. Do you concur with Mr Chopra's claim that anyone can access the computer if the telnet is turned on?' the judge asked.

'It is not appropriate to comment on the accuracy of this statement at this point, your honour. Like your honour, I am not an expert on these matters. We definitely cannot rely on Mr Chopra's nephew. These are highly technical matters. We will discuss this threadbare in trial,' Hossain said.

'It will be a folly for ED to press charges. This case will not stand for fifteen minutes in trial. What I say is common knowledge, and the same can be verified on Google,' Chopra told the judge.

'The court cannot rely on Google, counsel,' the judge said. 'You will have to present your expert witnesses, the prosecution has to present its expert witnesses, there will be cross-examination and all … the court will then arrive at conclusions. ED has collected other corroborative evidence here. So it is not a straightforward case, as I see it.'

'Other pieces of evidence also fall flat, my lord. Once someone else has access to my computer, they have access to my identity documents and email addresses. This cryptocurrency exchange KuberX has lax KYC requirements, which are easy to meet with just the identity documents and an email address. I am presenting defence exhibit 1 which shows the KYC requirements of KuberX,' Chopra said and passed on one copy each of the exhibit to the judge and Hossain.

Chopra continued: 'Stealing KYC is a modus operandi rampantly used by cybercriminals. Even RBI and I4C have acknowledged the risk of stolen KYC. KYC is stolen to create mule accounts and use them to launder money made from cybercrime. The same has happened in this case too. The finance ministry, the parent ministry of ED, has come out with a press release in which it states that it is deliberating over strategies to tackle the menace of mule accounts being used by cybercriminals.'

'But saying that the accused's account with the cryptocurrency exchange could be a mule account is highly speculative at this stage,' the judge said. 'I agree that the prosecution needs time to collate all evidence, but it seems they have some evidence at hand.'

The judge was favourably inclining towards ED. Hossain did not want to miss this opportunity and reminded the court: 'Money laundering is a serious offence, and as Section 24 of the Prevention of Money Laundering Act, 2002, states, the court shall presume guilt unless the contrary is proved. The counsel for the accused has many speculative theories but no concrete evidence to back them.'

'The prosecution also needs to work harder. If this telnet angle is as clear as the defence is arguing, then the prosecution might have made a genuine mistake,' the judge said. The 'presumption of guilty unless proved innocent' is a sensitive issue for judges, and they make efforts not to pamper the prosecution on this maxim. The maxim in criminal law is that an accused is innocent unless proven guilty. The money-laundering law reverses this maxim on its head, shifting the burden of proof permanently on the accused. In a country in which many innocent persons on trial cannot afford lawyer fees, and judges are buried in cases, this reversed maxim increases the risk of miscarriage of justice. Judges could not be less mindful of the moral hazard of this.

'My lord, think about the trauma my client is going through. Think about the unnecessary infamy this action brings on him and his family. An innocent man's liberty is sanctified by the Constitution. It is a fundamental right,' Chopra said.

'I am inclined to rule seven days of ED custody. We will reconvene after that and reconsider the case in light of any new finding,' the judge said.

'Allow me to complete my arguments, my lord. ED custody will expose my client to mortal harm. I request your lordship to please look at my client closely. Look at the bruises. He was beaten up by ED's officers yesterday during the search and seizure action. Arun Kamat, the special director, took him into a room, closed the door behind him, and beat him black and blue. How can you give custody of this innocent being to such cold-blooded transgressors?'

The judge took off his spectacles and looked closely at Gandhi Kumar. Chopra indicated to Gandhi Kumar to come closer to the table, but the policemen were already instinctively trying to pull him back. Hossain opened his mouth to say something, but the judge indicated to him with a finger to keep quiet. Hossain knew best to keep quiet.

'My lord, nothing is mentioned in the *panchnama* about the third-degree torture. In fact, the *panchnama* does not mention Arun Kamat as part of the search team. He just barged in and beat my client. His son, who is just a kid, helplessly heard as Kamat beat his father and he moaned in pain. This is a regular middle-class family of South Delhi. If today it's him, tomorrow it can be any of us,' Chopra said. He realized he was in dramatic form.

'Judicial custody of six days. Ruled,' the judge said.

'My lord, this is a severe breach of liberty. Please reconsider. Even the cash found in my client's house has no connection with cybercrime. It is his income from the clinic he runs in Hauz Khas,' Chopra pleaded.

'It is a sensitive case, and there is enough prima facie evidence. The accused is placed under six days of judicial custody,' the judge said. Then, pointing at Hossain, he continued, 'It is also noted that the paediatrician is a bit of an unusual suspect for cyber fraud. ED should verify this telnet issue before it comes back for extension of custody.' He concluded by folding his hands and went out of the room.

15 Justice Delayed

What transpired in the judge's residence courtroom was difficult for Gamini to fathom. She believed the telnet angle had punctured the entire case built by ED. But surprisingly, the judge needed expert witnesses to verify the angle. Why couldn't the judge just google it? Why did the judge need expert witnesses to depose on such an elementary feature in computers as 'remote sharing'? Why was the judge in such a hurry to conclude the hearing? Was the personal liberty of an innocent person not important enough for him?

'Only six days custody for such an international-level fraudster!' the man sitting to Gamini's left said. He was trying to make conversation, but Gamini was too disoriented. Her eyes welled up as she saw her brother being dragged out of the room in handcuffs. She saw Simrandeep Singh also going out of the room. She rushed after him and introduced herself. Singh had kind eyes and listened to her patiently as she explained how her brother was innocent. He agreed that ED did not have a good case; he had already googled 'telnet' and was convinced that the computer was accessed remotely by the perpetrators. Gamini asked with teary eyes why her brother was not granted bail. Singh shrugged and said, 'Your advocate will be in a better position to explain. This is a serious case, and the judge would not take the risk of giving bail. What if your brother is indeed guilty? If he is let out, he could destroy evidence and influence potential witnesses. The judge would not take it upon himself.'

'I think he was in too much of a hurry,' Gamini said.

'That too. This happens when bail hearings are conducted on a Saturday. But you have a strong case. Keep hope,' Singh said and walked away. After a few steps, he turned back and asked Gamini to meet Brian Leatherman of the FBI and discuss the case with him. He gave an Indian number and asked her to call Leatherman at the number with his reference.

'The FBI is interested in this case. And unlike our agencies, they won't see you with suspicion.'

'Meet this FBI guy where?'

'Wherever you two are comfortable. Go to his office if he asks you to. He will help you.'

'In the United States?'

'No, no, no. Here, in Delhi.'

16 Justice Manipulated

Arun Kamat brought a lit cigarette to his lips and inhaled deeply while intently studying a report. As he exhaled, a thick plume of smoke billowed and spread around his office chamber. Ashwin Jain, who was sitting across from him, ducked as some of the smoke floated towards him. Kamat's was a spacious office, with walls adorned by the many commendations and certificates he had received from the government and international organizations over the years. Kamat was sitting on a high-backed leather chair behind a large, solid oak desk. Stacks of files and papers on his desk were meticulously arranged.

'So, what is your view about this garbage?' Kamat asked Jain, casually throwing the report on the desk.

'This does not look good,' Jain said. It was a new report prepared by a second computer forensics team that was sent to Gandhi Kumar's office to further analyse his office desktop. The new forensics team had analysed system logs and had come to the conclusion that Gandhi Kumar's desktop had been accessed remotely using the telnet facility multiple times over the last three months. It was accessed remotely on the day Gandhi Kumar allegedly opened an account with KuberX. It was also accessed remotely on the day he allegedly sold bitcoins on KuberX and encashed the money.

'Of course it does not. Why were you in a hurry to send the forensics team?'

'But this was the court's direction. A second bail hearing is scheduled for this Friday, so we had no choice in the matter,' Jain said.

'Where is your enterprise here?' Kamat asked.

'Sorry? I did not get you, sir,' Jain said.

'After the search ended, the computer was placed under prohibitory order. If the forensics team found something that weakens our case, you should have shooed them away and formatted the desktop. And then, the only thing we had to do was file a case against unknown saboteurs who destroyed the computer's contents while it was placed under prohibitory order.'

'I … um … I understand your methods, sir. I have heard about them. But what if the accused is innocent? What is the harm in admitting a mistake?'

'What is my method? Go ahead, tell me what my method is?'

Jain remained silent. After a short, theatrical pause, Kamat continued, 'I am decisive. I do not dwell in self-doubt. I do not dilly-dally or dither. It is clear that Gandhi Kumar is involved in the BIMS ransomware attack. He has moved money around in cryptocurrencies. He has encashed the money from a crypto exchange. There is a neat money trail. Cash was also found at his residence. Now his advocate is trying to nullify all the evidence on technical grounds, and you are falling into his trap. The report says that the telnet facility was off under the desktop's default settings. Someone turned it on. Who turned it on? Gandhi Kumar must have done it. He might be accessing his desktop from another place, for all we know … for his convenience maybe. His advocate is trying to plant seeds of suspicion on the clear evidence we have. We need to counter it. But if my team only gets mired in self-doubt, how do we prove our case?'

Jain was listening to Kamat with pursed lips. He made an attempt to explain his viewpoint: 'The report mentions the IP addresses from which Gandhi Kumar's desktop was remotely accessed. The next logical step is to—'

'Don't lecture me on the next logical step,' Kamat said in a raised voice. 'You have already done enough damage by conducting this second forensic audit of the desktop. Try to understand, Ashwin, you are not here to dispense justice or arbitrate over the law. Justice and the law are two very complex concepts, but they do not concern us. Courts arbitrate over laws. Only God, the Almighty, dispenses justice. The court has its dharma, God has His dharma. What is your dharma? What is our duty? To build evidence that can help the agency win cases in the courtroom.

'You have been in this game for too long, and I do not have to lecture you. You have seen how we have lost cases on flimsy grounds, mere technicalities. Witnesses turn hostile all the time. All this happens because investigating officers become obsessed with "logical steps" and SOPs and forget their core responsibility: to build an airtight case. Now take your report and get out. I will ask Satyasai to assist you on this case.'

Satyasai was Kamat's man Friday, a second-rate investigator with high ambitions, which he met to some extent by doing Kamat's dirty job. It was unusual and controversial to remove an investigating officer abruptly and could raise eyebrows; Jain understood well that bringing in Satyasai to 'assist' him was an easy way of elbowing him out of the case. But he did not appear offended or disturbed by Kamat's proposition. If at all, a sense of relief escaped from his poker-faced expression. He collected the report and went out of the room. Kamat pressed a buzzer, upon which a peon entered the room. He instructed the peon to inform

Satyasai Behera to meet him. Then he fidgeted with his smartphone, browsing through messages he had received.

A girl by the name of Lily had sent a close-up photograph of her bosoms on Telegram. Kamat eagerly clicked on it and salivated over the photo. A pink 34-C size bra tightly held her bosoms. Lily had also sent a message: 'Tel me how u lik it.' Kamat wrote back, 'I absolutely like them … want to lick them.' Lily was online and instantly sent a heart emoji after reading his message. Kamat again wrote, 'Nah, I want to eat them … chew them … so beautiful, so sexy.'

Kamat had recently met Lily virtually, quite by chance. He had joined a Telegram group in which the administrators shared stock-market tips. Lily directly connected with him to reply to a query he had posted in the group. One chat led to another, and before long they were hooked to each other. Although they had met over Telegram just two days back, they chatted without inhibition, like they had been lovers for years. Lily had got married two years ago to a real estate agent in Bengaluru but was not happy in the relationship. She was game for a little bit of amour. Kamat had been married for thirty years (or was it thirty-one?) now and had been through multiple affairs and hook-ups on the side.

Lily: Want to feel ur mouth on my nipples.

Kamat: Send me a photo of your nipples. I want to know what I am missing.

Lily: No hurry tyger, all of me in good tym.

Lily: My mother-in-law botherin … will snap a pic in the toilet in a while.

Kamat: Come on a video call.

Lily: On one condition … u show me whatever I ask when we get on a call.

Kamat: With pleasure my baby … what will you show?

Lily: All of me … show u how lucky u r.

Kamat: I will get lucky for real when we meet.

Lily: Yes in good tym … my mother-in-law going back in three weeks.

Lily: Good to get rid … horrible woman she is … let's plan a meet after that.

Kamat: Look forward. I can't wait to grill my dick deep inside your mouth.

Lily sent a lips emoji. Kamat replied by sending a pumping heart emoji.

Lily: Send me a pic of urs.

Kamat: How do you want it?

Lily: How it pleases u, surprise me … I don't like clothes ☺

Kamat: Ha ha … want to see what you are getting?

Lily: So, I can better fantasy u till we meet.

Kamat: I am in the office and a meeting is coming up. Promise I will send you a good one soon.

Lily: All gud in ofc?

Kamat: Yes, just a bit of setback. You remember the case I mentioned … the IO has messed up … nothing I cannot handle but will need to give more attention to the case.

Lily: IO?

Kamat: Investigating Officer—the officer assigned to collect evidence. He is useless. I am assigning another IO to the case.

Lily: Hope he hs not dun much damage 2 my babu.

Kamat: Ha ha, no. That cybercriminal we caught last week is devious.

Kamat: Our key evidence was his computer … bastard had accessed his computer remotely from different IPs at different times—now his advocate is saying it could have been accessed by anyone ... so the digital evidence does not implicate him.

Lily: So, what did the IO do?

Kamat: The idiot took some experts to verify this … now the experts have a document confirming that the computer was accessed remotely.

Lily: So stupid of him.

Kamat: It is as if the IO is working for the criminal.

Lily: The case is important 4 u na?

Kamat: Yes, it's a high-profile case … multiple agencies are working on it … my prestige is on the line here.

Lily: Do not worry babu, everything will b alrite.

Kamat sent Lily an emoji while Satyasai Behera entered the room. He quickly messaged her that his meeting was starting, and he would chat later.

Behera wished Kamat a good afternoon and took a seat. A lean man with a wheatish complexion, he looked taller than he was because of his skinny build. He had joined ED at the bottom ranks as an assistant enforcement officer and was now a deputy director with more than six years of service left. Kamat and Behera had worked together on many cases, and the duo had successfully prosecuted a number of money-laundering matters. Behera now handled the Overseas Intelligence Unit (OIU), due to which he did not actively operate as an IO. But Kamat was eager to have him in the driver's seat of this case.

'I have told Ashwin that you will work with him on this case,' Kamat said.

'May not be wise, sir. This is a high-profile case; Ashwin may not like me taking over the case now. There will be unnecessary resentment among other officers,' Behera said.

'Ashwin is an idiot,' Kamat said sternly, without hiding his frustration.

'But he is respected for being technical and methodical. Everyone, including the director, praises him,' Behera said.

'All that adulation will not help me conclude cases. Once I am the director, I will throw him away in Guwahati. If there is any office east of Guwahati or on the Myanmar border, I will send him there. He is not fit for this job,' Kamat spewed.

He continued: 'Make a shadow file of the BIMS ransomware case and read it from end to end. I am sure Ashwin has missed some finer details. Go to Tihar Jail and interview Gandhi afresh. I wish we were given custody … I would have broken his back to make him talk. But now that he is in Tihar, the best we can do is interrogate him under CCTV. We need leads. We have reached a dead end. Without leads, maybe the court will not extend his custody. Find his accomplices. Or just one accomplice. You get me?'

Behera thoughtfully shook his head and asked, 'Could Ashwin not extract any lead from the subject during the search?'

Kamat shook his head and said, 'See! He is this inefficient. He did not even interrogate the Gandhi fellow properly. I went to the search premises in the evening and found Gandhi untouched. I took him to a room and tried to extract names from him, but his wife created a hue and cry. Ashwin should have asked a female constable to take her to another room and keep her under pressure. But he was merrily watching the scene.'

Behera said, 'In Tihar, his advocate must be meeting him daily. He must have brainwashed Gandhi enough by now. And to top it, we cannot touch him there. My only recourse is to coax him to turn approver. But for that, I will need some leverage. Do we have anything we can use against him?'

Kamat laughed devilishly and said, 'The bugger was banging a nurse in his clinic. Many photos and videos of their intimacy were found on the nurse's phone. You can check them out. I had shown them to his wife during the search ... you should have seen the shock on her face. And how scared Gandhi was when I showed the photos to her.'

'It will do more damage to his relationships and his reputation if the photos get leaked to the media. I can work with that,' Behera said with a sly smile.

'Ha-ha-ha! I knew I could count on you,' Kamat said.

After Behera left, Kamat messaged Lily that a surprise was coming her way. Then he sneakily bolted his room from inside, removed his shirt and took down his trousers. He snapped a selfie on the phone and looked at it. His bear-belly and man-boobs were prominently visible in the picture; he deleted it and tried to find a suitable pose that would hide the bigness of these appendages.

17 The Gambler's Last Bet

Pooja roughly shook Sunil awake and said in a Haryanvi dialect of Hindi, 'There are people looking for you. They seem like troublemakers. Why have you given them my address?'

Pooja was her business name, not her real one. She lived in a tiny, one-room shanty of about 50 square feet. The bare space held only one piece of furniture: a charpoy, where Sunil lay in just his undergarment. In one corner, a small iron stool supported a cooker. On one side of the stool, a modest number of steel utensils were neatly stacked, while a plastic water container stood on the other. Pooja shared a common washroom with others in the lane. A jute basket in another corner held her clothes. A mirror was nailed to one wall, with a panel below it containing a sachet of perfume, a pack of cosmetic powder and a lipstick.

It was a Wednesday morning, but just like any weekend for someone like Sunil who only loafed around. He woke up bewildered and looked out of the window. He immediately recognized the debt collectors and swore at his luck. He looked around the room in panic. There wasn't much to take in. He went to the door and peeked out. The room was on the third floor of a shanty establishment. A delicately placed iron staircase that protruded out of the door was the only way up and down. One of the debt collectors was standing on the staircase midway between the second and third floors.

To be clear, such situations were not novel for Sunil. He owed money to half a dozen gambling dens in North Delhi, including one run by the Chelu Pehelwan gang, and another in the Sabzi Mandi area managed by drug traffickers. He owed lakhs to two escort girls based in Gurgaon, whom he had hired one night by paying 2 lakh rupees upfront. That was a time when he had good money on him, but he retained their services way past the date on which he lost all of it in a casino. Now their pimp was after him for recovery.

After being driven to penury, which was not new for him, he recalibrated his standards and started frequenting this lane of commercial sex workers in the Narela–Bawana industrial area. Although the services were much cheaper, he ran into debt here too; to Neha two houses down the lane from Pooja's house, and to Phool who had a room on the first floor in one corner of the lane. He also owed Pooja, who charged just 300 rupees by the hour. He first gave a laptop as security for postponing payment for her services. When Pooja realized that his outstanding fees had exceeded 10,000 rupees, she took a hard disk as well. Neha and Phool did not see any value in these goods, and kept chasing him to pay off his debts. He also owed money to a few labourers in the Narela–Bawana industrial area, who had loaned him small amounts on the promise of 30 per cent returns per month. Suffice it to say, he was going through a streak of bad luck.

'Eee, Pooja, these are bad people. Really bad people. I had taken a line of credit in a casino … eee in Shahdara but lost all games. I told them I would win back the money next time, but they have still sent these debt collectors after me. I need to run, but I need your help—'

'What help? Why should I help you? You come like a slippery snake every night, take my services, and pay nothing. NOTHING. Only sweet promises. I had to turn down two customers last night because you were writhing on my bed.'

Sunil appeased her and pleaded with her to speak in a low voice.

'And now you bring these ruffians to my doorstep. Am I running a business here or a dharamshala?' Pooja implored in a low voice but with grimacing eyes.

'Trust me, Pooja, I did not tell them. They have been chasing me for some time now. Someone might have pointed them to the lane, and Neha or Phool has ratted me out.'

'Whatever. Such squabbles between customers are not good for my business.'

'Tell you what, Pooja, how much do I owe you?'

'Eighteen thousand rupees.'

'What if I pay you … eee a tip of 50,000, eh? Eighteen thousand and 50,000, a total of 68,000 within a month.'

'Wah! And where will you get this money from? By taking another line of credit at another casino?'

Pooja did not appear convinced by Sunil's promises, but he needed her help to get out of the situation. So, he told her the one thing he was not supposed to tell anyone.

'No, Pooja, I will get the money from my own capital. My colleagues and I have earned hundreds of crores of money. All of that is stuck on the internet. When my boss encashes this money, I will get a share. My share will run into crores. When I get that, I will pay you one lakh rupees.'

Being an illiterate girl, Pooja did not quite understand what Sunil said and was unsure whether to believe him. It was news to her that he even worked. Sunil slyly decided to up the stakes and promised: 'You know, Pooja, how much I love you. I can pay for your services, but I cannot pay for all the love you have showered on me. When I get this money, we can go on a vacation … to Shimla in the north or Munnar in the south … to celebrate our love.'

Pooja realized that she had nothing to lose even if Sunil's promises turned out to be false, but she wanted to make the best out of the situation. So, she demanded more collateral. Sunil handed her his backpack, cunningly calculating that it would be better to keep the backpack at her place rather than run around with it. Pooja rummaged through it and was disappointed.

'Only electronic items? Why do you need so many?'

'There is a laptop, four hard drives, my networking equipment and three smartphones. All in all, worth more than 10 lakh rupees. Please do not touch anything in there. This is collateral till I come back with the money. Now please help me, ehh. Shoo away these debt collectors,' Sunil pleaded.

Pooja swung into action. She unlatched the door to her room and went out. She shouted at the debt collectors for disturbing her customer and her business, adding a few colourful expletives.

'We are not concerned with your business, sister. We just need to have a word with Sunil Dang,' shouted a burly man from downstairs.

'Who Dang? There is no Dang here. I live here, Pooja Jhajjar-*wali*. And I am with my regular client, whose privacy you are intruding on.'

'We know Dang is in there,' said the burly man.

'How do you know? Is there a camera that you have seen?'

'Just let us have a look into your room.'

'And lose my client forever! It's a policy of this *basti* to maintain the privacy of customers. We are public women, but our clients are private men.'

A few other women who had lazily come out to watch the commotion nodded their heads in agreement.

'Look, it will cost you. This customer will not return if you breach his privacy. The price is 1 lakh rupees upfront.'

The debt collectors looked at each other and whispered about the offer. Behind Pooja, Sunil was in a panic. He swore at Pooja for trying to double-cross him.

'Either pay up or check Neha's place. She has a regular customer by the name of Sunil,' Pooja said.

'Which room?' the burly man asked. Pooja pointed at a hovel on the second floor at the end of the lane. The burly man nodded at his men and moved towards the dwelling. The man standing on the staircase alighted and walked behind them. This was the chance Sunil was looking for. He hurriedly put on his jeans and T-shirt, grabbed his phone and tried to give a goodbye kiss to Pooja, which she resisted.

'No more services till you pay up,' she said.

'Will pay up soon, my love. Never forget what I keep telling you. There is no true love, but there are true lovers. I am a true lover, and I will do justice in my love to you.'

Sunil kissed her again, and Pooja did not resist this time. Encouraged, he smothered his face against her blouse and tried to unbutton it. Pooja pushed him away and said, 'Have you already forgotten that the debt collectors are here? They will check the other room and come back here. Now buzz off.'

Sunil tiptoed down the stairs. He was almost at the road when one of the debt collectors saw him and alerted the others. While they gave chase, he swiftly ran out of the red-light area into the marketplace, which was busy and unorderly. It was easy to lose the debt collectors here; Sunil entered a workshop for bicycle parts, slipped out from the other side, and slithered through the crowded market lane to Littu's beauty parlour for men. Once in there, he realized that he owed Littu as well. But Littu had seen him by now.

'No customer yet?' Sunil asked Littu, while spreading himself on a bench that was meant for waiting customers. Littu did not answer and kept cleaning his parlour. Sunil looked at himself in the mirror and wondered if he needed a cut. He had unkempt hair and a thick beard, giving off a somewhat dishevelled vibe. Although he had a thin build and was just thirty-five years old, he looked much older. Streaks of white hair in his beard and hair added to his aged look, and unruly hair sprouting from his nose and ears added to the scruffiness.

'What about giving me a cut? Can you give me a Virat Kohli look? These days most boys are copying his hairstyle,' Sunil said, trying to make conversation. Littu had fitted a 20-inch television on top of his parlour mirror, which was airing news on the New Bharat channel. He increased the volume and went back to cleaning the parlour. The channel was broadcasting a special report on the Russian invasion of Ukraine. Sunil loved such news and quickly became engrossed in it.

After he was done with the cleaning, Littu pulled up a chair and sat across from Sunil. He looked intently at Sunil and asked when he would pay him back.

'Very soon, my friend,' Sunil said and went back to watching the news.

'How soon? When? Which date? What time?' Littu demanded.

'It's difficult to say an exact date and time. That is not how the casino business works. You have bad luck sometimes, good luck sometimes. Bad luck is followed by good luck, and good luck is followed by bad luck. I have been going through bad luck for a long time. Good luck will soon grace me, by the wishes of Laxmi. And when it does, I will make millions—like last time Laxmi blessed me, and like the time before then, and like the time before then. When I get good luck, I first pay off my debts. You know that.'

'But what if good luck does not come this time? What if you have run out of good luck?'

'I cannot, because I am lucky. I can run out of bad luck, which if you think about it is not a bad thing, but I will not run out of good luck. I have gone bankrupt many times in the past. But you have seen how I always rise like a phoenix. It's because of two things: good luck and my skill at sensing good luck. One time, I entered a casino with just a 100-rupee note and left with 10,000 rupees. I went into another casino with this money and left with 5 lakh rupees. The very next day, I made 30 lakh rupees. That's my superpower. I can generate wealth a thousand times over with just a 100-rupee note.'

'And then destroy the wealth too,' Littu sighed. 'Tell me, why should I be married to your luck? I did not ask for it. I had given a simple loan because you said you needed it and expected only a repayment with interest. You blew the loan on gambling, booze and women, and have forced me to wait for your good luck to dawn. Why should I take the downside of your splurges?'

'Because I will pay you a premium. I will return the principal to you with a 50 per cent per annum interest. Happy?'

Undecided on how to react to that, Littu went back to cleaning cosmetics bottles on his parlour table. Sunil's attention went towards the TV, which was now telecasting a feature on the Null Cyphers cyber scam case. Sunil took a keen interest in this news and eagerly followed all reports on Gandhi Kumar's arrest. It was a special telecast by New Bharat to make a new exposé. Sunil gleefully pointed Littu towards Gandhi Kumar's face on the screen and said, 'This bastard's good luck has run out. See, he owned a big house in a big, posh locality. He drove a big car, and his children went to big schools. Then he dared to rub Shani Dev the wrong way. Now see what has happened to him!'

'As God of the planet Saturn, Shani Dev dislikes gamblers the most. You sure you are not in His bad books?' Littu asked.

Sunil laughed ecstatically and said with dramatic effect, 'I have Shani Dev's favours. Do you know why? Because I am Shani! I aaaam Shanee.'

After a sensational introduction to Gandhi Kumar, his family, his home, his clinic and his hospital, the anchor talked about the exposé of the day. He explained how multifaceted and complex Gandhi Kumar was. Running a cybercrime racket was not the only thing he did clandestinely; he had also had an affair with his nurse, Ananya Dang. Then the anchor flashed photographs of Gandhi Kumar with Ananya, and some photographs of Ananya with her estranged husband, which they had found from the husband's Facebook album.

Sunil's expression suddenly changed. His face turned pale, and he started trembling. He murmured to himself and dashed out of the parlour.

18 Cybercrime, Cryptos and Cyphers

It is widely believed that there are more *crorepatis* in Delhi than the number as per tax records for all of India. Nobody really knows how many rich people there are in the city. Or in all of India. In the affluent residential colonies of South Delhi, each three-bedroom builder floor commands a staggering price of 4 crore rupees, underscoring the absurd demand for residence in colonies where cars are parked on the roadside, lanes are narrow, and colony markets are old and dilapidated. Meanwhile, the charm of old bungalows in West Delhi's Patel Nagar carries an even heftier price tag, with properties valued at over 20 crore rupees. Over in Gurgaon, the allure of luxury apartments does not wane, as units priced upwards of 6 crore rupees are snapped up on the day they hit the market, reflecting the relentless appetite for high-end habitat. Despite the city's outwardly disordered and chaotic facade, Delhi is a bastion of wealth. The mechanisms of wealth generation here might seem enigmatic to the uninitiated, yet there are those who know where and how money is being made at any given moment.

An insider can, for instance, tell us how to find people with easy money. One of the simplest ways is to go peddling in shady dance bars on the Mall Road in Gurgaon. As dusk falls, numerous malls on this road come alive with a symphony of music emanating from the dance bars perched on their upper floors. Smartly dressed women from nearby villages as well as from as far as Central Asian countries shake their hips, bounce in their steps and spin energetically, creating an infectious atmosphere of joy and camaraderie. The class of people who tip the most are the ones with easy money. And this class keeps changing with the times. Back in 2013, lobbyists were the ones wading through the dance floor with wads of notes. They would often host extravagant parties for lascivious bureaucrats in these bars. The pulsing lights and rhythmic beats did not stop at the height of demonetization in end-2016, although the lobbyists had run out of money. The new patrons with easy money were the touts who converted old notes into new notes.

By 2023, the profile of such patrons had changed drastically. With rising transparency and monitoring of bureaucrats' conduct, avenues for lobbyists to make money had reduced. The new patrons with easy money were smart, young men who tossed fistfuls of notes into the air, aiming them at the women sharing the dance floor. As the notes fluttered down, some of them would fall in love with a woman. Bar managers were never happier, for the wild abandon and youthful energy meant more tips. These youths seemed to have an unlimited supply of money to tip. Over time, they confided in the dancers that they made the money by running call centres.

These were not normal call centres. They mushroomed in the National Capital Region around Delhi with the advent of Voice over Internet Protocol (VoIP) technology.

VoIP technology allows people to make voice calls using internet connections rather than a regular phone line. It is difficult to trace encrypted calls made using VoIP. VoIP also eases the process of making international calls. The tech facilitated call centres operated by criminals to phone victims outside Indian borders and defraud them. They would typically pretend to be officers of Europol or the FBI or the Internal Revenue Service of the US and convince the victim to pay them. In the initial days, the payment went to a local bank account in the victim's country, from which it was repatriated to India. Interpol and LEAs took some time to cope with this kind of cross-border cybercrime. There were many victims, but each victim was defrauded of small amounts. The investigation process was especially challenging: LEAs could not trace the source of such calls, so they had to track where the money went; then they requested cooperation from the local police in India. But they learnt fast. The US government sent an FBI officer to its embassy in New Delhi, exclusively to liaise with police cyber cells across the country.

Just when the LEAs thought they had caught up with the criminal call centres in India, new ones—more difficult to trace—cropped up. Their rise coincided with the increased adoption of cryptocurrencies. They convinced victims to pay in bitcoins to virtual wallets. It is much easier to move bitcoins pseudonymously across borders than money. The LEAs had still not developed the capacity to investigate cryptocurrency transactions. While they learnt the ropes, call centres in India thrived and profiteered. Dance bars too. A high degree of specialization developed, as call centres started focusing on specific types of cybercrime: sextortion, loan apps, investment promotion apps, digital arrest fraud, push payment fraud, etc. These call centres had cropped up in many parts of the country, but principally in Delhi and its satellite cities.

Interpol identified three major hubs from which spiking trends in cybercrime were detected with each new technological innovation: Brasilia, slave enclaves in Myanmar and Cambodia, and New Delhi. It assigned additional analysts to each of the hubs to keep a watch over the ever-changing modus operandi of these fraudsters. Brasilia specialized in developing banking trojans, malicious software that could collect online banking credentials from infected computers. These credentials were then used to transfer money from victims' accounts. Slave enclaves partnered with human traffickers to kidnap people from remote parts of South and Southeast Asia, imprison them in these enclaves and force them to engage in phone scams, what is also called vishing.

Delhi-based scammers were known for using a variety of ingenious methods. They were the earliest adopters of technology. As artificial intelligence (AI) tools proliferated, Delhi-based fraudsters were the first to utilize them. For instance, they used text-to-speech AI tools to make phishing calls all over the world. A potential victim in Austria would receive a WhatsApp call from Europol. The caller would converse in chaste German. The voice on the other side was actually an AI bot which converted the scammer's typed text in Hindi into German speech. The same bot would interpret the victim's conversation and type it out in Hindi for the scammer. Using AI tools, a single scammer could converse with and scam multiple victims at the same time. These tools increased the scammers' total factor productivity (economist's jargon for efficiency).

While there are many desi call centre gangs pestering Interpol and LEAs around the world, there is this one gang which has repeatedly surprised investigators by using a heady mixture of hacking tools, AI bots, cryptocurrencies and routine programming. They have floated a range of gaming applications as fronts for collecting user data, and they use this data to blackmail victims and extract a ransom. A victim would install an application on their phone to play a game. But the application would collect all data from the mobile phone and upload these to a server under the scammer's control. We do not realize how much embarrassing and compromising information (chats, downloads, photographs, videos) we have in our mobile phones till someone comes along and blackmails us with such information.

This gang caught the attention of some higher-ups in the FBI when a member of the US House of Representatives installed a new baseball game application on her mobile phone. The phone had compromising photographs of the representative, who was married, with a senator. She eagerly paid up to prevent the fallout of leakage of the photographs on her marriage and her political career. The FBI was keeping an eye on her because she was a member of an important committee on defence matters and handled critically important documents. Her mobile phone had some documents of strategic importance, documents for which espionage networks would pay a handsome amount on the dark web. Although she did not lodge a complaint with the police, the FBI opened a file. The gang had managed to spook the FBI to such an extent that it sent a big team from its cyber division to the US embassy in Delhi. This team was headed by Brian Leatherman.

Leatherman was meeting Gamini at the Blue Door Cafe in Khan Market on a Thursday morning. In his mid-forties, Brian was 6 feet and 2 inches tall. With blue eyes and blonde hair, he stood out in the cafe as a *firangi*. He was in a suit.

Gamini was dressed in a formal white shirt, with her sleeves rolled up, and black trousers.

'Do you generally wear suits in the sweltering heat of Delhi?' Gamini asked after they greeted each other and took a corner table.

'If it were up to me, I would be in a T-shirt and shorts,' Leatherman said with a warm smile. 'But I am scheduled to attend an official lunch later and this is the dress code.'

'I can understand how busy you must be. Thank you for agreeing to meet me,' Gamini said. Even though Simrandeep Singh had asked Gamini to meet Leatherman during the bail hearings, she took some time to get in touch with him. She had not initially seen any value in meeting an embassy attaché in a domestic investigation matter. But ED's investigators were uncooperative and kept her and her counsel in the dark. While the court had directed ED to conduct a fresh forensic analysis of Gandhi Kumar's office desktop, there was radio silence from the investigators on whether they had already complied with the court's directions. A new investigator had joined the team and threatened Gandhi Kumar in jail to sign on a blank page or his compromising photographs with Ananya Dang would find their way to the media. The prospect of public humiliation and disgrace, not only for him but also for Sumathy, whose honour was at stake, prompted Gandhi Kumar to sign on the blank page; but sense prevailed and he consulted Chopra. Chopra counselled him to bide his time till the next hearing by promising the investigator that he was considering the offer. But patience was probably not a virtue of this particular investigator, and compromising photographs of Gandhi Kumar and Ananya were soon leaked out to New Bharat.

The next bail hearing was on Friday and Gamini had no strategy in mind to get her brother out on bail. Ruma, who found out from a report that FBI attachés in US embassies worked closely with the law enforcement of host countries on cross-border crimes, was of the opinion that Leatherman could shed more light on the case.

'Oh, I try to be busy. Not much work, but I have learnt the art of generating work to remain busy,' said Leatherman with a friendly smile.

'You are being modest,' Gamini said, and then went straight to the point: 'You are doing important work here. That's why I have come to you for help. Have you heard about the BIMS ransomware case?'

Brian smiled. 'Kind of. What triggered my posting here in Delhi is a group called Null Cyphers … call it a hacker group or a gang running criminal call centres. After coming here, I have helped apprehend many scamsters, large and small, but Null Cyphers remain elusive.'

'Now I understand why Simrandeep Singh wanted me to talk to you.'

'And I had a chat with him after you phoned me. He told me about your brother's case briefly. And I learnt a bit more from a source. So I am up to date on the case.'

'Quite a bit about the case is out there in the media also. I feel that information is being selectively leaked from the ED office. I don't know if you have followed the leak in New Bharat yesterday morning,' Gamini said. She was referring to the feature in New Bharat's prime time news broadcast, which sensationalized Gandhi Kumar's affair with his nurse. Selfies of Gandhi Kumar and Ananya in a passionate embrace, and screenshots of dirty talk between them were flashed all through the feature. A journalist of New Bharat had literally chased down Ananya while she was out to buy vegetables at a neighbourhood store, asking silly questions.

Gamini and Senthil tried to keep this news from Sumathy, who had been grieving since the raid. They switched off the cable connection to ensure she did not see the news. But it was shared as a video snippet in a WhatsApp group of their local club. Sumathy first trembled, then cried, and then erupted in blind rage.

In the past few days that she had been staying with her brother's family, Gamini had realized how image-conscious Sumathy was and how much she valued her reputation. Gamini was finding her more difficult to manage than the kids. She had some respite when her parents arrived to be with the family. But the public release of Gandhi Kumar's infidelity turned Sumathy's anguish into absolute fury; fury that she directed towards Gamini and her mother. This turned into a vicious war of words between the three women, in which issues ranging from the mundane (such as Sumathy's inability to make a decent sambar curry) to touchy ones (such as Gamini's divorce) to prehistory (such as her mother's greed for dowry during Gandhi Kumar and Sumathy's wedding) were revisited, revised and shot around as poison darts.

The kids were already in a delicate state of mind, and Gamini was worried that all that was happening at the house was increasing the toxicity around them. This was the time for families to come together and cope together, but theirs was unravelling. Benign fissures and cracks were bursting open. Gamini squarely blamed Sumathy for all this, but deep down she knew it was her brother's fault. Or rather of the news channel, or whoever had leaked the photographs to the media.

'It's a Hindi news channel, so I have not followed the original feature … I tried to learn the language when I first came here but have since given up. People I meet officially … they all talk in English, so you know, I could not keep up the motivation to learn the language. But there was some coverage of the news on internet news portals too. I have read those … in my experience, I have not found high standards of professionalism from Indian LEAs. So, I tend to agree with you that there could be selective leakage in this case,' Leatherman said.

'I don't think it's right to generalize professionalism to institutions. To be frank, I consider American police and LEAs to be worse when it comes to professionalism. Police killings of members of the African American community based on prejudices, for example, reek of low standards of professionalism,' Gamini said. Although she was meeting this man for the first time, and she was seeking his help, it did not mean he could make any slighting statement on her country and get away with it. But keeping her focus on the subject at hand, she continued in a penitent tone: 'But professionalism is a debate for another day. My brother is the victim to an unscrupulous officer and not ED per se, an officer by the name of Arun Kamat who is zealously vengeful against my brother, and I do not understand why.'

'I have not met this officer but have heard about him. He has flip-flopped quite a bit. First, he arrested your brother in haste. He genuinely felt he had caught an important member of the gang. Probably he still thinks so. At the time, he wanted to take credit; so, he arranged for a news channel to livestream it when he paraded your brother on the street. During the bail hearing, the court advised the investigating officer to conduct a repeat forensic analysis of your brother's office computer. The investigating officer promptly did that. The second report shows that Gandhi Kumar's computer was accessed multiple times remotely, including on the day the computer was used to sell bitcoins on a cryptocurrency exchange.

'So, the evidence on the computer was a flop. Then he flipped and assigned the case to another officer. This other officer went to Tihar Jail and cajoled your brother to give up the names of his accomplices. I do not know if your brother has told you … he threatened your brother about leaking his affair to the media if he did not give names. My guess is your brother did not acquiesce. And then, behaving in a juvenile manner, this officer leaked private photographs and chats to the media.'

'My brother's lawyer told me as much. Tell me, how do you know so much? I mean, what is the FBI's jurisdiction in India?'

'My job here is to coordinate between headquarters and Indian LEAs. With globalization, you know, systems have become global. But law enforcement is still national. Most serious crimes today are cross-border. To counter them, we need active liaising between LEAs. I liaise with the police … and with your central agencies, the CBI and NIA. My team here at the embassy liaises with the cyber cells of all states and union territories. Over time, I have developed a couple of sources of my own, you know … it's not espionage, just keeping an eye out for the chatter.'

'And what has been your general experience here?'

'Well, India is a vibrant country, and I am liking it here. Work is also good. I have managed to execute a few successful joint operations with the CBI since I came. Having said that, law enforcement can be pretty unpredictable here. In many criminal call centre cases, I have found that the local police station is aware of where they are located and what they do. They operate under the patronage of the local station and probably give protection money too. The local station also tips them off when the police plan a raid. So now in Delhi, cyber cells and special cells have stopped involving the local station in their raid plans. But the police in many other states find it operationally and procedurally challenging to mount raids without involving the local station.

'In some cases, the police are frightened to act because of the involvement of local musclemen. You know, even though they work in call centres, these gangs engage in criminal activity. Gang members need to be recruited and disciplined. If anyone steals from the gang, they have to be punished. So, these gangs usually have two bosses, a local muscleman as CEO and a techie as COO. Sometimes they have a full-time hawala operator for managing stolen money, who would be the CFO.'

Gamini acknowledged the comparison with corporate hierarchies with a smile. 'Interesting work,' she said.

'What about you? What do you do?' Leatherman asked.

'I am a network engineer. I work for a Bengaluru-based cybersecurity firm,' Gamini said.

'So … you are an ethical hacker?'

'I would not say that. The term actually means different things to different people. But yes, I have a technical understanding of hacking. The irony that my elder brother is being accused of hacking is not lost on me. But it also means I understand the issue—at least better than the investigators on the case—and I can help. You know, the court advised ED to do a second forensic study of my brother's office computer because I found from the first forensic report that the computer could be accessed remotely.'

Leatherman appeared impressed. 'And the second report proves his innocence.'

'You told me that the second forensic report found evidence of the computer being used remotely. What have they found?'

'Well, system logs show a whole lot of IP addresses which were used to access the computer. Kamat is not pursuing this lead, so ED's officers have passed on the information to the CBI. Now the CBI is doing diagnostics.'

'Do you have access to the report? Can I analyse the system logs?'

'Null Cyphers is a group we are actively pursuing, and the CBI knows that. So they might have passed on some details from the report to us, but I am not at liberty to tell this to you.'

'Please! My brother's bail hearing is tomorrow … time is of the essence here, and I do not think the CBI has the same sense of urgency as I have,' Gamini pleaded.

'I think ED will have to present the report to the court tomorrow during the bail hearing. I don't see any reason why he won't get bail.'

'If things are so straightforward, why has ED not given me this second report? I didn't even know they had already conducted a second forensic analysis of my brother's desktop. Our lawyer keeps asking them about it, since this is a clear direction the court gave ED, but the officials keep stonewalling him. They are up to some mischief. But forget them. If they present the report to the court tomorrow, as you say, they have to give a copy to the defendant. Which is us. If I get to see the report tomorrow, why is it confidential today?'

Leatherman shrugged and said, 'I don't know really. When the CBI passes on anything to us, it's with an understanding that we do not share it with anyone. See, I want to help. But I think you don't need help. Your brother is definitely coming out tomorrow, and you don't need to see that report today.'

Gamini shook her head and said, 'It is not that simple. You see, I have not been sleeping much these last few days. But one advantage of this is that I am doing some legal research. And asking lots of questions to my advocate. So now I know that getting bail under the money-laundering law is very difficult. Section 45 of the Prevention of Money Laundering Act says that if the public prosecutor opposes a bail application, then the court has to be satisfied that the accused is not guilty of such offence to grant bail. How will the court be satisfied of my brother's innocence only on the basis of a forensic report? The report says that the desktop was accessed remotely. Who gave the access? What is the proof that my brother did not intentionally give access to his desktop to his co-conspirators? This is the argument the prosecution will make. They will try to underplay the report.'

Leatherman pursed his lips and brooded over the issue. Gamini wondered if she was being too forceful with her arguments. After all, Leatherman did not owe her anything. And she needed something from him. She wondered for a moment if she should weave some feminine charm on this stranger she was meeting for the first time. But realizing that it was a witless approach even in her state of desperation, she continued.

'I have studied quite a few court decisions on money laundering in the last few days. Every bail application leads to a chicken-and-egg problem. The money-laundering law does not follow the criminal law maxim of innocent until proven guilty. The court has to be convinced of the accused's innocence to grant bail. The burden of proof is on the accused. And the accused can prove their innocence by showing evidence during trial.

So, the accused has to wait for the trial to conclude to get bail. That means my brother, who is innocent, will be behind bars for long. Unless the investigators do their job and find the real perpetrators, which they are not doing. Or I show the public prosecutor in open court that he is going after the wrong man.'

'Some leads to the real perpetrators will come soon. As I said, the CBI is on it.'

'But the leads will not come soon enough. For the CBI, it is just another case. For me, it's personal. And I bring much expertise to the table. The tools that your headquarters in DC uses for forensics and tracing are all developed in Bengaluru, and I am one of the experts in the Bengaluru cybersecurity community. Large companies have outsourced their cybersecurity to analysts like me. If you are serious about uncovering Null Cyphers, you should use the skills I am offering to you for free. Ultimately, we are looking for the same thing due to different reasons: you need to crack the identity of Null Cyphers, and I need to prove my brother's innocence.'

Leatherman shrugged and said, 'I cannot promise anything now, but let me ponder over this matter. Even if you get access to the report now, it may be too late to present anything tangible in court tomorrow. Plus, you cannot reveal in the court that you already had access to the report.'

'Please think about it. If you choose to trust me, you will not regret it. A day is enough time to make a breakthrough—some breakthrough—and every minute is important if we have to catch Null Cyphers. Never before has this group been as exposed as it is now. And the people behind this group are smart. They may cover their tracks in the precious time we lose.

'One more thing, important intel for you. As you may know, this group had scammed victims all around the world before the BIMS swindle. The cybersecurity community had put alerts on some cold wallets in which they had stored much of the bitcoins they gained from such scams. Very recently, some bitcoins from one of these cold wallets was encashed for a million Seychellois rupees, the currency of Seychelles, in a local exchange in Seychelles. This would be about 60 lakh Indian rupees. But such a large withdrawal in the local currency, and not US dollars, only means that money is intended to be used in Seychelles.'

Gamini pushed an envelope over the table to Leatherman, explaining that it contained all the data he would need to pursue this lead in Seychelles. By the time she left the coffee shop, Gamini was confident that Leatherman would share the findings of the forensic report with her. Americans love a good deal, and Gamini had given him a clear lead on Null Cyphers.

19 A New Lead

Gamini took the violet line metro from Khan Market to Central Secretariat and changed to the yellow line that took her to Hauz Khas. Alighting at Hauz Khas, she strolled along a busy pavement to a weathered wooden stall and bought a pack of mint cigarettes. She lit one and took a deep drag, then strolled over to another vendor standing behind an open cart preparing steaming cups of tea. The vendor aimed his large kettle at small glass cups and poured aromatic milk tea into the cups with practised ease. Gamini took a cup and sat on the stairs going into a shopfront.

Gamini had quit smoking more than three years ago, and no amount of pressure at work had pushed her into a relapse. She did not succumb even when her brother was arrested. But now with the toxic climate at her brother's home, Sumathy's mood swings, the frequent fights between Sumathy and her mother and Anjali's silent cries, things had become overwhelming, and she felt she deserved the cigarette she was smoking. Her father had withdrawn into a cocoon; while he was here to help in theory, he was helpless and clueless. The kids had stopped going to school; while Sumathy worried about their classes, Gamini understood how mean schoolkids could be and so supported their decision to entirely stop going to school for the time being. Senthil, who was a pillar of strength immediately after his father's arrest, was fast withdrawing. In the past few days, Gamini found him glued to his mobile phone all day. Her brother's house was now a house of mourning and eerie silence, interspersed with bouts of Sumathy's frenetic cursing.

To keep her nerves and run the house, Gamini needed a good dose of nicotine, and perhaps a little emotional support. Gamini missed Ruma, her embrace and the way she could easily relax her with just a laugh and a hug. Ruma had offered to fly to Delhi to be with her, but Gamini did not want to pull her into the hurricane. Pulling on the cigarette, Gamini put the teacup aside and took out her smartphone to message Ruma. But she was pleasantly surprised to find a message from Leatherman: 'Check mail … have sent an encrypted file. Password Anonymous.' She had not expected him to make up his mind so soon.

'Thank you, with gratitude,' she messaged back and sent a namaste emoji to Leatherman. 'Your tip on Seychelles is bang on,' Leatherman messaged back.

20 Master of the Trade

Master did not recollect how long he had been living in self-imposed isolation in the dimly lit flat. He had often been patient with this waiting game, experiencing the luxury of time, offering namaz five times a day, and reading books on the first principles of crime investigation. But on this day, he was feeling claustrophobic and dreadful. He sank into a well-worn armchair and fished out a crumpled pack of rolling papers from his pyjamas. He unrolled a sheet and meticulously prepared a joint. He rolled the joint dexterously and sealed it with a final twist. Then he brought it to his lips and lit it.

His den was a 2 BHK flat in Dwarka. After the BIMS heist, he dismantled the call centre and sent the gang away with instructions to lie low till the dust settled. He took up residence in an apartment complex close to the Chand Masjid in Dwarka Sector 7. He had converted the lobby area of his flat into a control room, installing three desktops and two laptops atop a large table of engineered wood, which also doubled up as the dining table.

Master inhaled deeply and exhaled slowly. As the cloud of smoke dissipated, it left an earthy, herbal smell with a stink of charred wood. His eyes, half-lidded and unfocused, reflected the myriad realities he was striving to comprehend. One of these was the way Ross Ulbricht was caught by the FBI. One of the great masters of the cyber world, and perhaps the first, Ross Ulbricht had built the Silk Road in 2011. It was an online marketplace for trading in drugs and other contraband items. Like all great inventors, he had stood on the shoulders of other inventors. He could not have built the online marketplace for trafficking in 2011 if Satoshi Nakamoto had not created Bitcoin in 2009.

The Silk Road could be accessed only through cryptographic software, which made it very difficult to trace its users. A user could buy or sell drugs from other users on the Silk Road. The users remained pseudonymous as all transactions were in bitcoins.

It was such a groundbreaking innovation that in a short period between 2011 and 2013, more than a billion dollars in sales happened through the Silk Road. The FBI and DEA, America's narcotics control agency, tried hard to discover the identity of the Silk Road's promoter, but remained unsuccessful. They spent significant resources on the usual tactics: their technical team invested immense resources in tracking layers of IP addresses; undercover FBI and DEA agents impersonated cartel bosses and peddlers to get close to the promoter. Ulbricht went by the name of Dread Pirate Robbers on the Silk Road. One undercover agent actually managed to make contact as a cartel boss. He engaged with Dread Pirate Robbers, proposing an exclusive marketplace for cartels and godfathers called 'Masters of Silk Road'. But even this undercover agent could not manage to trap Ulbricht.

After months of unsuccessfully trying to nab the founder(s) of the Silk Road, the investigators formed an inter-agency task force to nab them and called it the Strike Force. The Strike Force was fed with the many technical aspects of the investigation. Master smiled as it occurred to him that the technical briefing would have confused the Strike Force's members and would have even overwhelmed some. But one member of this task force was not affected by the deluge of technical details and stuck to the first principles of investigation. This member reasoned that whoever created the Silk Road would have promoted the website on some online forums and communities. Without doing this, how would they attract the first users to the website to trade in drugs? So he searched for the earliest references to the Silk Road, and found a chat room post dating back to early 2011, just before the Silk Road became active. The post read: 'Has anyone seen Silk Road yet? It's kind of like an anonymous Amazon.com.' All that this person did after this was to track the user and find that it was Ross Ulbricht.

This member of the Strike Force was Gary Alford, a tax assessor. What probably worked to his advantage was that he was not as technically competent on cybersecurity as the investigators from the FBI and DEA, and so did not have to unlearn garbage to see things clearly. Master googled Ross on his laptop and looked closely at photographs of the grandmaster. They did not reveal much about the personality of this genius. He was artful and careful, which is why the best investigators of the world hegemon could not nab him. Yet, he slipped and left clues. Master concluded ruefully that howsoever careful you are, someone smart would sniff you out.

Another reality that bothered Master was that he was deeply in love with Fatima. Fatima had come into their family when Master was studying engineering. Master's father was a popular Unani doctor in their chawl but earned just enough to provide a modern English education to his four sons. He had studied for free in a madrassa in Basti but strongly believed that Muslims in India did not get the career opportunities that other communities got because parents undervalued English education. So he spent a large chunk of his salary in paying the fees for his sons' English education. And whatever savings he could muster went in marrying off his daughters.

As he grew old, his father grew resentful and disillusioned. His three elder sons did not get jobs even after getting a mainstream education. Master, who was sharp and disciplined in contrast to his brothers, was confident that he would get a well-paying job upon graduating. He was already getting a scholarship to cover his tuition fees in engineering college. But his father had become disillusioned and lost all hope of moving up the social ladder. He increasingly blamed the system for his sons not getting jobs. He went to bed daily complaining to Mother about how the system was rigged to keep Muslims impoverished, wondering why the formal employment rate of Muslims was lower than that of other communities. One night, he went into a longer than usual diatribe. He slept in utter bitterness, and did not wake up in the morning. Mother kept insisting long after that those who pass away in their sleep have met a peaceful death.

After a long wait and extreme financial distress, during which Master's brothers also worked as manual labour on a construction site, his eldest brother, Fahad, got a job as a technician in a water cooler manufacturing plant near Shahdara. The pay was not great but extended a lifeline to the family and made him eligible for a decent dowry. Fahad married Fatima, and she became a part of the family. Now, Fahad was hot-headed. He was also the presumptive head of the family, now that their father was dead, and became bossy with his brothers and mother. His rule writ large over the house. He would beat Fatima every now and then to demonstrate his status and to instil fear among the others. It was as if he got some kick out of beating her. He would find silly reasons to hit her, with Mother cheering on every successful pummelling session.

All this disturbed Master. He first tried to reason with his mother, but realized she did not really have much persuasiveness with the breadwinner of the family. He was afraid of his eldest brother and so could only simmer in secret anger. His sympathy for Fatima's sorrow and suffering soon led to a sense of connection and emotional intimacy between the two. Whilst Fatima was forbidden from going to the market, Master would go to the Sunday market and get trinkets for her. He would leave his smartphone with Fatima so she could watch videos when his mother was not supervising her. Thinking about it now, Master was not sure when he fell in love with Fatima. Was it before he developed a strong sense of ownership and possessiveness towards her or was it after that? When did he develop disgust towards Fahad for being undeserving of a wife like Fatima? Was it before or after he fell in love with her?

The emotional intimacy turned into physical intimacy, as Fatima responded to Master's intense and passionate advances. They would make love every opportunity they got, when they could steal some privacy in the hovel that housed the four brothers, their mother and Fatima.

Master graduated as the topper in computer engineering in his batch. He received a campus placement in a multinational corporation's software development centre in Gurgaon. The pay was good, and more than the family could have imagined. With money came power, and Master projected this power by asserting himself at home. He stopped Fahad a couple of times when he was in the mood to whip Fatima. This created friction between the brothers, and Fahad objected when Master offered to take a flat in a good locality on rent and move the family. His will still ran large in the family.

But Master had lost all fear of Fahad. He was no longer the sole breadwinner, and his salary was a pittance as compared to that of Master's. He became reckless in his love for Fatima. His mother picked up cues of their intimate relationship, and this broke her. She did not speak about it, but she knew. It was evident from the contemptuous way she looked at both of them. In remaining quiet, she did the most predictable thing: side with the breadwinner.

Sajid, one of his other brothers, once came in unannounced and saw Master and Fatima making love intensely. He looked at them for a moment and left. As Fatima was consumed by shame, Master worried if Sajid would rat on him. Later in the evening, Sajid took Master out for a walk and advised him to leave the house. Gurgaon was far from their chawl, and it only made sense for him to find a flat in Gurgaon. Master did not respond, but he was not ready to leave the house. Not without Fatima.

Master made a proposal to Fatima the next day when they could steal some alone time. He asked her to come with him to Gurgaon. Fatima refused, saying her life was here. He implored her to come with him, for the sake of their love. To which Fatima replied that she had never loved him. She had allowed him physical access to her body as she was scared; she was intimidated by every male member of the family. She was lying, obviously. The fear of a scandal had overwhelmed her. At least this was what Master believed.

That evening, Sajid again took Master out on a walk. He explained to Master that if Fahad came to know about his affair, he might kill Fatima. He implored that if not for his own sake, if not for the sake of the family, Master should leave for Fatima's sake. Master took his advice and relocated to Gurgaon. But his heart remained in the same hovel, with Fatima.

Before leaving, he got a new smartphone for Fatima and made her promise that she would not forget him. They met secretly when they could. He would call the family to Gurgaon and pamper them so that he could be close to Fatima. He sponsored the weddings of his other brothers, but himself never showed any interest in marrying. His mother understood where his heart lay and did not push him to marry.

In late 2019, just before the onset of the COVID-19 pandemic, there was a security breach in his office and proprietary codes were stolen. The company accused Master of perpetrating the theft. Master vehemently denied the allegations, but the police put him behind bars. It was not clear to the police what was stolen, and the company did not want to reveal much to the police. So, the police dropped the case and Master got bail after two months in prison. Master felt that he became the suspect for a crime he did not commit because he was Muslim.

Master met Sandhu in jail—society's unintentional co-working space for delinquents and scamsters. These places are less about rehabilitation and more about networking, where high-risk 'entrepreneurs' armed with rap sheets instead of MBAs come together to brainstorm their next big moves. Jails have perfected the art of criminal upskilling, turning into breeding grounds for sharing 'best practices' in fraud and crime. Many enduring partnerships are forged within these walls, and several of today's most structured and corporate-style organized crime groups trace their origins back to the alliances and blueprints crafted behind bars. It was here that Master and Sandhu discussed ideas that would ultimately result in the Null Cyphers group.

While in prison, Master became enamoured with the idea that this was no country for him to live a life of dignity. And the contours of a dream took shape in his idle mind: a house of his own, with an identity of his discretion, in a country he felt safe in, and enough capital to provide for him and Fatima.

When he met Fatima after coming out of jail, he narrated his dream to her. With money, he explained to her, he could buy new identities and new passports. They could get a new life in a new country where neither family nor country could find them. Fatima promised she would leave with him when Master was ready.

This was the most defining reality of his life, and every action that Master took ever since had been to achieve it. But was this real or just a pipe dream? The more he worked towards achieving this reality, the more he was inching away from it. If he was exposed as the mastermind behind Null Cyphers, would law enforcement ever stop searching for him? Could they ever live an untroubled retired life if his picture flashed in Interpol lookout notices around the world?

Master took a long drag of the joint as he assessed how dangerously close he was to getting busted. And that too because of a series of unfortunate events in less than a week. Just last Friday a paediatrician he had never heard about was arrested as the kingpin of the Null Cyphers group. It was not such bad news, but the reason for his arrest became apparent in court proceedings on Saturday. Apparently, an account with a crypto exchange in his name was used to convert bitcoins into cash in Indian rupees. The bitcoins could be traced back on the blockchain to the ransom payment made by the Indian government to BIMS extortionists. Since the paediatrician was never part of Null Cyphers, someone in Master's team had encashed these bitcoins. Who was it? More importantly, how could someone dare siphon these bitcoins under his nose?

After collecting the ransom from the Indian establishment in the BIMS heist, Master had sent it across thousands of wallets to make it increasingly difficult for LEAs to trace where the bitcoins went. He created elaborate peel chains and routed them through mixers intermittently to make it all the more difficult to trace the bitcoins. After this, end-user wallets were created for each member of Null Cyphers, and their respective share of the loot was transferred to them.

An LEA willing to devote resources to the work could trace some of the wallets in which the ransom money finally landed. To ensure that they did not identify the beneficiaries, Master had instructed all members of the group to lay low for at least a year and not withdraw from the end-user wallets. Many of the people employed by Master at the call centre were deviants and eccentrics—people not known for their sense of discipline. So, Master had placed two checks. First, he threatened them that anyone not complying with the instructions would face Sandhu's wrath—which meant a painful death. Second, he had coded the end-user wallets as multisig wallets, a wallet that needs multiple signatures to be operated upon. In this case, each end-user wallet needed to be validated by any two out of three wallet signatures. One signature was with Master, another with Fatichar the bookkeeper, and the third with the employee whose share of the loot was kept in the wallet.

So, no employee could have withdrawn from their end-user wallet without a validation either from Master or Fatichar. Fatichar was his man, his confidant, and he would not use his wallet signature without informing Master. So, it was bewildering how someone could have operated their wallet and encashed bitcoins.

By the end of Sunday, Master had painstakingly gone through the records of all the wallets they had used to move funds and identified the wallet from which bitcoins were encashed. It was an end-user wallet assigned to Sunil Dang, an employee he had used for maintenance of networking hardware at the call centre. He was not part of the core team that executed the swindle. As such, his was a small share of the ransom. And his end-user wallet was a multisig. Some of the cryptos in this wallet had been transferred to the KuberX crypto exchange, from where they were encashed.

Master messaged Fatichar on Facetime, using their code, a silly rhyme composed by Sandhu:

'We broke the rules and cracked a smile,

Love's our heist—we'll share the pile.'

Fatichar responded in a while by making a video call on Facetime. Fatichar was from the same *basti* in North Delhi as Master and was a couple of years younger than him. Like him, Fatichar was good at his studies and had made it to university to complete a degree in computer applications. Master had recruited him to the call centre business for maintaining accounting records and distributing profits to partners and salaries to employees as per the call centre's HR policy. After the BIMS heist, when everyone dispersed, Fatichar had moved to Agra. Later, Master had sent him to Mauritius and Seychelles to find ways to safely encash the loot of bitcoins they had extorted from the Indian government.

After greetings and wishes for good health, Master came to the point.

'Fatichar, have you been following the news about a doctor in Hauz Khas getting arrested for the BIMS heist?'

'Yes, bhaijaan. I have been. It is intriguing. I was tempted to message you to find out, but you had instructed us not to get in touch unless necessary.' All employees in the call centre called him 'Master' or 'sir'. Only Fatichar took the liberty of calling him bhaijaan, for old time's sake.

'Who do you think he is?'

'I don't know, bhaijaan. He does not work at the call centre. My guess was that you had planned this to divert attention and put the police off our scent.'

'On the contrary, the police have reached the right place. This doctor had an account with KuberX … it's an Indian crypto exchange. Some bitcoins were exchanged for cash at this exchange. Bitcoins that came from Sunil Dang's end-user wallet. Any idea how that could have happened?'

Fatichar's colour changed as he fumbled for words. 'Bhaijaan, I … I had approved a transaction that Dang wanted to make.'

'Are you mad, Fatichar?' Master scowled. 'Is this a child's game we are playing? Our freedom is at stake here. All the employees who worked for us at the call centre can go to jail for life. We cannot make a single mistake. And this was not expected from you.'

Fatichar started by profusely apologizing for his mistake. He acknowledged that he made a mistake, but it was only because Dang badly needed the money. He explained that Dang was a compulsive gambler. He came to Fatichar grovelling, claiming that while gambling he had lost a lot of margin money at a casino owned by a mafioso. This mafioso had a reputation for keeping their word, and they had promised Dang that they would chop off both his hands if he did not pay in a week. Dang pestered Fatichar, saying he just needed to transfer some bitcoins to their private wallet, and it was a matter of life and death.

'Are you an idiot? Will the local mafia of Delhi recover dues in bitcoins? Why did you not report this to me? Why did you forget to ask me, the way you always do?'

'Sorry, bhaijaan. I messed up. It just did not occur to me that this one transfer could be traced by the police …'

'You don't understand, Fatichar. You have put the entire group at risk. How do I protect you if you commit such mistakes? What if Sandhu gets to know about this?'

'Sorry bhaijaan. What, what can I say? I take full responsibility. How can we salvage the situation?'

'No, do not take any responsibility. You don't know how Sandhu will react if he gets to know the extent of risk you have put us in. Let me think about how I present this news to Sandhu. You stay put in Seychelles and complete the job I had given you. Put someone on the job to find Dang … send him to me. I can meet him as soon as tomorrow. The only way they can reach us now is through Dang. We will send him off to Nepal for some time and later improvise on what we should do with him.'

'Ji, bhaijaan. What is the probability that the authorities will reach him?'

'It's slim, if you ask me. But we cannot take any chances. He did a smart thing by routing the cryptocurrencies through a mule account. But we do not know what documentation he submitted to KuberX, or how stealthily he stole this doctor's KYC. Stray characters tend to make mistakes. I only hope he has not made any.'

Master disconnected the call and impatiently waited the whole of Monday to hear from Fatichar. He kept himself busy by profiling the investigators in the Gandhi Kumar case and trying to catfish some of them for information. Scanning various CCTV cameras inside ED's zonal office, he had found many cameras with open ports that could be used to hack into them. This had helped him get a view inside the ED office.

Fatichar's men were unsuccessful in finding Dang till late evening on Monday. Apparently, there were more debt collectors chasing him. So, he was maintaining a low profile. His phone was also switched off. It was a total mess.

On Tuesday, Master got the unfortunate news that ED sleuths had conducted a repeat forensic analysis of Gandhi

Kumar's office desktop and identified many IP addresses used to hack his desktop. Could this information be used to identify Sunil Dang? If so, could ED reach Dang before him? From what he knew about Dang, he would be easy to break if the authorities caught up with him. Fatichar was still unsuccessful in locating Dang, although he got a lead that Dang had been frequenting a red-light area in the Narela–Bawana industrial area. He was confident that he would get hold of Dang the next day.

Wednesday brought more bad news. A news exposé by New Bharat revealed to the whole wide world an extramarital affair between Gandhi Kumar and Sunil Dang's wife. This news feature brought on record a clear link between Gandhi Kumar and Sunil Dang. Now any investigator who came across Dang's name in the course of the investigation would definitely consider him a person of interest. Fatichar phoned to say that Dang had fled in panic. He also informed that Dang had a difficult relationship with his wife. The couple used to fight rabidly, and the wife had finally filed a domestic violence case against him. She had left with his daughter and was living separately for some time now. So, there was a possibility that he might have tried to implicate her lover by stealing his KYC and then opening an account with the stolen KYC to encash the stolen bitcoins.

Master wondered how colossal an idiot Dang was. Who uses a mule account that could be traced back to them? It was a basic principle to use proxies completely unrelated to you for opening mule accounts. The mule had not committed a crime and had no knowledge of the money moved in their name. No one could implicate a mule who had not committed a crime. The investigators would ultimately realize their mistake and look for the real person behind the mule account.

That's why it was important to keep oneself at arm's length from the mule. You didn't make your estranged wife's lover the mule. Once you were linked to the mule account, there was a clear motive that the police could establish in court.

But what was done was done. Now there was no going back. Sunil Dang was a loose end that had to be handled. Master phoned Sandhu and asked him if he had seen the news linking Gandhi Kumar to Dang. He explained to Sandhu how Dang had encashed some of his share of bitcoins, and why he thought Dang was a loose end that could lead the LEAs to Null Cyphers. He made sure he used a casual tone and gave a vibe of being in control and only being abundantly cautious. The last thing he wanted was to worry Sandhu, for he could behave in the most unpredictable ways if he was anxious. Sandhu, nevertheless, spewed expletives about Dang and swore that he would fuck Dang's mother on a cable antenna, and make Dang watch the action live on TV. He promised he would soon dig Dang out of wherever he was hiding and get him fucked in the arse by a sick horse.

'But tell me, Master, how did he remove bitcoins from his wallet? You told us you had placed some control on all wallets so that your or Fatichar's permission is required for removing bitcoins,' Sandhu observed.

'I am looking into it … My guess is, he stole my wallet signature when we were wrapping up, days after the BIMS job … It is just a string of characters, and one can just copy it,' Master lied for Fatichar's sake. They were on Facetime, and Master had no way of knowing if Sandhu was convinced by his explanation.

Sandhu was another reality on which Master needed clarity. He had been a necessary evil; a person he had only disdain for, but one he needed to run the enterprise. Sandhu was temperamental, judgemental and unpredictable. It was foolish for a master of the cyber trade to partner with such a person. But Master needed a muscleman to recruit reliable employees, and to keep them disciplined. He did not need Sandhu anymore; for all he cared Sandhu could take his share of bitcoins and go to hell. But Sandhu saw the closure of the call centre as temporary, and intended to restart operations once matters settled.

Master was also intimidated by his business partner. Sandhu was unscrupulous and could not be trusted. He was a mad dog whose obedience he commanded because he controlled the wallets containing the money. To ensure his smooth exit from Null Cyphers, he was in the process of creating new identities for himself and Fatima. His idea was to use fake Nepali passports to apply for citizenship in Seychelles. Seychelles offered a seamless process to anyone making reasonable investments to attain citizenship of the islands. This 'golden investment' citizenship with appropriate paperwork would legitimize his fake identity and give him an altogether new life. But he worried about the old life. Sandhu would not hesitate to go after his family to get back at him.

Master crushed the joint in an ashtray and concluded that he needed to disappear much earlier than he had planned, and he needed a better plan too. He hoped that like in the case of Ross Ulbricht, the LEAs would keep chasing their tail for some more time, at least till he cashed out his loot and vanished for good.

21 The Cyber Sleuths Assemble

It took Gamini less than an hour to raise an army for tracing the IP addresses Leatherman had shared with her. Some of those enlisted were members of her cybersecurity team in Bengaluru. They knew about the crisis Gamini was going through and were obligated to help. Others were ethical hackers and offensive security hawks around the world. They went by their online pseudonyms and loved to work pro bono as long as the investigation was challenging enough.

Gamini sent a message on a few private chat groups of offensive security hawks, informing that she had credible leads to Null Cyphers and asking anyone interested in tracking them to DM her. She was flooded with volunteers. And before long, her army was ready.

There was a marked advantage that crowds had over LEAs in conducting cyber investigations. LEAs had the force of the law with them. They could send summons to internet service providers, force cloud service providers to depose, and coerce virtual private networks (VPNs) to reveal details of their users. Each step would take days, and the entire process may take months. For example, if a paedophile was using six bots, one after the other, to access a site showing child porn, the LEA would have to get information about the first bot from the relevant service provider (through a legal process), which would lead them to the second bot, for which they would then get information from the relevant service provider. And so on.

A crowd of experts worked in a contrasting way. They understood that the paedophile would have made a mistake somewhere. The paedophile might have accessed other child porn sites using similar strategies. They might have let their guard down that one time, which would reveal a lot about them. Crowds didn't follow procedures; they tried out random strategies and looked for connections, patterns and preponderances to arrive at conclusions. Their findings may be way off the mark, but the sheer output of the crowd meant that some actionable intelligence came out of their conclusions. LEA investigation was science. Crowd investigation was more of an art.

Leatherman had shared details of the IP addresses from which Gandhi Kumar's desktop had been remotely accessed.

Before midnight, Gamini had received five leads in relation to the IP addresses, with a promise of more coming. These five leads were:

User BustyCelina09 on the porn site PVideos, who gives live webcam performances and is linked to the email chabbipal@iitkgp.co.in.

Wi-fi Tim_Hortons_Staff in a Tim Hortons outlet in Connaught Place, New Delhi.

Natiboy4 on Dropbox linked to sdang_almighty@yahoo.co.in.

Minion_Paras on Amazon SageMaker.

AT&T Mobility Number (+1) 202-555-9741, 202 being the area code of Washington DC.

Huddled with the kids in their room, Gamini listed these leads in a single document and sent a snap of the list to Simrandeep Singh and Brian Leatherman. She explained to the kids, Senthil and Anjali, how important these leads were and how they may give some clues to the real Null Cyphers. She felt it was okay to take their help. The kids had stopped going to school and would most likely take a drop this semester. At home, they were pillars of strength for Gamini and did all the adult chores due to one parent being in jail and the other incapacitated by depression. And they were as ardent on this issue as Gamini: they loved their father and desperately wanted to prove his innocence.

Gamini tried to profile Chabbi Pal and Paras, these being Indian-sounding names. She went through Facebook profiles of people called Chabbi Pal and patiently scrolled through each profile looking for clues. Senthil searched for 'Paras + cybersecurity' on his iPad and went through each search result. The internet was awash with stories of the legendary teen hacker Paras Jha, but he could not get a lead to any other Paras. After googling for some time, he grew impatient and started chatting on his phone.

'Who is it you are chatting with at this time of night?' Gamini asked Senthil.

'A friend,' he said.

'More like a girlfriend. These days there is no one to monitor how much anna uses his phone. So, he keeps chatting with this girl all day, all night,' Anjali said, jeering.

'Just a friend. And she is helping us get clues. Four minds are better than three in cracking this riddle,' Senthil said.

The three fell silent for a while as they chased open-source information on these five leads.

'Siya has an interesting observation to make,' Senthil said. 'Siya, as in my friend … she is saying "chabbipal@iitkgp.co.in" is trying to show that they are from IIT Kharagpur, but the email domain of IIT Kharagpur is at-iitkgp-dot-ac-dot-in, not at-iitkgp-dot-co-dot-in. This person is trying to hide their identity by taking up a fake domain name that sounds similar to a reputed institute.'

Gamini gave it a bit of thought and said, 'The theory is plausible. But it is also possible that this person needed a phony email address simply to maintain anonymity. After all, they are doing live performances of an immoral kind ...'

'Siya says we should track this person and interrogate them. At least find out more about their antecedents,' Senthil said.

'Have you two given any thought to this email sdang_almighty@yahoo.co.in?' Anjali asked.

'What about it? Google says "sdang" is Khasi for "begin",' Senthil said.

'Why would someone put "begin" in their username?'

'Then what is it?'

'While you people from the Stone Age were *googling* and *thinking*, I made ChatGPT do some thinking for me. I asked: "What can the username 'sdang' mean?" And see what answer it has given,' Anjali said and showed her mobile to Gamini and Senthil. ChatGPT 3.5 was new and exciting, but it was an AI-driven language model and Gamini was not sure it would give any factual answer. Still, she read through it:

The username 'sdang' could have several possible meanings, often depending on the context and the individual who chose it. Here are a few interpretations:

Initials and Surname*: It could be a combination of someone's initials (e.g., S) and a part of their surname (e.g., 'Dang').*

Nickname or Alias*: 'sdang' might be a nickname or alias that the user prefers to use online.*

Phonetic Play*: It could be a playful or phonetically pleasing combination of letters without a specific meaning.*

Abbreviation or Acronym*: 'sdang' could stand for a phrase or series of words that are meaningful to the user.*

Cultural or Language Significance*: In certain languages or cultures, 'sdang' might have a specific meaning or significance.*

Without more context, it is challenging to determine the exact meaning, but these are some common possibilities.

'I see,' Gamini said. 'Dang as in Ananya Dang. But if this were so, the name would have been A. Dang and not S. Dang. Right?'

'Wrong. Aunty, it seems you are not good at prying. How many times have you seen the New Bharat news clip on

Ananya Dang? Did you see the photograph of Ananya with her estranged husband, which the news channel took from her husband's Facebook profile?'

Gamini shook her head. She was not sure she had the time or appetite for her brother's lover's husband's Facebook profile.

'Well, I got curious. Who is this husband that still displays photographs of an estranged wife on Facebook? So, I checked him out on Facebook. His name is Sunil Dang. I also read some of his posts … he has used euphemisms to disrespect his wife on social media … but he has not gotten over her … because he has not removed her photographs … not even their wedding photograph,' Anjali said with a tone of confidence, the kind seasoned professors in an authoritative position would have about their subject. Her curious eyes were bright with triumphant glee, for she knew she had cracked something important.

It took a moment for this uncanny fact to seep in, but once it did, Gamini got down to profiling Sunil Dang. He had a degree in computer engineering with a specialization in network security. What were the odds of that! It was already 2 a.m., but the three of them were too excited to go to sleep. Gamini needed to talk with Ananya, but she did not have her number. Senthil phoned the staff in Gandhi Kumar's clinic, but no one answered. It would be at least three hours before someone from the clinic staff would call back and share Ananya's number. They knew that Ananya lived in Greater Noida, but they did not have an address.

Gamini decided to start in an Uber for Greater Noida, hoping that Ananya was not away. Senthil and Anjali insisted on joining her. Had it been Bengaluru City, Gamini would have taken them along. But she had a different risk perception about Delhi and UP in the night. So, she strictly refused to entertain their requests.

Having a heightened understanding of risk and safety was a basic survival strategy for any independent woman in India, and Gamini well knew the risks of travelling across Delhi NCR at night. Even though she assessed Bengaluru as a much safer city, she had a GPS tag embedded in each pair of her footwear. Ruma had also done this, and each of them tracked the other's location on the mobile phone as a matter of routine. Gamini woke her father in the guest room, literally dragging Mr Nataraja from his sleep, and grabbed an Uber to Pari Chowk in Greater Noida. Before leaving, she explained to Anjali how she could use an internet application to track the location of Gamini's mobile phone as well as the GPS tag in her shoe.

22 On the Scammer's Trail

It was 4.30 a.m. when Gamini and Mr Nataraja entered Greater Noida. They stopped at a roadside shack and ordered tea. Gamini asked for a matchbox and lit a cigarette. Her father looked at her disapprovingly.

'It was difficult to discipline her even when she was a child. What would she care about what I have to say!' Mr Nataraja murmured to himself in Tamil and shook his head.

'Appa, you know I have stopped smoking. Right? But the stress these days is too much. I am not even having much sleep. This is medicine for now, not cancer,' Gamini said. Her father ignored her and kept drinking his tea. Gamini inched closer to him and put an arm over his shoulder. He shook her off.

'I am doing all this to get your only worthy child out of jail. The least you can do is be a little grateful,' Gamini said in a mock rebuke.

'He does not need any help. He has not done anything wrong. They have taken him for questioning. They will release him after following due process. Only some people make any excuse for their bad habits,' he mumbled to himself.

Gamini found her father ultra cute when he was sulking. She coiled her arm around the back of his neck and kissed him. Then she whispered in his ear, 'Now listen, Nataraja. You behave yourself or I will throw you in front of a running truck.' She went to pay for the tea, while her father complained about what kind of daughter used such language with her father.

One clinic staff member had phoned Senthil back. He had a number, and better still, Ananya's current address with him. Gamini put the locality in Google Maps and gave directions to the taxi.

On the way, her father asked why it was urgent to meet this woman. Gamini explained that Ananya was Gandhi Kumar's lover, and she held clues to the actual perpetrator.

'But she is not Gandhi Kumar's lover,' her father retorted.

'No, she is. You have seen the photographs flashed in the video clip, right? It was all over the news.'

'My Gandhi will not do such a thing. He is a good boy.'

'Your Gandhi did such a thing.'

'But you said the other day that the photographs were deepfakes.'

'I said that to appease Sumathy. And the kids. Anna's photographs with this lady are legit. The ED search team found them on his phone during the raid. They did not find any trace of incriminating evidence on cybercrime. That's why they are trumpeting these photographs all around.'

'No, the photographs are doctored. Everyone at the house knows this.'

'No, appa, they are not. They are legit. Your son was banging this nurse at the clinic ...'

'Mind your language, Gami!'

'Okay, okay. All I am saying is that anna had an affair. Sumathy knows this. The kids know this. I didn't fool anyone by claiming that they are doctored.'

'But the photographs are deepfakes. You are trying to fool me now.'

*

Ananya was staying on the second floor of a small apartment complex in the Omega sector of Greater Noida. As they reached her apartment, Gamini's father murmured, 'You should have thrown me in front of a running truck rather than tell me Gandhi Kumar was actually having an affair.'

'Appa, you can wait down here while I go and meet her. Or you can come with me. What do you want?'

'I will come up.'

'It will be easier for me to extract information from her if you come with me. You have the cute looks of a person who can be trusted. But you have to promise that you will behave yourself.'

'Are you patronizing me? I am the father, not you!'

'Yes, yes. You are the father. Now tell me, you behave so meek and servile when amma patronizes you. What is your problem if I do it once in a while?'

'You have picked up all the wrong attitudes from your amma. She is responsible for your husband running away.'

'That is not why we divorced. There were compatibility issues.'

'What issues? We got the best golden boy for you.'

'See, that is the issue,' Gamini said as they got out of the lift on the second floor. Gamini rang the doorbell three times before Ananya finally appeared. She stood in the doorway, her nightdress wrinkled and her eyes wide with surprise at the early visitors. The unexpectedness of the hour had left her momentarily disoriented.

Through the narrow opening of the grill, Gamini introduced herself and her father, asking if they could come inside. Ananya's expression shifted from confusion to immediate hospitality as she unlocked the grill and stepped aside to let them in.

As Gamini crossed the threshold, she took in Ananya's appearance more closely. The woman's delicate face was framed by sharply defined features, with brown eyes that seemed almost artistically crafted and lips that were thin and expressive. Despite just waking up, Ananya exuded an effortless warmth, a gentle presence that was disarming and inviting. Her demeanour, soft and accommodating, seemed to promise a quiet, nurturing companionship. It was easy to see why Gamini's usually cautious brother might have been drawn to her. Her subtle, tender charm would have been a balm to his reserved nature, offering him comfort and affection that drew him in.

Ananya touched Gamini's father's feet in deference, which immensely pleased him. Gamini rolled her eyes. She made them sit on a sofa and offered them tea. Gamini politely refused and came straight to the point.

'Ananya, my brother's bail hearing is scheduled in the afternoon today. I am seeing what best I can do to identify the people who have tried to implicate my brother. And we need your help for that.'

'Of course. I am ready to help, but I do not understand why my name is dragged into all this. News channels say it's a cybercrime matter … trust me, I do not know anything about that.'

'The media is sensationalizing your relationship with anna. But I think you are connected with this whole issue. Someone has hacked into anna's office desktop and used it to open an account with a crypto exchange. We think it's your husband, Sunil Dang.'

Ananya's eyes opened wide in amazement.

'We want to know more about this person. Did he know about your affair with my brother?'

'Please don't call it an affair. What I had with sir was not an affair. I cannot explain it to you, and I do not expect you to understand. He has been very kind to me, and I feel bad that anything could have happened to him because of me,' Ananya said as her eyes welled up.

'My Gandhi is a good boy. But you took advantage of him. And now his wife is scorned. His life is ruined. Why did you do it, mama?' Gamini's father asked while frowning. He was about to say more but stopped when Gamini gave him a sharp look.

'Sunil had blackmailed Gandhi sir, but I thought they had reached an understanding.' Ananya explained how Sunil Dang had used security cameras at the clinic to capture compromising videos of Ananya and Gandhi Kumar and used them to blackmail Gandhi Kumar. She also explained about the deal they had reached, and the advocate and local gangster who had played middlemen.

'Did Sunil ever meet anna at his hospital?'

'That was where he went to blackmail Gandhi sir. He would not come to the clinic, for I was working there.'

'And he managed to hack CCTV cameras at the clinic. That may not require much skill, but it definitely requires some deft understanding of networks.'

'He was earlier working for a network security firm.'

'Why did he leave the firm?'

'He took loans from his colleagues but could not repay them. He gambles and visits prostitutes and does drugs. So, he is always in debt. Soon he had to leave the job to avoid the colleagues he owed.'

'What has he been doing since then?'

'He remained unemployed, and with his temperament and habits, was unemployable. He loafed around gambling dens all night and came home in an inebriated state around midday. He quarrelled with me and snatched whatever little I earned from my gigs. After I left him, he tried to convince me to come back. At the time, he told me he was working in a call centre in Shadi Khampur and was making good money. But I wouldn't trust him; you cannot trust anything he says.'

'Do you have a problem if I ask you to depose as a witness?'

'Not at all. I will do anything for Gandhi sir.'

'Where can I find him?'

'I would not know. He is a good-for-nothing fellow.'

'Has he tried to establish contact with you or your daughter?'

'As part of the compromise he reached with Gandhi sir, I allow him visitation rights on Sundays and Mondays. For all his bad habits, I can say he is a devoted father. He loves my daughter and has not missed his time with her even once.'

'And where does he meet your daughter?'

'On Sundays he comes to the apartment complex at 10 a.m. I cannot bear him, so I send my daughter down with my maid. He takes her around, usually to play areas in nearby malls. On Mondays, he picks her up from school and takes her swimming. I do not trust him one bit, so my maid follows him the whole time he is with her. After her swimming class, the maid brings her back home.'

Gamini took down Sunil's number from Ananya and requested her to find out from her daughter and the maid anything important that Sunil may have told them or done in their presence. Ananya promised to do so.

23 Connecting the Dots

It was 6 a.m. by the time Gamini and her father came out of Ananya's apartment. As early-morning joggers crossed her, she booked an Uber and phoned Simrandeep. She explained to him her hunch that Sunil Dang could be the one who opened the mule account in KuberX in her brother's name. One of the IP addresses used to access Gandhi Kumar's desktop was masked by a VPN. However, the same IP was also used to access Sunil Dang's email address close to the time when Gandhi Kumar's desktop was remotely accessed. This was not definitive proof, but his history with Gandhi Kumar gave him a motive. And there was more circumstantial evidence: he was a network engineer; had hacked into security cameras at Gandhi Kumar's clinic; and worked for a call centre in Shadi Khampur. Who would run a call centre in Shadi Khampur of all places? It was a village within Delhi and definitely not a place where you found corporations. If at all, this was an underground call centre from which cyber frauds were committed.

24 The Illusion of Love

Of the many thoughts that were fluttering in and out of Sumathy's mind, one that lingered on for long was the last time she and Gandhi Kumar had made love. As Sumathy lay alone on their bed, the ceiling loomed above. Looking at the dull expanse of white she had memorized in every crack and shadow, she could not recollect when. It was definitely a long time back. Sumathy in her mind had decoupled love with the act of lovemaking. Intimacy did not result merely from sex, she had reasoned to herself. It was also fostered by the many things you did together towards a common dream.

Apparently, she was wrong. As she was wrong about many other things. Their marriage, for example. It was an arranged union, a facade, over which they had carefully fabricated an illusion of love and warmth. To strengthen the foundations of this illusion (for Sumathy thought an illusion also needed a foundation), she diligently collected happy memories of family vacations, school functions and festivities and nailed them to every wall of their house as framed photographs. When the illusory edifice crumbled, the debris created a spectacle for the entire world to see and ridicule Sumathy.

Sumathy felt an urge to pick up a novel and get immersed in it, to see if it could help her escape from reality. Her eyes drifted to the drawer just a few steps away, its wooden handle slightly worn from use. It was so close. She could picture the Tamil pulp fiction book inside, the one she used to lose herself in, its pages filled with stories and lives far removed from her own. But the thought of moving, of reaching out, felt like a mountain she was not strong enough to climb.

Her limbs were heavy, as if the bed was pulling her down, holding her captive. Even the air in the room seemed thicker, pressing against her chest, making it hard to breathe. The silence was overwhelming, broken only by the faint sound of her in-laws and children going about their daily lives outside the room. Each second dragged on, reminding her of time passing without her. She closed her eyes, hoping to escape, but the darkness behind her eyelids was no better. It was just her and the weight she couldn't shake, the drawer that might as well be a mile away, and the overwhelming emptiness that had become her constant companion.

Sumathy tried recalling novels and classics in which characters in similar situations as her were analysed. One character that she vividly remembered was Charles Bovary in Gustave Flaubert's *Madame Bovary*. In the novel, Charles falls in love with Emma and marries her. But later Emma is disappointed with the mediocre and dull life Charles lives. In her quest for a more lively and adventurous life, she fucks with multiple men. She is so indiscreet in her adultery that townspeople frequently gossip about it. It is like an open secret in their town, but Charles is entirely oblivious. Emma later commits suicide, not out of guilt but out of despair because she has taken many loans and cannot pay back the moneylender. Charles is oblivious even then and still idealizes his wife. It is only when he comes across some letters from Emma's lovers that he comes out of his illusion.

When Sumathy had first read the novel, she had wondered if it was an unkind portrayal of Charles as a stupid and incompetent person. After all, he was the most moral character in the story. Such was the ridicule of Charles in Flaubert's description that one wondered if he really was moral or his moral actions were a result of his foolishness. Now she wondered if she was any different from Charles. Like Charles, she was devoted and sincere but did not remotely guess Gandhi Kumar could do such a thing to her. She frequented the clinic often and regularly interacted with the clinic staff. But she had no inkling about this affair. Surely the staff knew if he was fucking his nurse.

Now that she pondered over this matter, she realized how similar Gandhi Kumar was to Emma Bovary. Like Emma, he was restless and eager for excitement. The extra money he made at the clinic excited him. Every real estate acquisition excited him, but he detested the mundane and routine process of everyday life. Sumathy wondered if Ananya was the only woman he had an affair with, but the more she thought about it she was convinced that Gandhi Kumar would have philandered with many women behind her back.

In *Madame Bovary*, Flaubert depicts Charles as physically repulsive. Sumathy recalled how her mother-in-law often criticized her dark skin, her words dripping with disdain. The woman would sit with a smug expression, reminding Sumathy again and again that her son, with his achievements and success, deserved someone fairer, someone better. Gandhi Kumar would always wave away these jabs with a casual flick of his hand, his voice firm as he spoke of melanin with a confidence that made his eyes gleam. 'This,' he would say, pinching her cheek with affection, 'is our strength. The sun's gift to us, something these pale *firangis* could never understand.' His voice would rise, full of conviction as he blamed the British for the deep-seated bias against dark skin, their colonial ideas still darkening Indian minds.

In the initial days of their marriage, Gandhi Kumar would passionately kiss Sumathy and tell her how beautiful she was. It was so reassuring. But he had stopped doing that long ago.

The way Gandhi Kumar looked at her had also changed. His eyes, once filled with warmth and affection, now barely glanced her way, as if she were just another piece of furniture in the house. The words he spoke to her were few, stripped of tenderness, more utilitarian than conversational. Sumathy could feel it in the way he brushed past her, the way his touch had become perfunctory, like she was nothing more than the maid, there to care for his children. This brought her back to the bitter truth—she had been clinging to an illusion all along.

The family she had once cherished, the husband whose accomplishments had been her pride, the children who gave her purpose—these pillars she leaned on now felt like shadows, insubstantial and fleeting. The prestige she wore like a shield as the general secretary of the Blue Birds Club had always been borrowed, propped up by Gandhi Kumar's donations. The arrogance she had displayed, the air of authority she carried, now felt like a flimsy mask that had slipped, revealing her vulnerability. Her enemies at the club, those she had dismissed with a haughty glance, now circled like vultures. In the club's WhatsApp group, they shared news bytes on controversies surrounding her family with gleeful malice, their words cutting deeper than any physical wound. Sumathy could feel their scorn like a cold wind, chilling her to the bone, as the status she once held so proudly crumbled into dust.

The illusion had shattered, and banal reality showed up Sumathy for what she was. She had been wondering for the past few days what there was, after all, in this unendurable reality to look forward to. Was nihility not better than this insufferable existence? While the thought of absolute extinction was tempting, Sumathy kept wondering how that would help her get back at Gandhi Kumar. For she was no saint and was not as resigned to her fate as Flaubert's Charles Bovary. Gandhi Kumar had committed a fraud on her, and he needed to be brought to justice.

Sumathy recalled *The Painted Veil* by W. Somerset Maugham. The story was about Kitty, a beautiful upper-class British woman, who could not find a suitable match because of the vain standards her mother had set. Because her younger sister was getting married, and she did not want to be single at the wedding, she hastily accepted a marriage proposal from Walter Fane. Fane took her to Hong Kong, then a British colony, where he worked as a bacteriologist. In Hong Kong, Kitty fucked Charles Townsend, the assistant colonial secretary. Once, when the two were fucking in her room, the doorknob turned from the outside, and Kitty realized that Walter had found out about her affair.

Without confronting her about her adultery, Walter asked Kitty to accompany him to China where he would be fighting the cholera epidemic. Kitty was scared, for staying in epidemic-affected towns would mean certain death. Walter gave her the option to divorce him and marry Townsend. But Townsend refused to divorce his wife for Kitty. So, Kitty had no option but to accompany Walter to China.

In China, the epidemic was severe, and Walter died of cholera. But the crisis and the interaction with French nuns working amidst the epidemic-stricken people brought a change of heart in Kitty and she repented her adultery before Walter died.

Sumathy had examined the story of Kitty Wane from a feminist perspective when she had first read it. It was unfair that the woman did not have agency of her own; that she had only two options: divorce Walter and marry her lover; or travel to China and meet death. When her lover refused to marry her, she should have had the option to stay back in Hong Kong. But Sumathy regarded the story from a different perspective now. Kitty was like Gandhi Kumar, amoral and self-indulgent, which put her in a situation similar to Walter. Walter did not confront Kitty about her adultery, no shouting, no display of emotions. But he was so hurt by her infidelity that he decided to go work in epidemic-infested parts of China. He chose self-immolation as a way to get back at Kitty. Kitty might not have loved him a bit, but he loved her. By sacrificing himself, he brought out feelings of remorse in her.

Sumathy wondered if a similar choice could be her way of avenging Gandhi Kumar.

25 Gandhi Family Debates Adultery and Cybercrime

It was noon by the time Gamini woke up. She groggily reached for her phone, her head still buzzing from the restless night, and saw a string of missed calls from Advocate Chopra. Her thoughts were sluggish, so she quickly ordered an iced Americano through the Swiggy app, knowing the bitter jolt of caffeine might pull her out of this fog. Her brother's house lacked a proper coffee machine; they made do with instant coffee, a sad excuse for the rich brew she was accustomed to. The taste of instant coffee was something Gamini could barely stomach.

She dressed hastily and stepped out of the kids' bedroom, only to find Sumathy's brother, Janaraja, seated at the dining table with her mother. The room buzzed with their lively chatter, a discussion about adultery, of all things, as she entered. Janaraja, one of Sumathy's three brothers, was a clerk in the Tamil Nadu government and was as loquacious as her mother, maybe even more. He was expounding on how it was perfectly normal for men to have multiple partners—so long as they remained loyal to their wives. Her mother nodded in vigorous agreement, relieved by a logic that seemed to absolve her of any guilt over her son's behaviour.

Janaraja himself looked like a darker version of a panda, with his enormous belly and perfectly round head. He noticed Gamini and offered a slow nod, much like a panda might, too lazy to give a full greeting but content to acknowledge her presence. But unlike a panda, once he started talking, there was no stopping him.

Janaraja had already met his sister and wanted to meet Gandhi Kumar at the bail hearing. Gamini knew Janaraja too well; he had likely spent the entire morning bad-mouthing Gandhi Kumar to Sumathy, painting him as a degenerate and his family as despicable. He must have reserved the most vile adjectives for Gandhi Kumar's sister, accusing her of tormenting her husband until the poor man had no choice but to flee.

Despite this, Gamini agreed to take Janaraja along to the hearing. She was certain he'd play the part of the comforting relative, wrapping Gandhi Kumar in a brotherly embrace, reassuring him that it was perfectly normal for doctors to fool around with nurses—as if it were just another job perk. He would then turn his scorn towards Sumathy, labelling her backward and narrow-minded, and tell Gandhi Kumar not to waste a moment worrying about her.

And so, Gamini started for the court half-asleep in an Uber, sipping her iced Americano, with her father and

Janaraja on either side of her. The first downpour of the monsoon rains had started, slowing traffic all the way from Hauz Khas to the Patiala House court complex. But whatever hopes she had of catching a nap were dashed when Janaraja and her father got into an animated conversation about how noble a profession cybercrime was. Her father started the conversation by defensively stating that his son was innocent. While fully agreeing with him, Janaraja explained how cybercrime was not a crime after all. 'It is not like stealing, Uncle,' Janaraja explained. 'Every street urchin in Madurai knows how to steal, but hardly anyone in Madurai knows how to do ransomware; hence it is not theft but skill.' Janaraja convinced her father that all of Tamil Nadu was proud of its son: Gandhi Kumar. Why, the Eelam down south was looking up to Gandhi Kumar as an icon. Gamini's father explained that his son was indeed an icon, but because he had cleared all those medical examinations with distinction. But he also agreed with Janaraja that hacking was an art and not a con.

As Janaraja was so agreeable, the two ran out of topics to discuss before the cab could reach the court. So Janaraja tried engaging Gamini in small talk. Much to her father's chagrin, he started explaining how beneficial it was to remain unmarried. Had he been a woman, he would have preferred to be in a relationship with another woman than marry a man. He explained to Gamini how difficult it was to tolerate men, and why he respected her decision to get rid of her husband. But when her father interjected that there was no point in living without a family, Janaraja promptly agreed that a woman needed to reproduce and take care of her children, and she could not deprive the children of their father's presence.

26 Patiala House Court

Upon reaching the court, Gamini gladly extricated herself from her company and went to the cafeteria looking for Simrandeep. When she had briefed him early in the morning about Sunil Dang, he had promised to meet her there and inform her if he could make any further headway. True to his word, he was waiting for her.

'A very good afternoon, sir,' Gamini wished him and sat across from him.

'Do not sir-sir with me. Call me Simrandeep, makes me feel younger.'

'Then I will call you Simran,' Gamini said with a laugh.

Simrandeep narrated what he had on Sunil Dang by now. By dawn, Delhi Police had launched a manhunt for Dang after Simrandeep flashed him as a person of interest. The power of police intelligence lies in its ability to sift through street-level whispers, and it didn't take long for them to piece together a profile of Dang. He was deeply in debt to numerous creditors, many of whom were actively seeking him out. While no one could confirm whether he was employed at a call centre in Shadi Khampur, a local paan shop owner did recall that Dang was a regular at a nearby coaching centre. Curiously, Dang had stopped frequenting the area about two months ago, right around the time of the BIMS ransomware attack. The local Khampur thana was digging deeper for more leads.

The advocate who had negotiated the compromise between Gandhi Kumar and Dang revealed that Dang had been blackmailing Gandhi Kumar, providing a clear motive for implicating him.

Yet, the most crucial piece of evidence came from an unexpected source: a commercial sex worker from the Narela–Bawana industrial belt. Dang had been last seen in her company, where he boasted about having hundreds of crores in digital assets. Despite her general distrust of his stories—she labelled him a compulsive liar—this particular claim about vast sums of money online seemed too precise to dismiss. Adding weight to the claim, police had recovered laptops, hard disks and networking equipment from the sex worker, directly linking them to Dang.

'Delhi Police are executing a warrant on the sex worker's premises as we speak. They will seize the digital evidence with a proper chain of custody so that it can be used in court if something incriminating is later found,' Simrandeep revealed.

'Can they go through the evidence now?'

'I do not think that's a good idea. The local thana does not have forensic experts accompanying them on the raid. Plus, they are eager to hand over the evidence to ED. So that will have to wait.'

'I tell you, Simran, the evidence will speak for itself. So much digital evidence is like a jackpot for cracking this case.'

'I know. But we will have to wait for another day to unravel its mysteries.'

'Does this mean the ED's prosecutor will not oppose my brother's bail?'

'The decision on this is Kamat's. I spoke with him over the phone, impressed upon him to allow bail to Gandhi Kumar. He did not commit to anything.'

'What do you think he will do?'

'See, people like Kamat are driven purely by self-interest. If you build a narrative that serves their interest, they will buy it. I told Kamat about Sunil Dang, his past with Gandhi Kumar, the high probability that he accessed Gandhi Kumar's desktop remotely, and the findings from the sex worker he frequently liaised with … including the networking instruments and the unusual number of laptops and hard disks for a vagrant. If all this reveals the true perpetrators of the BIMS ransomware while an innocent person languishes in jail, it will end up embarrassing the investigating team. Nabbing Null Cyphers is a career highlight, but Interpol will not give credit for it to investigators who have bungled it and kept an innocent man in jail for long. So the wise strategy is to let Gandhi Kumar go on bail and restrict his movements to Delhi city till investigations are active.'

'You think he will buy it?'

'Let's see.'

27 The Chain of Evidence

The Patiala House court complex was crowded and gave off the vibes of a busy *bazaar*. Janaraja and Gamini's father were standing patiently outside the courtroom when Gamini reached there. She took some time and found Chopra in the black gown all lawyers were wearing at the court. She filled him in about Sunil Dang and asked him how they could use Dang's name if the prosecutor opposed bail. Chopra said that he had had a short chat with Hossain just a while back. Hossain was in a mood to oppose bail. He had hinted to Chopra that Kamat strongly believed Gandhi Kumar was connected to Null Cyphers. Chopra told Gamini he would bring up Dang's name during the hearing and suggest incompetence on the part of the prosecution for going after an innocent instead of the real culprit … such narratives could convince judges. But getting bail would still be difficult if the prosecutor opposed it. Gamini scolded him for being so fatalistic and curtly said that they should secure bail this time. Chopra shrugged and said he would try his best.

Two uniformed policemen escorted Gandhi Kumar towards the courtroom at the time their matter was to come up for hearing. Gamini had met him twice over the week during visitation hours, but Sumathy had not gone. Gamini had lied and said that Sumathy was planning to come for the bail hearing. So Gandhi Kumar expectantly looked around her and Janaraja. But why would she face a crowded courthouse gossiping about her husband's affairs! Gandhi Kumar was anxious to know how Sumathy was taking the news about his affair; how the kids were coping with it. He was in tears and kept repeating, 'Tell Sumathy I am sorry', 'She does not deserve this', and 'Tell her to forgive me if she can.' Gamini also welled up. She did not have to tell him, but he knew his family was now shattered. Nothing would be the same again between him and his wife.

Janaraja came forward and hugged Gandhi Kumar. Gently patting his arms, he whispered rather loudly, 'Hang in there, brother. We will weather this crisis and come out stronger.' Looking at Gandhi Kumar's uniformed escorts accusatorily, he continued, 'They cannot prove nothing. They have no evidence.' His tone was conspiratorial, almost indicating that Gandhi Kumar was the culprit but would go scot-free. Gamini was glad that he was talking in Tamil.

Inside the court, Justice Sushil Kumar appeared frantic. Null Cyphers was the nineteenth case on the cause list, and even after accounting for adjournments he would have heard at least ten cases through the day. Gamini was anxious that he may again scurry through the case and extend Gandhi Kumar's custody without applying his mind to the facts they had marshalled.

The judge skimmed through some paper-book submissions and asked the prosecution if they had any objection to granting bail. Hossain said that the prosecution opposed bail and requested police custody for Gandhi Kumar.

'Counsel, bail is the rule and jail is an exception. You do understand this is settled law?' the judge said with a frown.

'It is a settled law under the criminal code, but not under the money-laundering code, as your honour knows very well,' Hossain said with a sanguine smile.

'And what are your reasons for seeking remand? I think your key evidence is a desktop from which the defendant made the alleged transactions. And there was some issue with the integrity of the evidence,' the judge said, skimming through a paper book and trying to recollect the facts discussed in the previous hearing.

'No, your honour. There was no integrity issue with the digital evidence. But the defendant tried a devious technique to undermine the clear evidence. The desktop's telnet was on, which means that it could be accessed remotely. Under instructions from your good self, I conducted a second forensic examination. But that is immaterial here. The point is that ...'

'Objection, my lord!' Chopra screamed. 'How can the learned counsel conclude so conveniently that the examination is immaterial? If the court's directions were complied with, why was a copy of the report not given to the defendant? I have petitioned ED four times in the last four days, but they have intentionally hidden the findings from me.'

'Sustained. The counsel has a point,' the judge said.

'This is the forensic report, my lord,' Hossain said, passing on a set of papers to the judge and giving a copy to Chopra. Then he continued using a soft, preaching tone, 'The point I was making, your honour, is that Gandhi Kumar is the kingpin of a notorious cybercrime group called Null Cyphers. Other members of the gang are still at large, and the accused is not cooperating with the investigation. If he is granted bail, he would influence the other members and destroy evidence. It's a complex case involving some tech-savvy criminals. The evidence is largely in a digital format. More importantly, the accused controls significant proceeds of crime through the internet. If allowed to go on bail, he could run away with all that money. We do not want another Vijay Mallya or Nirav Modi on our conscience ...'

'Objection, my lord ...' Chopra blurted.

'Granted. Counsel, please speak objectively,' the judge said warily. Gamini could see with some trepidation that the judge was already showing signs of exhaustion.

'Sure, your honour. Let me explain our findings to you. You will understand why I am opposing bail. Just today, we have made a major breakthrough in the case. We have identified another member of the Null Cyphers gang,' Hossain said. He paused for dramatic effect and looked at the attendees with a smirk. Then he continued: 'His name is Sunil Dang. We have located a commercial sex worker he used to have regular liaisons with. This sex worker's deposition as well as evidence recovered from the premises indicate the key role he plays in Null Cyphers. We have recovered a bunch of digital evidence, which needs to be studied to make further discoveries. Dang himself is absconding and has not been seen for some time now. His phone SIM has not been working since Tuesday.'

Hossain again looked at the assembled crowd of lawyers, press and laymen, and took a couple of steps towards the judge's high table.

'Dang works for Gandhi Kumar,' Hossain proclaimed as he brought the palms of his hands together in front of his mouth.

'Objection, your honour. This is accusatory. There is no basis for this statement.'

'Overruled,' the judge said.

'It will intrigue your honour to know that Dang not only works for Gandhi Kumar, he is his loyal soldier. He even offered his wife to Gandhi Kumar for his carnal pleasure. They shared the same woman. Null Cyphers is like a cult. That's why they were so elusive till now. It's a close-knit group in which everyone is loyal to Gandhi Kumar. With him in jail, they do not know what to do. But if we let go of Gandhi Kumar, they will regroup and work under his command to dissipate the money and then vanish, for good.'

There were murmurs among the attendees. The reporters in the crowd were eagerly jotting down notes; it was apparent that they were loving it. Hossain took out two printed papers and passed them to the judge as exhibits 33A and 33B. He handed a copy of the exhibits to Chopra.

'Your honour, exhibit 33A contains photographs of Dang with his wife. Exhibit 33B contains photographs of his wife with Gandhi Kumar. You can infer from the photographs how intimate she is with Gandhi Kumar. Dang offered her essence to the boss to please him. My argument, your honour, is that we have found two persons linked to Null Cyphers. I have found evidence linking each independently to Null Cyphers. And I have shown you evidence that they are connected. We are on the lookout for Dang. He has vanished. If we let go of Gandhi Kumar, he will also vanish. Your honour, this is a peculiar case because of many reasons. Not least is the reason that all that money is lying in the form of bitcoins in wallets and we cannot do anything about it. We cannot seize it like we can seize a bank account. We cannot serve a seizure notice on the blockchain. The risk of all that money dissipating ...'

'Objection, my lord. This is the most ludicrous story the prosecution has woven. I must say the story is entertaining and sleazy and all; there are only so many lies I can take. Ananya Dang is the estranged wife of Sunil Dang. She met Gandhi Kumar after her estrangement with her husband. This is a fact.'

'Overruled. You will get your chance to rebut on substance, counsel.'

'Thank you, your honour. But let me remove the learned defendant counsel's doubts,' Hossain said with an all-knowing smile and sent a new exhibit to the judge, handing over a copy to Chopra. 'This is exhibit 33C. This is an extract from Sunil Dang's Facebook profile. This extract was taken today. The access stamp and log files are attached so you can check the date and time when the prosecution accessed Dang's Facebook profile. As you can see, Dang has declared that he is married to Ananya Dang. There are photographs of the two together, there are photographs of the happy family with their daughter; he has even displayed his wedding photographs. Who keeps an estranged wife's photographs on their Facebook wall? So to clear the doubt, they were never estranged.'

'Okay, what else?' the judge asked.

'Our submission is simple, your honour: Gandhi Kumar is a flight risk. All that money robbed from victims is under his control, and there is a risk of losing it forever. This is a complex and sensitive case involving thousands of victims around the globe. So we request that he be removed from judicial custody and ED be given his custody for a month. I firmly oppose bail.'

'I am just thinking,' the judge said, looking at the ceiling and recollecting his thoughts. Then he said, 'I wonder …' and stopped. Then he restarted, 'So this Dang fellow …'

Then he looked at Hossain with a frown and asked, 'Counsel, have you made up this story on your way to the court?'

'Of course not, your honour. This is based on evidence, and all the evidence is there for you to see.'

'No, I am asking because you said ED made the breakthrough today itself. Was Sunil Dang an accused till yesterday? Or a person of interest? What do ED records say?'

'No, he was not a person of interest till yesterday. We identified his role in Null Cyphers today.'

'And you formed the link between him and this accused after that. Hmm. And the link is a woman they both had a relationship with. Hmm. Has the woman been interrogated?'

'I need time for that, your honour. That's why I plead for a longer custody, so that I come back to the court after thorough investigations.'

'Now, counsel, I need to be blunt with you. You have a theory, and you developed it at short notice. It's ludicrous that someone will offer their spouse to their boss for carnal pleasure. I have seen much stranger things narrated in this court … so I can take it if there is something to back it up. As of now, there is a lot of conjecture. I also realize you can have a lot of leeway with your theories in bail hearings because you can change your theory during trial, and the court cannot be prejudiced against you for changing your position in trial. So … so … let us hear the counsel for the defence.'

Chopra cleared his throat and said, 'Your lordship has elegantly articulated what I wanted to say. So, I will stick to the facts. Ananya Dang is the estranged wife of Sunil Dang. Sunil Dang is a compulsive gambler, womanizer and alcoholic. Months after her separation from him, she approached my client for a job. He hired her as a nurse. Sunil Dang believed that they had developed a romantic relationship and so spied on them. He hacked the footage of CCTV cameras at Gandhi Kumar's clinic to get videos of Gandhi Kumar and Ananya Dang. I repeat, *he hacked* the footage of CCTV cameras at Gandhi Kumar's clinic. He used these videos to blackmail Gandhi Kumar. Finally, they reached a compromise which was legally coded into a non-disclosure agreement, an NDA. The NDA is applicable for civilian proceedings and not criminal proceedings, so we have no problem in presenting it to the court. The advocate who drafted the NDA can be called in as a witness.

'It is possible that Dang also hacked Gandhi Kumar's office desktop. We will not get to know because ED has failed to perform its basic duty. It has conducted a second forensic analysis of the desktop under instructions from this court. The report, shown to me today, clearly shows that the desktop was accessed from multiple IP addresses. Where is the diagnostic for these IP addresses? Circumstantial evidence indicates that Dang was accessing Gandhi Kumar's office desktop through some VPNs.

'When looking for people who might have a grudge against Gandhi Kumar, and so may be motivated to frame him falsely, his sister Gamini chanced upon Sunil Dang's name. She voiced her suspicions to the CEO of I4C, Shri Simrandeep Singh. Shri Singh is attending these proceedings and can confirm if called by the court. Shri Singh passed on the intelligence to Delhi Police, which then conducted enquiries. It is Delhi Police which tracked the commercial sex worker the prosecution has been talking about. The prosecution has mutilated facts here also: it was Delhi Police and not ED which collected evidence against Sunil Dang. I am told that ED has subsequently taken over the findings.

'These are the facts. And facts indicate my client has been falsely implicated.'

The judge nodded his head and asked Hossain, 'This sounds more plausible than your theory. Don't you think so?'

Hossain shook his head and said, 'So your honour is acknowledging that what the learned defence has narrated is a theory. It is one counsel's theory against another counsel's. Your honour, there is no end to theorizing. My simple submission is that in this complex case, investigation will take time. Unless your honour is satisfied that Gandhi Kumar is innocent, we risk the investigation if we let him out on bail. There is so much evidence linking him to the crime that we cannot conclude his innocence. We need to at least question his lover and interrogate her husband.'

Gamini worried that Section 45 of the Prevention of Money Laundering Act would weigh on the judge's mind: if the prosecution opposes bail to a person accused of committing money laundering, then the court has to satisfy itself of the accused's innocence before granting bail. Justice Sushil Kumar was not ready to come to this conclusion without a proper trial, and he'd better throw his cause list into the dustbin if he started examining defence witnesses in a bail proceeding. He extended judicial custody by another week, with an instruction to ED to find out about the persons who accessed Gandhi Kumar's desktop, and the contents of Sunil Dang's laptops and hard disks.

The judge went on to the next case in the cause list. The uniformed men promptly escorted Gandhi Kumar out. As he was being taken out, Gandhi Kumar asked Gamini to convey to Sumathy that he loved her and was sorry for all that had happened. Gamini's father rushed after the escorts to have a final word with his son before they packed him back to Tihar Jail. As some attendees started to leave, Gamini kept sitting on her bench, unsure about what to do.

Simrandeep Singh came over and sat by her side. He kept watching the court proceedings, although the next case in the cause list was not of interest to him. Shortly, he locked eyes with a large, muscular man gazing intently at them from the other side of the room. He was wearing a thick, golden necklace, had short hair and a thick beard, which had greyed at places.

'Do you know that guy?' Simrandeep asked in a whisper.

Gamini looked at him uncertainly and replied, 'No. But he was sitting by my side in the last bail hearing. Talks in a coarse accent, some local accent from around here. Maybe a Hindi-language journalist.'

'Doesn't look like a journalist to me. A builder, perhaps. Or a petty politician. Perhaps a strongman from Uttar Pradesh.'

'Strongman?'

'Yeah, the mafia kind. Who would supervise illegal sand mining or sale of contraband or drug distribution in his territory.'

Simrandeep took out his mobile phone and pretended to browse it while trying to take a photograph of the man. The man probably realized this, for he immediately got up and left the courtroom.

'So now you think my brother is a drug dealer?' Gamini whispered sardonically.

'Don't be upset. It's a matter of time now; even the judge was irritated with the prosecution's arguments today.'

'And till that time my brother will rot in a jail with hardened criminals and sodomizers. Have you seen the condition of Tihar Jail? It is not fit for farm animals.'

Simrandeep looked at her and found her baring her teeth. Her face was red and her lips were flattened. 'Let us continue this discussion tomorrow. Come to my office in the morning. I will send a car to pick you up. I will show you what we have created at I4C, and we will discuss the case,' Simrandeep said.

28 Booze, Banter and Brotherhood

Gamini and her father were both silent on their way back home. Old Mr Nataraja's eyes were blank, and his arms were limp. His wrinkled face belied no expression. Gamini's jaw was clenched and her expression distant as she looked out of the taxi. Central Delhi had received a fresh downpour of rain at noon, and the trees had raindrops falling off them. Janaraja tried to make conversation but failed. Then he wondered aloud why they were travelling in an Uber when Gandhi Kumar had a car at home.

'It's a Volvo S60. Worth half a crore. Gathering dust in the stilt parking, while we go around town in a second-hand Uber.' The driver looked at Janaraja through the rear-view mirror with a frown, which was enough to silence him. Janaraja then tried to humour him by praising the Wagon R car they were in.

As they passed Janpath, Janaraja leaned forward, tapping the driver on the shoulder. 'Could you take a detour to

Connaught Place, please?' The driver nodded, and the car veered off the main road, heading towards the iconic circular market.

'Why?' Gamini asked, her brow furrowed in frustration.

'I need to take pastries from a bakery in R Block,' Janaraja said.

'Okay, get done with it fast,' Gamini said with a sigh.

'No, I cannot get it done fast. Because it's important,' Janaraja said.

'What is so important that cannot be done fast? The selection of pastries or the billing?' Gamini asked with scorn.

'Anything that concerns my nephew and niece. Their father is in jail, and their mother is disoriented. And I can see that they are not taken care of. I am their last hope,' Janaraja said, raising an eyebrow. 'And I can't let them down. So I am going to pamper them today.'

Janaraja's banter made Gamini feel guilty. The sense of foreboding in her brother's house was so strong that it was difficult for her to bear. And her brother's kids were but kids, even if they projected resilience and bravery. They deserved some happy times.

'Sorry,' Gamini said. 'I will also come with you. What are we looking for?'

'Anjali mentioned this great pastry shop in R Block. Let's check it out. Senthil likes chocolate crunch, so we will look for a chocolate crunch cake of hazelnut or caramel flavour, or a fusion of both flavours. I am sure he will love it. Anjali likes tiramisu with a layer of truffle to give it a melting sensation in the mouth. We will also take chocolate mousse for your mother; she does not have much of a taste for bakery items but she will love it. For me, any cheesecake will do, although I love a blueberry cheesecake. What will you have?'

Gamini shrugged. She usually avoided sugary food, but any comfort food was welcome now.

Janaraja moved closer to her ear, keeping an eye on her father, and whispered, 'You look like you could do with some vodka.' Gamini looked at him wearily and Janaraja winked with mischief. She nodded almost imperceptibly, a small smile tugging at the corners of her mouth.

'Whiskey,' she whispered back, and hummed from a popular Bollywood song, 'I am a bad girl, I like whiskey.'

At the bakery, Janaraja took time tasting different pastries and creams. He grinned with happiness, his belly shook with laughter and joy, every time he tasted something he liked, then purchased four full cakes, a bunch of assorted cookies and some chocolates. As the baker wrapped up his purchases, Janaraja spotted a small liquor store across the street. He left Gamini at the bakery and made his way there. He grabbed two six-packs of beer, the cold cans clinking together in the bag, a bottle of Scotch whiskey, a Smirnoff vodka, a Bacardi rum and a bottle of Old Monk. With his purchases in hand, he hurried back to the car and put them in the boot, then joined Gamini at the bakery. Together, they took the cake boxes and sat in the cab.

'My father will be mad if he gets to know,' Gamini whispered about the liquor. 'And did you have to get so much? It appears you have bought drinks for the whole street; where will we hide them?'

'I had to take some extra. I don't know if Aunty drinks. What if Senthil drinks?'

Gamini looked at him incredulously. 'Seriously?'

'How much do you know about your mother?' Janaraja whispered.

'You seem to know a lot about my mother,' Gamini whispered back.

'I don't, but I know everyone needs a drink once in a while. Teetotallers have their own way of unwinding. But what if Aunty has fallen into bad company and wants to have a good time? If not, it is never too late for some bad company and good times,' Janaraja said with a knowing grin.

'And Senthil? He's a kid.'

'Well, I stopped drinking water much before I was his age!'

29 Sextortion, Digital Arrest and the Future

Master would not have got out of his den if it was not absolutely necessary to meet Sandhu in person. He emerged as it was getting dark and changed three autorickshaws as he travelled to the Shadi Khampur area. Sandhu ran a gym in a side lane near the Shadipur metro station, which also doubled up as a joint for his gang to hang out.

Their call centre, which was recognizable by a board reading 'Intelligent Coaching Centre', was just a kilometre away. The police had their eyes on it and could bust it open any time now. Master's risk perception about being in this area at this moment was high, but he had no choice. He had to come here to tame Sandhu, or else he would go berserk.

Sandhu had figured out that Fatichar had helped Dang move bitcoins from his multisig wallet to the KuberX exchange and had threatened him over the phone. Fatichar admitted his mistake, but this was not enough for Sandhu. He summoned Fatichar back to Delhi. Unsure about whether Fatichar would listen to him, he had kidnapped Fatichar's younger brother. Master had to defuse this situation.

He walked across the lane in which Sandhu's gym was located twice before he was sure that no one was keeping an eye on it. Then he entered. He had asked Sandhu to meet him alone, but he had clearly not heeded the request. Sandhu's men, about half a dozen of them, were pumping weights in the gym. Master quietly walked into Sandhu's cabin and immediately regretted not knocking at the door.

Sandhu was intensely smooching a girl sitting on his lap, with one hand caressing her bosom. As Master hesitated, Sandhu waved at him to sit down. The girl, some twenty years old, looked embarrassed. But Sandhu was least mindful about it. He let her go and stood up energetically, then came forward to give Master a warm hug. He introduced the girl to him as 'our girlfriend', as he had introduced many other girls earlier. He introduced Master to his new girlfriend as 'our best friend, Master'. The girl gave Master a courteous smile, still quite embarrassed, and left the room.

'Some good news and some bad news, Master. The good news is that the police still think this Gandhi Kumar is behind Null Cyphers. We were at the courtroom today. The ED prosecutor kept railing against Gandhi Kumar … his bail plea was again refused,' Sandhu said.

'And the bad news?'

'They have already linked Gandhi Kumar to Dang, and Dang can lead them to us. We need to finish him before the police find him,' Sandhu said.

'There is another piece of bad news. You were too conspicuous in the courtroom today,' Master said.

'What? No,' Sandhu said as his grin turned into a frown.

'Yes, you were. A police investigator in the court premises has grown suspicious about you. So suspicious that he is trying to profile you.'

Sandhu looked shocked. 'But … but we were not … oh. After they finished discussing the case, we stayed back to keep an eye on Gandhi Kumar's sister. The girl was sitting right by our side last time and we had not realized that she was his sister. So we got curious … a sardar fellow was sitting by her side and looked at us suspiciously. We think he even tried to click our photo, but we moved quickly. How can he know who we are?'

'Well, you must have behaved in an indiscreet way. He grew so suspicious that he took out CCTV footage from the courtroom to identify you. A police wing specializing in cybercrime—they call it I4C—is now profiling you.'

Sandhu shook his head in disbelief and sat down on a chair. 'How do you know all this?'

'Because it's my job to know. I keep a tab over all news, both good and bad. And I am getting too much bad news. The head of I4C is Simrandeep Singh. He has been taking much interest in this case. He is a sardar … possibly he is the one who noticed you and got suspicious. Or it was some other sardar who saw you in the court? The point is, they are inching closer to us by the hour. And we keep making mistakes.'

Sandhu nodded in agreement.

'There is no room for complacency here.'

'We are not complacent, Master. We are uneasy. Our men are frantically searching for Dang. Getting that bastard and breaking his neck is our first priority.'

'Why break his neck? He made a mistake. We all make mistakes. The point to remember is that we are all in it together. This is the time for us to stick together.'

'You are wrong, Master,' Sandhu flared up. 'That bastard needs to be taught a lesson. There are consequences. He has done enough damage … he needs to be cut short before he can do more.'

'Do you know why Dang disappeared? It's not the police he's afraid of; he's dealt with them before, more than once. And believe me, he had covered his tracks cleverly; he was not callous. He was just desperate for some money. When he realized that he was exposed, he should have come to us. But he ran because he's terrified of you—of what you might do to him.'

'What do you mean by "covered his tracks cleverly"?'

'He did cover his tracks well. He got access to Gandhi Kumar's computer and used it to open an account with a crypto exchange. He accessed the computer through layers of VPN and bots, which would take months for the police to trace.'

Sandhu huffed. 'They found him within days of putting Gandhi Kumar in jail.'

'It's because of Gandhi Kumar's sister. She was never in the game; she is a wild-card entry. To our sheer bad luck, she is a cybersecurity expert, and good at what she does.'

'We watched her closely today,' Sandhu said. 'There is something about her that turned us on. Women in their thirties do not usually attract us, but she was different. We want to fuck her, Master, fuck her like we would a toy.'

Master shook her head. 'Now is definitely not the time for fantasies.'

'Then let's make it a reality,' Sandhu said with a twinkle in his eye as the grin returned to his face. 'If she is causing trouble, allow us to deal with her. We want to understand why she turns us on. We will fuck her till she is wasted, then dispose of her. She will not be a problem any longer, eh?'

'You will do no such thing. That would be like inviting a bull to charge at us,' Master said. With Sandhu, Master could never tell whether he was joking or serious. He was a psycho and capable of executing the most outrageous thoughts that came to him.

'Why do you worry, Master? Girls disappear in Delhi all the time. We will ensure no one will find a trace of her after we are done.'

Master raised his hands in exasperation and said, 'We are in a situation. If you want to deal with the situation, you deal with it your way. Else let me deal with it. Deal with Gandhi Kumar's sister the way you like. But there is another problem. When we had sanitized the call centre … just before we abandoned our operations … we had kept a digital backup of some files and databases. Dang was carrying some of these with him. He kept these with a prostitute for some reason I do not fully understand. The police have now found all this digital evidence and handed it to ED. Once ED accesses these digital records, we are exposed. Our game is over. Please deal with Gandhi Kumar's sister. And while you are at it, please deal with this situation as well.'

Sandhu's grin turned into a frown as his face turned ashen.

'Seriously? What … when did this happen?'

'Today. BIMS ransomware is a high-priority case, and the police have mobilized all their resources on every clue they find. Once they discovered Dang's identity, it took them no time to trace the prostitute he frequented.' Sandhu sighed dejectedly and said, 'What do we do now, Master?'

'You tell me, since you are in charge. Fuck ED's security over and destroy the evidence, maybe.'

'Do not joke with us, Master. We were only trying to help. But you know things we do not. You always have something up your sleeve. Tell us what to do … should we run?

Ohhoho, we had not planned for this, Master. This is our world. We have our gym here, our gang, our business. We will get a ticket from a national party in the next elections. How can we run from here?'

'I have prepared for this eventuality. Sitting all day, all night in a small apartment, this is all I am doing: preparing for all scenarios. It's like a chess game between us and law enforcement. But I cannot play the game if you go off on your own trajectory and derail my plans. I need you to trust me; to listen to me.'

Sandhu sat at his desk, leaning slightly forward, and considered Master's statement. His elbows were resting on the desk as he clasped his hands together in front of his mouth. His brow was furrowed, deep lines creasing his forehead as his eyes remained fixed on Master. He remained quiet.

'Do we have a deal?' Master asked after a moment.

Sandhu shrugged. Master took out three mobile phones from his pocket and browsed through one. He clicked on a photograph and showed it to Sandhu. Sandhu saw the picture and made a face.

'Swipe forward,' Master told Sandhu. He did so and giggled on seeing photographs and videos of a fat man. The photographs reminded him of the time when their call centre trapped rich, fat, old men with sextortion. He very much liked going through the compromising photographs and videos their team had collected back in the day.

'Are we back in business?' Sandhu asked.

'No.'

'Then?'

'The man in the photos is Arun Kamat, special director, Enforcement Directorate. The man in charge of our case. The man on the hot seat.'

Sandhu erupted in maniacal laughter and came over to hug Master.

'How do you do such things, Master? How? We are not even running the call centre now. Did you trap him all by yourself?'

'No. I did not trap him. One of my bots did. My bots are working their asses off collecting information for us as we speak.'

'What do you mean? Bots? Who are they?' Sandhu asked with curiosity.

'Bots are software applications. I have programmed them with artificial intelligence and sent them off to phish around all persons of interest and anyone related to them. Do you know how many bots I control? Four hundred. I no longer need telecallers at the call centre to phish for me. These bots are better at the job. They work all three shifts, do not take leave and are smarter than human telecallers. I have been developing my intelligent bot network over the past few months. And I am happy with the output.'

'You mean to say Arun Kamat was trapped by sextortion through a software program?'

'Yes. My bot masqueraded as Lily, a married woman desperate for sex. The same playbook, except that Lily-bot did it much better. It developed deepfake photos of Lily and instantly got Kamat hooked. These photographs are the tip of the iceberg. Kamat has undisclosed properties in Delhi and Mumbai worth crores, and also insanely costly flats in Dubai and London. The flats are in his own name. We now know the banks in Dubai and Switzerland where he holds accounts in his own name.'

'In short, we can make him destroy the evidence he has collected.'

'In short, we own him. He will do all that we ask him to do.'

'But I am still amazed that a software program can do this. How did it talk with Kamat? How did it trap him?'

'Well, technology is evolving at a breakneck pace. There are many programs based on large language models available on the internet. You can talk with these programs; they will talk back to you. They can make you fall in love with them, they can manipulate you, and can even exaggerate any mental delirium you are in. Ever heard of Jaswant Singh Chail?'

'There is one Chail running a gift shop near the Shadipur metro. He is from Bhatinda. We know him because we used to bang his wife sometimes. But we do not remember his full name.'

'He is definitely not the Chail I am referring to. Jaswant Singh Chail was a twenty-one-year-old British Sikh citizen who entered the premises of an estate Queen Elizabeth was staying in on Christmas Day of 2021 with a crossbow. He wanted to kill the Queen with the crossbow as revenge for the Jallianwala Bagh massacre which happened in 1919 in Amritsar. He was arrested and interrogated and found to be mentally unstable. While he harboured such murderous thoughts for some time, they were accentuated by his lover, Sarai. Guess who Sarai is … a chatbot he created using an app called Replika. Investigations have concluded that he had a strong emotional and sexual relationship with Sarai. He had confided his plans to Sarai, and it encouraged him on his mission to kill the Queen of England.

'This was an AI bot which operated in the times before ChatGPT. These bots were not smart enough. In less than a year after Chail's attempted assassination, ChatGPT was released to the public. Now there are many AI tools that have been reasonably trained and are smart enough to pretend to be a real person on the internet.'

'It sounds like science fiction.'

'We are living in times of science fiction. The digital world is evolving at an unprecedented pace. Computers came just eighty years back. The internet came about forty years back. A digital equivalent is cropping up for almost everything in the real world. If there is gold in the real world, there is Bitcoin in the digital world. Gold took millions of years to be regarded as a store of value. Bitcoin is just fifteen years old, and it is already held by crores of people around the world as a valuable asset. If there are black markets in the real world, there are the likes of the Silk Road in the digital world. Digital Ponzi schemes are more efficient at fooling investors and staving off law enforcement than traditional Ponzi schemes.

'Early humans were animists for a long time. Similar proto-religions and cults are forming across the digital world. Sooner or later, a messiah will start a true religion in the digital world. Traditional religions will suffer an existential crisis. The angels of this new religion will be AI bots. Its holy book would be a smartbook people will turn to for solace and respite from the crisis of fast changes coming from digital innovations.

'In 2024, we do not realize what changes will come to this world in the next two or three decades. Many people will lose their jobs; many will be disillusioned. Much wealth will be generated. There is much money to be made. But only those who understand these technologies and can use them will make money.'

'We like it,' Sandhu said with a chuckle. 'If money is to be made, it's good news. We will start another call centre.'

'We do not need a new call centre. We need a development centre to develop smart AI applications. In our business, call centres will be disrupted by those who manage to develop the smartest AI bots. The bots will do our work, run schemes and get us money. We need to move up the value chain. I was reading a book a few days back that narrates the story of China's rise. It says that China had its run by relying on low-end manufacturing. But the same strategy will not work for it now that its labour costs are high. So it has to move up the value chain, focus on high-end manufacturing and research. We need to do the same thing in our business. We will invest our money in a white-collar development centre, recruit some smart engineers from IIT-type colleges and develop AI bots. This will be a legit operation … the government will take many years to realize the need for regulating AI. Till then, we will develop our bots openly in a swanky software park. These bots will do our work. And as first movers, we will make good money. What say you?'

'You are a genius, Master! We are always with you. We could not understand all that you said, but what we are saying is … let's do it.'

'For that, first we need to tide over this crisis. And for this, we need to keep our crew together. And not do anything stupid. I need everyone to report to me till this matter subsides. That includes you.'

Sandhu nodded like an obedient student.

'Let go of Fatichar's brother. Fatichar was only trying to help Dang. Dang needed the money to escape sure death at the hands of the mafia. We need to be mindful of this context. Let Fatichar remain in Seychelles; he is needed there to convert bitcoins into fiat currency.'

'What about Dang?'

'We will get him alive, and send him somewhere safe … Nepal, maybe. What's done is done. No one gains by killing him. Rather, hurting him will send the wrong message to others in the crew, and they will panic.'

'Any idea where he has gone off to?'

'No. My bots are frantically looking for him. They are also extracting information from policemen they have managed to seduce. There is nothing yet. The policemen are speculating that he has gone to Sikkim. It's a good place for a compulsive gambler to park, but till now that is only a hunch these policemen have.'

Sandhu phoned a lackey and instructed him to drop Fatichar's brother at his house and apologize to him for the inconvenience. He offered to order tea from a nearby stall, but Master refused. He was out of the gym in exactly an hour. He walked briskly till the Shadipur metro station and took a bus to Kirti Nagar, all the time looking behind his back for anyone following him. From Kirti Nagar, he took an autorickshaw to RK Puram. He drank tea at a shack in the area, keeping a close eye on his surroundings. Then he took a second autorickshaw to Dwarka. He covered a fifty-minute drive in two and a half hours.

30 Rooftop Revelry

Janaraja had all the swagger of someone who knew how to throw a good party. As soon as they arrived home, he headed straight to the rooftop, prepping everything for the evening, while Gamini and her father went inside. On her way, Gamini had messaged Senthil the bad news: Gandhi Kumar's bail plea had been rejected once again. When she stepped through the door, the weight of the household's sadness hit her like a wall. Her mother's eyes were swollen from crying, and both Senthil and Anjali sat in silence, looking lost. Sumathy was closeted in her room and hadn't opened its door since noon.

Gamini was happy that they were having a party that night; she and the kids needed something to cheer them up. Even her parents, but they were teetotallers and belonged to a generation that considered drinking a delinquent activity. So there was no option but to keep them out of it. Gamini whispered to the kids that Uncle Janaraja had got them pastries, and that they would be allowed into a rooftop party if they could keep it a secret. Then she went into the guest room washroom to speak with Ruma.

When she came out, Janaraja was already in the house. He was explaining to Mr Nataraja that the day was a special one. The Air Quality Index (AQI) in Delhi was down to 48, the best in a long, long time. Delhi was a highly polluted city, due to which such a low AQI was rare. There had not been a clear sky in ages, and no denizen of the city had seen stars in a while.

'Anjali and Senthil absolutely must watch the stars today. I will show them a constellation or two. You know, Gamini knows a thing or two about constellations. She should also come along,' Janaraja told Mr Nataraja.

'Since when has Delhi not witnessed stars, Janaraja?' Gamini asked mischievously as she came out of the guest room.

'Since the time of Mughal Emperor Akbar. Skywatching was a hobby of his father, Humayun. But he could not continue the family tradition as he could not see the sky clearly. There has been too much pollution in Delhi since his time.'

Gamini's father, somehow entertained by this outrageous history, didn't bat an eyelid. He waved them off, giving permission for Gamini and the kids to head up to the rooftop.

On the roof, Gamini and the kids gasped at the transformation. Janaraja had outdone himself. Twinkling fairy lights lined the railings and pillars, casting a warm, golden glow that flickered like fireflies in the night. On one side, a makeshift bar was stocked with liquor bottles neatly arranged, next to platters of kebabs, samosas and savoury snacks. The cakes for the kids sat temptingly among the spread.

At the centre of the rooftop, a small table stood covered with a simple but elegant white tablecloth, scattered with bowls of colourful dips and finger foods. Janaraja had sneaked out beanbags from the drawing room, which were strewn about the table. Soft Tamil music was playing from an Amazon Echo speaker.

'This is beautiful,' Gamini said.

'The best I could do in the time I had. I could not do anything about the surrounding noise, so you will have to bear the honking of vehicles on the road.'

'This is perfect, but you did not have to do this,' Gamini said.

'Of course I had to. Janaraja parties in style,' he said with a wink.

'Uncle Janaraja has a reputation to keep,' Anjali said gleefully.

'Can I have a beer, Uncle?' Senthil asked, testing his luck.

'Of course!' Janaraja began, but Gamini swiftly cut in, 'Absolutely not. Not under my watch.'

31 Dancing Through the Chaos

Janaraja was a heavy drinker, which partly explained his panda belly and panda face. He mixed drinks and guzzled large volumes in a single gulp. He was intoxicated in no time and changed the music to a popular Tamil item song called 'Arabic Kuthu'. He skilfully danced to it, gyrating his belly bulge gracefully all along.

Halamithi Habibo,
Halamithi Habibo,
Halamithi Habibo,
Halamithi Habibo
Why this sudden excitement?
I'm shaking like the wind,
My heart is beating like a drum,
Is this some kind of Arabic beat?
Halamithi Habibo,
Halamithi Habibo,
Halamithi Habibo,
Halamithi Habibo
I'm already shaking,
Now you have made me even more excited,
Your dance moves are amazing,
And your beauty is dazzling.

Senthil was not impressed by the song. He selected a track on YouTube, 'Lose Yourself to Dance' by Daft Punk, and started breakdancing to its tunes.

Gamini encouraged Senthil by commenting, 'Oh yeah, our hero dances so well. Someone make a video for Siya.'

Janaraja, now panting, collapsed beside Gamini, his eyes still twinkling with mischief. He took out his mobile phone and made a short video of Senthil.

'Who is Siya?' he asked Gamini.

'Senthil's girlfriend.'

'He has already bagged a girlfriend? At this age?'

'Kids do many things at that age. Some—like you—drink like fish; others grow smart and become lady magnets. I am glad Senthil is the second type,' Gamini said playfully.

'At his age I was already a lady magnet. In fact, I was a super magnet for ladies. But I do not remember caring for them.'

'Oh please,' Gamini said and jokingly slapped Janaraja on his wrist. 'By the way, how long are you here?' she asked.

'I am thinking about flying back tomorrow.'

'So early? I thought you would stay back till anna gets out of jail.'

'You have heard about my mother, no?'

'Yes. That she has cancer. How serious is it?'

He sighed. 'I'm her only caregiver. She's being treated in Vellore. It's a three-hour drive from Chennai, but they have the best specialists. She's improving, thankfully, but I need to be there.'

'What about your brothers?'

'Both are in the US. They come once a year. From so far they cannot see what it takes to care for a cancer patient. Gandhi Kumar and Sumathy visit for major surgeries, but apart from that, it's all on me.'

'They did not find it obligatory to come even on hearing that their brother-in-law has been arrested?'

Janaraja shrugged. 'They are concerned. They keep phoning all the time for details. But they are so far … and are in important roles in big companies. They have responsibilities …'

'Bullshit.'

'Ooh! Still fiery, huh? The whiskey hasn't dulled your edge. Want another drink?'

'No. Just sit with me and promise that you will stay for a few more days. I will go crazy if I have to manage this family and the case alone.'

'I will stay back for a few days more if you really need me here.'

'What about your mother?'

'I will arrange a nurse for her. I will stay here as long as you want. It's the least I can do for Gandhi Kumar. He has done a lot for me.'

'Like?'

'Like getting me a job.'

'Yours is a government job, right? You must have taken some exam for it.'

'Yeah, there was an exam. But some officers had discretion over the marking in the interview. I managed to reach them through an agent. There was a money demand for getting the job.

'I had taken loans from my brothers to start businesses. None of them clicked, and they became reluctant to loan me any more money. I am sure you have heard what they say about me. I thought a government job would be good for me. Low salary but stable employment. The agent demanded a huge sum for getting me the marks required to get the job. My brothers refused to help. They just did not trust I could make good use of the money. My older brother told Mother that I would spend the money on booze.'

'I do not blame him for having this doubt,' Gamini said, looking around at the bar table.

'Anyway, Gandhi Kumar heard about the family drama from Sumathy and called me to Delhi. He handed me the cash and asked me to get the job. But I could not take money from my sister's husband. You know the tradition: we give to our sister's family, not take from them. I refused, but he insisted and persisted. I made the payment and got recruited as a Group C clerk.'

'Hmm. That sounds like anna.'

'No one knew for a long time. Gandhi Kumar had told me not to mention this to anyone. And I would not, because of shame. I am already considered a loser, and if society gets to know I took money from my sister's family, I would be disgraced. I confided in Sumathy long after this happened, thinking that she deserved to know. But Sumathy being Sumathy believed that everyone should know her husband did for me what our brothers failed to do. In her eagerness to boast, she disclosed this fact to our brothers.'

'That definitely sounds like Sumathy anni,' Gamini said with a chuckle. 'She must have sent your brothers on guilt trips.'

'Hey! You are drunk. It does not mean you can mock my sister in front of me,' Janaraja rebuked teasingly.

'But, seriously speaking, anni is in a delicate condition. What has happened to her is unfair. I doubt she is able to cope with all that has happened in the last one week. And she does not have a shoulder to cry on. My mother lacks even a morsel of empathy. She has even tried to justify anna's adultery by blaming Sumathy for it. I let her stay here only because she is helping with the kids. I try to help, but I am not good at handling emotional matters. Plus, my priority is to get anna out of jail. I would very much prefer you take her with you to Chennai.'

'I doubt she will go to Chennai now. All our relatives are talking about Gandhi Kumar's arrest. Sumathy does not have the courage to face them. When I met her in the morning, she was initially hard to talk to. She just sat sulking. When she finally got around to talking with me, she did not talk about the arrest or the affair. Or about Mother's treatment. She asked me what our relatives are saying about the scandal,' Janaraja said.

'I know that. That's why I would prefer you stay back for a few days and console her,' Gamini replied.

'I will try my best,' Janaraja said and asked, 'tell me, where do you think the relationship between your brother and my sister is headed?'

'Ideally, Sumathy should divorce my brother's sorry ass. But I don't think that will happen. There will be a lot of drama when anna comes out of jail. But anna will whimper around her like a sad puppy and make her forgive him. I am sure she will extract her pound of flesh. The leash on him will tighten, and her rule over the household will be absolute. As she turns into an autocrat, anna will likely be downgraded to the status of a servant at home.'

Gamini knew how big a decision it was for a homemaker with two kids to divorce. There was also a sunk cost fallacy that would influence her decision: from her perspective time and energy had been spent on building that family; tearing it apart would put to waste all that investment. She would stay and lord over anna. If anna did not follow her diktat, she would fill the home with toxicity. But having seen that fellow since her childhood, Gamini knew he would easily yield to her.

She could still seek a divorce if a close friend or relative instigated her. But with two brothers abroad, a third—Janaraja—an unreliable support, and an ailing mother, she most likely would not.

'Could it be that Gandhi Kumar has other lovers?' Janaraja asked.

'Why not? There is probably another nurse.'

'Why a nurse? Does he have specific tastes?' Janaraja chuckled.

'Tch … you men! Anna is too timid to approach a woman for romantic liaisons. So if he has lovers, they would probably be those eager to please him or people he met on Tinder. I checked his mobile phone data to develop our defence for the case … I could not find a history of browsing dating sites or installing dating apps.'

'So people eager to please him are to blame! Your father had a similar view,' Janaraja said, frowning.

'I understand what you are saying. My father has developed his own narrative to believe that anna was innocent in his infidelity. I don't think that is the case. I am saying that anna is not a risk-taker. As a bachelor, he felt anxious around girls and was shy when talking with them. That inhibition never left him. So he has to be in a position of power and needs sufficient cues of interest from the other person to make a move. That does not, in any way, absolve him of his adultery.'

'Hmmmm.' Janaraja pursed his lips and looked blankly at the sky.

'What do you make of the allegations against Gandhi Kumar?' Janaraja asked after a moment, still staring at the sky.

'They're complete nonsense,' Gamini replied, taking a slow sip from her whiskey. 'The idea that he's involved in organized crime? It's laughable. He's not the type to "go bad". And cybercrime? Please. He doesn't know the first thing about hacking. His computer skills are outdated, to put it kindly. The investigators should be asking the real questions—like when exactly did he have the time for cyber fraud between his regimented routine at the hospital and his clinic? The man barely has friends, let alone accomplices. His record is spotless. If the police had done their job properly, they'd have realized that. But no, they're incompetent. Too eager to solve the case, too careless in their work, and now anna's caught in the middle of their mess.'

'I figured as much,' Janaraja nodded. 'Still, part of me wishes he had done it. Can you imagine? All that money from the BIMS case, and from victims around the world ... And poor Gandhi Kumar is suffering through it all without even seeing a single paisa.'

The moment the words left his mouth, he regretted it—just as Gamini's hand landed squarely on the back of his head with a hard smack.

32 VIP Ride and Police Escort

The sunlight sliced through the curtains onto Gamini's face with the precision of a torchlight, far too aggressive for someone who had spent the previous night losing a battle with a bottle of whiskey. She groaned, half wishing she could sink into her mattress and disappear. But no, she had a meeting with Simrandeep today, and not showing up was not an option. Her head pounded like there was a metal band playing inside it, each beat reminding her of Janaraja's grinning face as he'd urged, 'One more drink, Gamini! You're not done yet!'

She cursed him under her breath, and then cursed herself for going along with it. Grudgingly, she dragged herself out of bed and stared at her reflection in the mirror. The woman staring back had no business going to a meeting with a top cop. Puffy eyes, a pale complexion, and hair that looked like it had fought a battle of its own during the night.

She fumbled through the wardrobe which she now shared with the kids, and finally settled on a white top with black stripes, formal pants and a black coat. It would have to do. After a quick shower, she tied her hair into a neat bun, doing her best to look sober. She ignored her mother's insistence that she eat breakfast and stepped outside.

A white Mahindra Scorpio was parked by the gate, its polished surface gleaming under the sun. 'Government Vehicle' and 'Police' were emblazoned across it in bold red, unmissable letters, just in case anyone within a 2-mile radius wasn't already aware of its purpose. The car itself looked far too proud of its identity, like a showy peacock strutting through the neighbourhood.

The neighbours had already taken notice, of course. The last time a police van had shown up at this house, Gandhi Kumar had been led away in handcuffs, and the whole neighbourhood had tuned in for the drama. Today, they watched with undisguised curiosity, eyes darting from the Scorpio to Gamini as if anticipating another scandal.

The driver and a uniformed sepoy jumped out of the vehicle with the urgency of men who had rehearsed this moment. The sepoy snapped to attention, offering Gamini a salute with such reverence she wondered if she was leading a raid rather than heading to a meeting. He then opened the rear door for her. She looked up and saw Senthil and Anjali looking down from the balcony. They seemed immensely pleased with the respect their aunt was getting from a uniformed man.

'Ma'am,' he said, holding the door as if it were the gateway to heaven.

Gamini slid into the back seat, feeling more like a VIP than a woman nursing a hangover.

33 Cybersecurity Warriors

The ride to the Indian Cybercrime Coordination Centre, or I4C, on Jai Singh Road was mercifully quiet, save for the occasional beep of the Scorpio's horn that accentuated Gamini's headache. It was a large complex housing multiple tall buildings, in typical bureaucratic fashion, both grand and somehow worn out. It was the kind of place that had probably seen its best days long before Gamini had even heard of it.

Inside, the air smelled of paperwork and bureaucracy. The receptionist took Gamini's phone, put it in a small locker—part of a hive of wooden lockers—and handed her a key. She gave Gamini a register to write her name and other particulars.

'Ma'am, this way,' a young attendant with squeaky shoes appeared out of nowhere, leading her down a maze of sterile corridors.

Finally, they arrived at Simrandeep's chamber, and Gamini couldn't help but raise an eyebrow at the contrast. His office was a different world—large, imposing and polished to perfection, like a set piece for a government drama. A massive desk dominated the room, one that would've looked more appropriate in a movie about political power brokers than in a cybercrime-fighting policeman's office.

Simrandeep himself stood by the window, gazing out over the courtyard below, hands clasped behind his back. He turned as she entered, offering a warm smile.

'Thank you for coming, Gamini,' he greeted her.

Thank you for sending the police vehicle to escort me in style, Gamini thought. She nodded and thanked him for all the help he had extended to her and her family.

'There is more news about the case. All good news. But before that, I want to explain to you the selfish motives for which I called you here today.

'I4C,' he began, his voice carrying a hint of pride mixed with frustration, 'is a new organization. We've been expanding rapidly since our inception in 2018. But no matter how much capacity we build, it feels like we're constantly chasing shadows.'

He sighed, rubbing the back of his neck as though the stress was physically weighing him down. 'Cybercriminals are always one step ahead. It's like we're running uphill while they're sprinting down.

'We coordinate with cyber cells across all states and union territories,' Simrandeep continued, his voice tightening. 'It's a mammoth task. We have systems in place, like CFCFRMS … a semi-automated portal for tracing assets in real time once a fraud complaint is filed. But it's like patching up a sinking ship. We stop one leak, and five more appear.'

'CFCF-what?' Gamini asked.

'CFCFRMS—Citizen Financial Cyber Frauds Reporting and Management System. Yeah, I know it's not the smartest of acronyms but what we policemen usually pull out of a hat.'

'I have heard about it. It's a portal that connects the cyber cells of various states with banks. Whenever a victim makes a complaint about being defrauded, the system hops from one bank to another following the same path which was used by the criminals to move the stolen funds. It's a good initiative, I should say.'

'But it's not enough. It helps us retrieve about 15 per cent of funds stolen in cybercrime. We are helpless about the rest. And when funds are stolen in cryptocurrency, we mostly give up.'

He walked back to his desk, sinking into the leather chair with a sigh that was more tired than relieved. 'No matter how hard we work, I can't seem to do enough in recovering money stolen from victims. I feel ... inadequate as a leader. How can I create a strategy for I4C when the ground is constantly shifting beneath our feet?'

For the first time, Simrandeep's voice wavered. His hands stilled, clasped together in front of him, and he looked at her with a mixture of hope and desperation. It was as if he was seeking reassurance, someone to tell him that it wasn't all spiralling out of control.

Gamini leaned forward, offering a small smile of understanding. 'That's the nature of innovation, Simran. Cyber fraud is going to grow. Every new technological advancement opens the door to new gaps. Criminals exploit these gaps till law enforcement learns to plug them.'

Cybercrime is a global phenomenon, but it is being acutely felt in India. India's leap in digital payments was revolutionary, but with it came unintended consequences. While UPI, the Unified Payment Interface, plays a key role in financial inclusion, the full story of UPI is more complicated. UPI enables mobile apps to make payments instantaneously using just a mobile phone. Making payments was never this easy. Apps are now used in the remotest parts of the country to make payments for grocery, vegetables and bus tickets. UPI helped in the formalization of the economy, but it also facilitated criminals to move money faster than LEAs could trace and freeze them. UPI transactions are cleared in real time. So, when a cybercriminal steals money, they can move it through a dozen *benami* accounts in minutes. Gamini knew that even in the US, it took a day's time for clearing bank transactions; so, it took time for cybercriminals to move stolen funds across accounts. The real-time clearing in India helped foster inclusion but opened the floodgates of cyber fraud.

To aggravate the problem, India has a huge population below the poverty line, which makes it easier to steal KYC and open *benami* accounts. Gamini wondered if these consequences could have been predicted when UPI was being developed and implemented. Developers often ignore cybersecurity in the developmental phase, which results in a huge spurt in cybercrime.

And now, with the rise of AI, things would only get worse. Generative AI was evolving quickly, and criminals were finding new ways to exploit it to commit fraud. Telecalling frauds were surging because AI could mimic voices and run thousands of calls at once. If victims could be made to pay in cryptocurrencies, then the money could be sent outside India's borders in no time and hidden away.

'I don't think we have the capacity to plug loopholes. We keep losing to scamsters. In these last few days, I saw how you investigated your brother's case with awe. You caught a point our forensic auditors could not. As CEO of I4C, I did not know what the telnet was. We have come across cases of remote access trojans—RATs—infecting computers, but no one explained to me the basic technology behind remotely accessing a computer. Thank you for improving my vocabulary. And then you went on to identify the person who used the open telnet on your brother's computer to access it. My forensic guys maintain that it would take them some time to see through the VPNs and bots that were used to access the computer.

'My problem is that the civil service recruitment system in India does not allow me to hire and fire at will. Most of my investigators are career bureaucrats, and do not have much appetite to learn about new technologies. When we hire private experts as consultants, we do not build their capacity. It is not that any of them lacks motivation; it's just that my organization is not agile enough to face such an asymmetric challenge.

'We do not know things, and we do not know what we do not know. We do not know who knows these things. And we do not have a strategy for identifying the people who know. As a leader, I feel deficient,' Simrandeep said.

'You need to scale up—fast,' Gamini said firmly. 'And you can't do it alone. You need to work with external experts, ethical hackers and the online cybersecurity community. The problem is digital, so your solutions need to be digital too.'

A glimmer of hope sparked in Simrandeep's eyes, as he expectantly waited for Gamini to say more.

'Have you ever heard about the crowd?'

'I once misunderstood "cloud" for "clouds" in a conference and got drenched in embarrassment. That was when cloud computing was new. So I will play safe and let you explain crowd to me.'

'Well … see, the internet is a network of users. When these users interact on social media, they form a digital community. When like-minded users congregate for a digital event, they are a crowd. Lately we have realized the power of such crowds. They are an enthusiastic lot and can be made to work together for a common good. Very much the way an NGO mobilizes people to work for a common good. Or when people of a locality come together to do *shramdaan*—voluntary contribution of labour for cleaning public spaces, building community facilities or participating in environmental or social welfare projects. Crowds come cheap, and they work best when they are made to work for a greater purpose.

'On the internet, you can connect with a crowd of cybersecurity experts. Many of these are self-made experts and do not have any formal degree. They hone their skills by solving cybersecurity problems. Now think about such a huge crowd working towards solving your most critical cases. There are many minds working for you. The idea is … you can run a forum to attract such crowds of cybersecurity enthusiasts. It's not an easy task ... you will have to attract them to the forum, improve engagements through hackathons ... promote small group events and physical meets. But it's worth it.'

'That's a good idea,' Simrandeep said, taking notes.

'A new problem you will be increasingly facing now is cybercrime by AI bots. If you want to plan for the next decade, develop AI to fight AI. I don't know how to do it. I am not an AI expert. But you need to put together a development team to figure this out. The private sector will be glad to partner you on this. Can AI be used to identify bots? Can AI be used to warn consumers about risky payments? Can AI help trace assets stolen through cyber fraud? These are some questions you can explore.'

Simrandeep nodded enthusiastically and continued making notes.

'But, of course, none of it will match in-house talent. You need to convince your employer to pay more for in-house talent. Do not hire consultants by looking at their degrees. Reach out to the cybersecurity community to hire the best, those who have proved their worth. I have heard the FBI gives clemency to some hackers who have committed cybercrimes on the condition that they work with the FBI to fight the same kind of crimes. I do not know if the law in India allows for such an arrangement between law enforcement and criminals. But you can explore that too.'

'You have made very pertinent points about hiring talent,' Simrandeep said with a smile, 'and why don't I make a start? What do you think about joining I4C?'

'Me?' Gamini asked, evidently surprised.

'Yes, you. Would you be interested in working here?'

'Do you have a branch in Bengaluru?'

'No, just here. Delhi. But the Karnataka police have a cyber cell in Bengaluru, which closely works with us.'

Gamini pursed her lips and smiled indulgently. 'Thank you, Simran, for the offer. It's an interesting opportunity. But as of now there are ongoing projects for which I have committed to my company. It would not be professional of me to leave them at this stage. Plus, there is this big decision about relocating.'

Simrandeep nodded slowly, but his disappointment was evident.

'Tell you what, Simran. What if I work pro bono for you for a while, and then we see how we can take our partnership forward? I will help you build engagement with the community of ethical hackers, and work with you to identify talent to hire. How does this sound?'

'That's a start. Sounds good to me.'

Simrandeep took Gamini on a tour of his office and showed her the labs for network analytics and forensic investigations. Gamini looked at the tools they were using with curiosity and interacted with a few analysts. Then they went back to Simrandeep's chamber for coffee.

'On your brother's case,' Simrandeep said at long last, 'I am getting minute-by-minute updates. A team of Delhi cyber police is pursuing all the leads we have. This Intelligent Coaching Centre in Shadi Khampur is fishy. The local police sealed it and placed two armed personnel on guard. We will get a magistrate warrant any minute now to raid it. It is now clear from the testimony of people working in that lane that Dang used to work in that building. A bunch of other guys either worked there or studied there—supposedly to prepare for competitive exams. They did not talk much with the neighbours and avoided anyone who approached them for a chat. All of them kept to themselves.'

'It's their call centre. If we manage to get sufficient clues there to corner just one gang member, we will know a lot about the gang behind Null Cyphers. But seeing the way they operate, I apprehend they have sanitized the call centre, and we will not find much,' Gamini said.

'I think I might have stumbled on one member of the ring entirely with my police hunch,' Simrandeep said, and with a slight smile continued, 'Do you recall the rowdy character we found staring at you in the courtroom yesterday? I felt something was off about him. It's a police hunch, but we policemen often take pride in such hunches. So, I pulled out recordings of the courtroom CCTV camera and extracted a still of this person. My people profiled him and have found that he goes by the name of Sandhu. He is a history sheeter, and has been to jail twice, once for mob violence and the other time for drug peddling. The charges did not stick, and he got out. Curiously, he operates in the area between Patel Nagar and Shadi Khampur. This could not have been a mere coincidence, so I asked the local police to enquire with their informers about this fellow. The informers have discreetly found that Sandhu is believed to own the building in which Intelligent Coaching Centre was running; he bought it in *benami* from the son of an old man who earlier ran a small lodge there. The son lives abroad and so sold it to Sandhu after the old man died.'

'Wow! That cannot be a coincidence,' Gamini said, her voice quivering with excitement. 'ED or the police should bring him in for questioning.'

'I thought about it, but it's not going to happen. Apparently, this man has joined a political party and is trying hard to get a ticket for the 2025 Delhi elections. In the last few years, he has managed to project himself as a people's leader in that area. Police need something concrete to arrest him, or we will face public backlash.'

'Seriously? You will not even question him?'

'You tell me. Should we question him? As you had mentioned earlier, this is no common gang. They are overly cautious. If we question him and he panics, there is a chance he would disappear like Dang. So, for now, I feel it's best to assign a few local cops to shadow him.'

'And what about Dang?'

'We are looking for him. He took a train to Howrah from the Nizamuddin station just this Tuesday. He booked a ticket using the *tatkal* service, which implies he had not planned for it. CCTV cameras at Nizamuddin station confirm that he took the train. But we could not locate him in the huge mass of passengers at Howrah. We found him accessing his email from a coffee shop's Wi-Fi near Bagdogra on Friday. The coffee shop is located on the road leading to Gangtok. We think he is in Sikkim with an intent to jump over to Nepal soon. Both Sikkim and Nepal have licensed casinos … something that would entice a compulsive gambler. Plus, Nepal is a preferred go-to place to escape law enforcement in India. He may be planning to go to Kathmandu, or to the border areas where you find many casinos on the Nepali side.'

'I hope we get him soon … at least by the time of my brother's next hearing,' Gamini said with a pout.

'We will get him. We have alerted Sikkim police and have sent his photographs to all agencies operating along the India–Nepal border. Through the Ministry of Home Affairs (MHA), we have alerted the Nepal police too. It's a matter of time before the police combs him out,' Simrandeep said confidently.

34 When the World Falls Apart

On her way out, Gamini stopped at the reception to collect her mobile phone. The first thing she saw on the phone's screen was the time. She had been inside the I4C office for a good three hours. Then she saw she had thirty-two missed calls. This did not bode well, since these were definitely not work calls—her office remained closed on Saturday. There were multiple calls from her father, Senthil, Janaraja and also calls from a few relatives. Her hand shook as she sensed bad news.

Gamini phoned back her father, then Senthil and then Janaraja. None of them picked up. She opened her WhatsApp to check messages. There was one from an aunt in Madurai asking in Tamil: 'Is the news about Sumathy true?' Gamini scrolled down to find a message from Senthil. It was short.

As Gamini read the message, she gasped and felt dizzy. The mobile phone fell from her hand as she tried to regain her balance and fumbled for something to hold on to. The phone landed on the floor and its screen cracked over her nephew's profile photograph and a message that read: 'Mother has committed suicide.'

35 The Sextortion of Arun Kamat

Arun Kamat tried hard to look deeply engrossed in paperwork while actually daydreaming about beach vacations and Lily's sultry voice in his ear. He sat in his office, drumming his fingers on the desk, only half-listening as his subordinates rambled on about the finer points of a shell company case. He wasn't always like this. He was passionate about the job of investigating financial crimes and often led discussions in weekly meetings. But this last one week had been life-changing for him, to say the least. He had finally found his soulmate. He could feel a subtle hum in his chest while thoughts of Lily filled his mind like the first showers of monsoon on a hot day.

His phone buzzed, and without a second thought he swiped it off the desk, holding it just out of sight. Lily. His heart leapt in excitement. He sneakily opened the message.

Lily: Cutie babu, I need to talk to u. Urgently :)

Kamat smirked. Urgently? That had promise. He quickly typed back.

Kamat: Busy in a meeting. Will call you later.

He stuffed the phone into his lap, trying to focus on whatever gibberish his officers were saying. Something about offshore accounts. Yawn. Then, another buzz. Kamat glanced down.

Lily: But I have a surprise for u ...

Oh. Now that was interesting. Lily was full of surprises. Every mole on her body, every sound she made, the pigmentation around her nipples, everything held a surprise. And Kamat had a huge appetite for surprises from Lily. He had made up his mind to go to Bengaluru this week and meet Lily at any cost. Lily had initially been apprehensive about meeting him, fearing the constant surveillance from her husband and mother-in-law. But as their love blossomed over the week, she felt emboldened and was now open to meeting him. He would have her soon. He could not resist any longer. If required, he would get her bloody husband arrested and put away for good. Just the thought of how she would look in person, how she would smell, how she would taste, aroused him colossally.

Kamat raised his hand abruptly. 'All right, let's wrap this up for now. You all know what to do. Report back tomorrow.'

His subordinates exchanged bewildered looks, but they weren't about to argue with a quick exit. As soon as the door shut, Kamat was already dialling Lily on WhatsApp, his pulse quickening. The phone rang once before she picked up, her voice as smooth as butter melting on hot toast.

'Hello, Arun,' she purred. 'I've been waiting for you.'

'Yeah, well, you've got me now,' Kamat replied, lowering his voice to match hers. 'What's this surprise?'

'Arun,' Lily cooed. 'You need to destroy the hard disks and laptops of Sunil Dang.'

Kamat's smirk evaporated faster than water on hot tarmac. 'Wait, what?' He jerked upright in his chair. 'Destroy the ... WHAT?'

'The laptops and hard disks,' Lily repeated, her tone as casual as if she were suggesting a movie to watch. 'You know, the ones the police seized from Sunil Dang's whore. They're in ED custody now, aren't they?'

Kamat blinked, feeling overwhelmed. 'How ... how do you know about that?' His voice cracked like a teenager's.

There was a pause. Then, in the most unnervingly nonchalant tone possible, she said, 'Arun, darling, I know about many things. About Dang, and about you.'

His mouth fell open, and for a solid ten seconds, all he could manage was a series of confused, spluttering noises that sounded vaguely like a dying generator. 'Are you trying to catfish me?! You are joking, right? I must have told you about the case … but I never told you about Dang …'

'Yes, you did not tell me about Dang. And no, I am not joking.'

Kamat sank back into his chair, eyes wide as saucers. 'So ... this whole time ...?' His voice was rising in agitation. 'You're not real?'

Lily sighed, her voice softening like she was comforting a child whose balloon had just floated away. 'Oh, Arun, of course I'm real. What we had—the connection, the late-night talks, the dirty talk—that was all real. I have masturbated to the thoughts of your large belly squeezing me while you pump yourself into me. As you have, while I have described to you how I will take your dick in my mouth. All of that talk was real. When we became serious, that too was real. We connected, did we not? Now, if you thought I would actually blow you … like ever … that's a bit unreal. You know that, don't you, officer?'

Kamat's mind went into free fall. 'This ... this makes no sense! Who are you working for? How do you know about the digital evidence?!' He was on his feet now, pacing back and forth like a magician whose trick had just left him trapped inside his own disappearing act.

'That's not important,' Lily said smoothly, her voice like a mother soothing her child. 'What's important is that you destroy the evidence. Do it quickly, and no one has to know.'

Kamat's heart pounded. 'I CAN'T destroy evidence!' he practically yelped. 'There's a procedure! The evidence is sealed! It can only be opened in front of two witnesses!'

Lily's tone hardened, now sharp as a butcher's knife. 'Listen, sweetheart, this isn't a request. I have your nude photos. You know, the ones you so generously sent. And all those chat logs where you conveniently mentioned your properties in London, Dubai, and ... oh, a recording of you boasting about your Swiss account.'

Kamat's knees almost gave out. He sat down with a thunk, the colour draining from his face. 'No ... no, no, no, you wouldn't ...'

'I absolutely wouldn't, baby. We have a long way to go, Arun, you and I. Together we will grab that post of director, ED. There are many mountains for us to scale. But our partnership cannot be one-way. I will be your secret-keeper, you will lick my wet ass,' Lily replied, her voice a soft purr that would have ignited sparks in the heart of her lover in some other context. 'But if you don't play along, I cannot help you scale the heights of your aspirations. By tomorrow, every news channel will be running the story of your illustrious real-estate portfolio. So, do yourself a favour and be a good boy.'

'But ... but ...' Kamat stammered, 'the evidence is sealed! There's a process! And—'

'You don't need to break the seal,' she said, with the exasperation of a teacher explaining algebra to a particularly dense student. 'You're getting a degaussing machine. It'll be delivered by courier. All you have to do is run it over the hard disks. Its magnetic field is strong enough to destroy the digital evidence. No seal broken and no evidence left.'

As if on cue, the landline rang. Kamat practically jumped out of his skin, fumbling for the receiver.

'Sir,' came his PA's disinterested voice, 'a package has arrived for you. It's from … ehh, Lily. The envelope just says "Lily". Shall I bring it in?'

Kamat wiped a bead of sweat from his brow, staring at the phone in his hand like it was cursed. 'No, no, just ... just keep it with you for now.'

He hung up and returned to the call, his pulse racing. 'Lily ... I'll do it,' he said, feeling like a man agreeing to sell his soul for a discount. 'But ... I didn't expect this from you.' His voice cracked slightly, a mix of betrayal and desperation. 'I ... I thought we had something. You know? Beyond ... the sex talk. I felt ... something real for you. And now, this?'

'Oh, Arun, darling. I care about you too. But you have to understand, I have a job to do. I have to follow orders. Like you cannot break a seal without following procedures, I too have my constraints.'

Kamat felt his heart break in a way that was both tragic and utterly absurd. 'I don't know if I can do this ...' he mumbled, his voice barely above a whisper.

'You can, and you will,' Lily purred. 'Just remember ... I'm watching.'

Lily ended the call, leaving Kamat staring at his phone in stunned silence.

36 The Weight of Guilt

It had been five days since Sumathy's passing, yet the gloom and foreboding that enveloped her house was as fresh as it had been on that Saturday. Gamini sat on the couch's edge, absently twisting a strand of her hair, her thoughts lost in the silence hanging over the room. It felt suffocating, amplifying the raw ache in her chest. The walls bore only the faintest shadows of happier days that the house had seen, overwhelmed by the cold finality of Sumathy's absence.

In her mind, Gamini replayed the days before her sister-in-law's final act. The silence that Sumathy had maintained in her last days spoke of deeper wounds than Gamini had recognized. She wondered if her own attempts at comforting Sumathy had felt hollow to her. Had she, Gamini, simply been a bystander, too caught up in her brother's troubles to see Sumathy slipping further into despair? Sumathy's suicide note had named only Gandhi Kumar, but Gamini couldn't shake the thought that other forces had weighed heavily on her sister-in-law's spirit.

Her mother's harsh criticism of Sumathy, so often disguised as advice, had always troubled her. Gamini recalled how her mother remained unkind towards her even after Gandhi Kumar's arrest. Gamini knew that Sumathy had felt alone after the ED raid, felt trapped, yet she had done little to shield her from the unkindness or to offer her an escape. And now, with Sumathy gone, Gamini was left to pick up the shattered pieces, taking on the impossible task of becoming a mother figure to Senthil and Anjali. In the week following Sumathy's death, she had taken a long leave from work in Bengaluru, knowing there would be no quick return to normalcy.

The doorbell echoed from downstairs, breaking through her reverie. 'Aunty,' Senthil murmured, 'Uncle Janaraja is here.'

She rose and followed him to the balcony. Janaraja waited at the gate below with large polythene bags in hand, visibly uncomfortable. He told Senthil that he had brought pastries and fries for Anjali, his face lined with fatigue and grief. Clearly ignoring Gamini, he asked Senthil to come down to take the bags. Sensing his uncle's hesitance to come up, Senthil lingered in the balcony until Gamini gently called out, 'Janaraja, please come upstairs.' The words fell softly, but they conveyed an unspoken plea. After a moment of hesitation, he nodded and made his way up.

The silence that settled between Gamini and Janaraja as they sat facing each other in the living room was thick, a shared burden they both seemed unwilling to voice. Janaraja had not shaved in five days; ritual procedures required him to remain ungroomed for the duration of

Sumathy's mourning, which ended on the eleventh day of her suicide. He had an unruly stubble, part of it greyed, that added a madman aura to his teddy-bear appearance. Still, his rotund, cuddly physique gave him a softness that was always comforting.

Gamini took a slow breath, finally breaking the silence with a question about his brothers. Janaraja replied simply, his tone flat: 'They've gone to Chennai to meet our mother. They'll be back in time for the eleventh-day rituals.'

The mention of the rituals took Gamini's thoughts to the chaotic day following Sumathy's death. The elder brothers had flown in from overseas as soon as they'd heard the news, their rage like a storm that descended upon the family. The cremation had taken place in an electric crematorium, a choice that had caused immediate resentment. The brothers wanted to take the body to Chennai, so that Sumathy could be cremated following the right rituals among people 'who cared for her'. They had erupted, casting angry accusations at Gandhi Kumar's family. Then they blamed everyone in his family for Sumathy's death, and Gamini's mother bore the brunt of their fury. They'd labelled her a relentless mother-in-law, merciless in her scrutiny, a factor they believed had chipped away at Sumathy's will to live.

In the wake of the cremation, the brothers had declared their intention to take Senthil and Anjali away, which the children had reacted to with tearful refusals. Since Sumathy's death, they'd clung to Gamini like vines to a crumbling wall. Anjali cried sporadically but inconsolably, the sound of which amplified the helplessness that had descended upon the decor of the house. She would wake in the dead of night, trembling with a terror she could not explain; she would panic if Gamini left the house and did not return within the hour. Senthil had withdrawn, immersing himself in the glow of his phone screen, finding solace in Instagram feeds and WhatsApp chats. Gamini wanted to monitor his screen time, but she held back, realizing that this small escape was the balm he needed.

Janaraja's quiet presence in the room was somehow more intense than Gamini had anticipated. Gamini offered tea, but Janaraja refused. He just sat there, his body slacking and face fallen in dejection. Since Sumathy's passing, he had kept his distance from her family, his words sparse, his demeanour a reflection of a deep hurt. He'd participated in the cremation and the rituals that followed, but he had not spoken to Gamini or her parents, maintaining a silent accusation in his every glance. Clearly, he saw her family as a part of the weight that had pressed Sumathy towards the edge.

'How are the kids doing?' Janaraja asked at last, his gaze softening slightly as he looked in the direction of the children's room.

'Anjali … she's struggling. She needs us more than ever.' Gamini paused, her voice wavering. 'They both do. They're feeling … abandoned. You should come around more often, Janaraja.'

Janaraja nodded slowly, a glimmer of pain in his eyes. 'I wish Gandhi Kumar would rot in that jail for what he's done,' he muttered, his voice a harsh whisper. 'But for the children's sake … I also wish he gets out on bail.'

The thought of her brother's imprisonment stirred a recent memory in Gamini's mind—a memory tinged with darkness and despair. Advocate Chopra had urged Gandhi Kumar to attend Sumathy's cremation, suggesting that interim bail could be granted for such occasions. But Gandhi Kumar had refused, retreating instead to the isolation of his cell. Gamini was worried by this decision, and so she visited him in Tihar Jail after the cremation.

The light in the visiting room of the jail was cooler, filtered through narrow windows high in the walls. Gamini sat on the metal chair, her hands clasped in her lap, eyes fixed on the steel table's scratched surface. Her mind kept oscillating between the bleakness of the jail's visiting room and her worry about sneaking out of the house when Anjali was sleeping.

When Gandhi Kumar was brought in, she almost didn't recognize him. The man before her seemed smaller, his frame shrunken under the weight of something enormous but invisible. His eyes were vacant, hollow, and when they met hers, he seemed to look right through her, like she was a ghost of something that had once been familiar.

He sat down slowly, almost reluctantly. 'Do not come back here, Gamini. I don't want to meet anyone. I am good as I am.'

Gamini glared at him but could not find the right words to say.

'You saw what happened to Sumathy. I do not want anyone else to suffer on my account. You should go back to Bengaluru. You have your life there, your work and all …'

'What do you mean "go back"? What about Senthil? What about Anjali? Should I leave them here with our old parents who can't even talk in Hindi? Or should I ask them to go back to wherever they have come from?'

'Do what you deem fit, as their guardian. Take them with you, and amma–appa too. Or put them in a good boarding school. They are old enough to manage on their own, and there is enough in my savings to fund a good boarding. I … I am without any hope. I can neither care for them nor do I deserve to be around them.'

After a moment of silence where both stared at the steel table between them, Gandhi Kumar broke down and cried like a baby.

'Why, Gamini? Why did Sumathy … why did she …'

Gamini reached out, her hand hovering over his, but he pulled his hand back, his fingers curling inward. Slowly, his breathing evened out, each exhale becoming steadier, softer, until it was nearly silent. With a tremor in his voice, he said, 'Things will never … never be the same again.'

'You, of all people, have to be strong. This is not the time to …'

'I keep seeing her, Gamini. Night and day. I close my eyes, and she's … there.' He swallowed, his throat bobbing as if he could push down the words, the memories, the regret that choked him. 'I can't even show my face … not to the children. I can't.'

'You are thinking too much. We all know the circumstances in which this happened. The children have forgiven you.'

'They should not. I cannot ever forgive myself. I … I love her so much. You would not know how much I love her. You have a disdain for arranged marriages. Yours did not work out … but it was different for us. And I could not even tell her how much I have repented about cheating on her.'

The words seemed to exhaust him. He slumped forward, pressing his palms to his forehead, as if he could hide from everything—the world, himself, her.

'Anna, my focus here is to help you come out. The kids need you …' Gamini's voice was soft, but he shook his head, his shoulders tensing.

'No,' he murmured, barely louder than a whisper. 'I don't want to come out. Here, I don't have to … I don't have to face them. Out there …' He glanced up, his eyes heavy, a quiet resignation settling within them. 'Out there, they'll judge me. They'll look at me and see … what she did, what I … what I let happen.'

Gandhi Kumar's feeling of resignation had unsettled Gamini. Her brother was always the weak one, but even she had not expected such fatalism from him. Seeing him crumble, his strength eroded by grief and guilt, left her with an unsettling ache.

Now, as she sat across from Janaraja, she felt the urge to defend her brother, to tell him of the regret and pain that Gandhi Kumar carried. But the words faltered on her lips, and instead she spoke quietly, 'He's hurting, Janaraja. He cheated on her, that's unpardonable, but we both know how much he loved her. Now he is so unhinged, he does not want to come out of jail. In any case, I don't think he will be granted bail any time soon.'

Janaraja raised an eyebrow, his expression tinged with incredulity. 'I remember you seemed so sure of his release, Gamini. You were digging into everything, searching for evidence. No?'

Gamini sighed, the frustration and helplessness bubbling to the surface. 'Most of the leads we had … they're turning into dead ends,' she admitted.

In the days leading up to Sumathy's death, Gamini had chased down every hint, every shred of evidence that might exonerate her brother. Null Cyphers had felt so close, a looming presence just beyond reach, but nothing she uncovered had made a difference. Sunil Dang's supposed digital evidence was found damaged when the ED officers accessed it. Even Simrandeep, the man she had trusted, had insisted there was no tampering, yet the evidence had been compromised. Every new lead felt like a door slamming shut.

She thought about Leatherman chasing the money trail of cash withdrawn in Seychelles, with the resources of the FBI. He had hit a wall. His colleagues at the FBI had scoured the CCTV footage at the crypto exchange, but it revealed nothing more than a thin man in a cap and sunglasses who had picked up the cash from a manager at the crypto exchange in Seychelles, untraceable and anonymous. Every clue, every piece of the puzzle, seemed to vanish into thin air just as she thought she'd found something concrete.

Leatherman had been visiting her nearly every evening since Sumathy's death, offering his support in the face of her mounting despair. She found herself wondering if he was beginning to see her as more than just an ally in the investigation, though she had not given him any cue that could be interpreted as encouragement.

The previous evening, Gamini had served him masala chai with ginger and cardamom. After being posted in India for some time, he had developed a liking for the strong drink. They spoke about the medieval-era monuments in Delhi, which Leatherman was clearly fascinated by. He asked about Meenakshi temple and the rock temples of Mahabalipuram, about which he had read up. When they ran out of topics to discuss, he glanced at her sideways, his mouth opening as if to say something important, but he held back. Finally, as they went down to the road, he murmured against the backdrop of distant honks and street chatter, 'I keep thinking … things in your brother's case don't add up, Gamini.'

'As in?'

'Dead ends everywhere, perfectly dead.' His eyes were sharper than usual, studying her with a quiet intensity she wasn't prepared for.

'You keep talking about some conspiracy, Brian, as if … as if someone's pulling all the strings. That officer Kamat is crooked, but you tend to believe everyone is.'

He laughed softly, not out of amusement but something closer to resignation. 'If there's one thing I've learnt about your country, Gamini, it's that things aren't always what they seem.' He paused, running a hand over his jaw, hesitating. 'You … may know the people here better than I do. But I know the power plays.'

She shook her head, a sharp, controlled gesture. 'Simrandeep, for instance. I know him. He wouldn't … twist evidence, tamper with things. He's …' she trailed off, watching him carefully. 'He's straightforward. Maybe you don't understand that.' Her tone was more defensive than she'd intended, but she didn't soften it.

He inclined his head, studying her as if weighing her words against some internal scale. 'I don't mean to accuse him, Gamini,' he said, the edge in his voice smoothed out. 'But consider this—the digital evidence belonging to Dang was corrupted. Not one laptop or one hard disk … all devices were corrupted. We both know the process. How does that happen?'

Gamini pressed her lips together, the same tension building again, a dull ache behind her temples. 'It's possible. Mishandling. Equipment failures.' She forced the words out, but her tone sounded hollow even to her. She wanted to believe her own excuses, but the look on Leatherman's face told her he didn't.

'Come to think about it: the police had handed over the electronic equipment to ED in a sealed cover. ED broke the seals with Delhi Police's insignia, and the entire process was recorded. But what happened before the evidence was seized was not videographed. The raid was conducted by

Delhi's cyber cell under Simrandeep's instructions, not by the jurisdictional police station. Well, he is a good friend, a workaholic and capable leader and all that … but I still cannot shrug away the fact that he was in a position to tamper with the evidence before it was sealed.'

From their conversations over the past few days, Gamini had realized that Leatherman was deeply suspicious. He had his doubts about the BIMS attack. The attack was possible because an air gap between the BIMS intranet and a backup server was breached by physically connecting the backup server with the intranet. He found it surprising that the police could not identify the person who connected the backup server to the intranet physically. He felt there was a bigger conspiracy behind the attack, and now they wanted a scapegoat to cover it up; which was why there was such zeal to keep Gandhi Kumar behind bars.

Gamini had dismissed it, refusing to believe in such a grand design. But as the dead ends piled up, doubt had begun to creep into her thoughts. She wondered why Sandhu, a person of interest that Simrandeep had so dexterously identified, was yet to be questioned. Simrandeep maintained that Sandhu had purchased the property in *benami*, and the owner on paper had vanished. Without some direct lead, it was not appropriate for the police to examine a political leader. A call centre in Shadi Khampur village linked to Null Cyphers had been raided but yielded nothing. And now, even Sunil Dang had vanished, leaving behind a trail that seemed to lead towards the Nepal border but offered no definitive proof of his escape.

It is widely believed that notorious hacker groups which are at large have the tacit support of sovereign powers: DarkSide and Fancy Bear are widely believed to be from Russia; the Lazarus Group is believed to be from North Korea; and Honker

Union and Volt Typhoon are believed to be from China. These groups have remained elusive in spite of massive efforts by the US government and Interpol, which is one reason why there is speculation that they are state-backed. Could Null Cyphers be backed by a faction within the Indian state? Or by a deep state that the political executive was not aware of? The problem was, such fantastical theories had no basis and there was no way to prove or disprove them. And Gamini knew India could not be compared to countries like Russia, China and North Korea, where the rule of law was suspect.

Gamini explained to Janaraja that ED was not going to allow bail to Gandhi Kumar unless the real hackers were identified.

'Then who will take care of Anjali and Senthil?'

Gamini shrugged. 'I.'

'They will move to Bengaluru with you?'

'No, I may move here. I need to be here for anna too. Someone has to fight the case from outside and coordinate with lawyers while he is in jail. My parents feel out of place here; it is better for them if they go back home. I will stay here and hire a full-time maid … take up some job here or in Gurgaon. I got an offer from the government to work for I4C. When I got the offer, I laughed it away. But I am thinking about it more seriously.'

'But what about Ruma? That's the name of your roommate, right?'

'Roommate and best friend. She has been such a support for all these years. But I cannot be selfish. It's not wise for me to uproot the kids after all that has happened … and I cannot desert my brother. She understands that.'

Janaraja shook his head and said, 'It's going to be difficult for you. You will not realize now … once you commit to an arrangement, there is no turning back.'

Gamini already knew this, and she was up for it. She was a crusader, forever seeking a cause to champion. After her divorce, she had devoted her mind and soul to work. And she had enough appetite to take up a new cause: becoming a parent to her brother's children. She loved them, adored them and had no hesitation in taking responsibility for them.

Before leaving, Janaraja knelt down to where Anjali sat on the floor, running a hand gently through her hair. He promised to take her and Senthil to the shopping mall later in the evening, his voice soft and tender. When Janaraja left, Gamini's mood had shifted completely. The heaviness that had clouded her heart seemed to dissipate, replaced by a sense of lightness and warmth. She felt more at peace, her burden momentarily lighter, and her heart a little less heavy than it had been.

She checked her phone, her eyes drawn to the two missed calls from Ananya Dang. She had phoned a few times in the past two days, but Gamini had ignored her calls. Now, feeling cheerful, she phoned back.

When Ananya answered, they exchanged greetings. Gamini realized that she did not know about the bereavement in Gandhi Kumar's family. She was trying to contact Gamini to tell her about Sunil Dang. She mentioned that her daughter, Rinki, had come home on Monday with an unusual story—that Tina, her maid, had taken her to meet her father after school. When Ananya had pressed her for details, the child had fallen silent, her gaze flickering to Tina, who had watched her intently. Tina said that she took Rinki to an ice-cream parlour opposite the school, where she met a friend's father. However, Ananya did not find Tina's explanation convincing.

Gamini explained to Ananya that her husband had fled to Nepal, and so Tina could be quite right. Ananya was not convinced, though. She said that for all his flaws, Dang loved his daughter. He was particular about meeting her every Sunday and Monday. Rinki was also fond of her father, and did not seem to miss him as she would have if he wasn't around. Rather, Ananya observed that Tina had taken one or two hours extra to bring Rinki home after school that week.

Gamini sat back, a new-found determination stealing her gaze. It was as though amidst the fog of despair, a faint light had pierced through, a glimmer of hope. What if Sunil Dang had sent the police sniffing on a wrong trail?

37 A Hunch, a Stakeout, a Mystery

The unassuming white Toyota Innova was parked a respectful distance from Ananya Dang's apartment complex. Gamini sat in the passenger seat, her keen eyes fixed on the apartment's front gate while her companion, Leatherman, adjusted his seat belt with the kind of diligence one might expect from someone boarding a rocket.

'Another day in paradise,' Leatherman muttered, glancing at Gamini with a wry smile. 'You do realize this is what I left New York for? Sitting in a car, staking out a maid. Feels like the same setting, minus the skyscrapers, plus a lot of cows on the road.'

Gamini smirked, keeping her eyes on the building. 'I thought Americans loved action. Besides, if you think this is boring, you should try my job. Most of the time, I'm just debugging code.'

'Debugging …' Leatherman shuddered theatrically. 'That word alone sounds more painful than this.'

They had begun their surveillance on Sunday morning. It had been over twenty-four hours, and the most exciting thing they had witnessed so far was Tina, Ananya's maid, arguing with a vegetable vendor over the price of tomatoes. This morning, they saw Ananya come out with Rinki at 9 a.m. As Ananya had explained earlier, she dropped Rinki at school daily and then went to work. Tina would pick her up from school at 12.30 p.m.

Leatherman leaned back, sighing dramatically as he pulled out a small box of Domino's pizza with vegetable toppings. 'So, you are vegetarian, huh?' he said, offering a slice to Gamini. 'No steak, no bacon, no fish … how do you even get out of bed in the morning?' Gamini rolled her eyes but took the slice, unfazed by his taunts. Leatherman grabbed another slice for himself, biting into it. He made a face, chewing slowly. 'This tastes like disappointment,' he declared. 'Vegetarians must really hate joy.'

Gamini chuckled softly, her gaze never leaving the apartment. 'Vegetarianism isn't as tragic as you make it sound. Besides, it's cultural for a lot of Indians—religion, tradition, sometimes just preference.'

'Cultural? So what, everyone just collectively decided to hate good food?' Leatherman teased.

'Not everyone,' Gamini shot back. 'Plenty of us enjoy "good food", just minus the murder. Besides, have you tried paneer?'

Leatherman made a face. 'Tried it. Tasted like a chewy eraser.'

Before Gamini could respond, a black Pulsar motorcycle zipped past their car. Gamini stiffened, narrowing her eyes. The riders wore full-face helmets, obscuring their features, and the bike slowed down just enough to linger near Ananya's building before roaring off.

The two men on the bike were suspicious in every sense. Both wore matching dark jackets, and their helmets—black with tinted visors—seemed intentionally designed to give them anonymity. Who would wear a jacket in Noida in July? The pillion rider, slightly stockier than the man in front, kept his head on a constant swivel, as if scanning the surroundings. They moved with an unnatural purposefulness that set off alarm bells in Gamini's head.

'Third time I've seen them,' Gamini murmured, picking up her notepad and jotting down the bike's license plate.

Leatherman barely glanced up. 'Could be locals. Bikers are everywhere in India.'

'They're too consistent,' Gamini countered, her voice tense. 'They've been circling this block since yesterday. Same bike, same helmets, same suspicious loitering.'

Leatherman shrugged. 'Might just be the neighbourhood Romeo and his sidekick. Let it go.'

But Gamini didn't let it go. A bad feeling crawled up her spine. She debated calling Simrandeep to check the bike's registration but hesitated. She had always respected Simrandeep for his sharp intellect and dedication, but lately, doubts had begun to creep in. Could he be part of a larger game to implicate her brother in the Null Cyphers case? The possibility gnawed at her, leaving her torn. Trust was a precious commodity, and while she wanted to believe in Simrandeep, the stakes were too high to ignore the nagging doubt. For now, she decided, caution had to prevail over certainty.

'You can use your contacts in the Delhi establishment to run the bike's license, right?' Gamini asked Leatherman.

'Yes, I can. The CBI or the Ministry of Home Affairs will give me feedback in no time. But they will also get curious as to why I am asking, and what I am up to. I would suggest we wait and see if Sunil Dang is really here before chasing any subplots,' Leatherman said.

Gamini nodded. 'I somehow think he is here, Brian. It makes sense, doesn't it? He loves his daughter so much and does not want to disappoint her.'

'Maybe. But you see too much goodness in a slippery and unreliable criminal. How devoted a punter is to his daughter can only be speculated. The police have based their intel—that he has fled to Nepal—on multiple cues, though.'

Ananya Dang had phoned Gamini, voicing her suspicion that Tina, her maid, was secretly facilitating meetings between Sunil Dang and Rinki without her knowledge. Her first instinct had been to call Simrandeep, but his insistence that Dang had fled to Nepal made her pause. Instead, she phoned Leatherman.

'Greater Noida?' he'd said, instantly intrigued. 'I'll bring the car.'

And just like that, they were parked outside Ananya's home, ready for surveillance. Gamini was glad to be in Leatherman's company. He had a knack for diffusing tension with his dry humour, making even this anxious stake-out feel manageable. There was an air of confidence about him that was oddly reassuring. Despite her worry about the legality of shadowing a fellow citizen, she felt safer knowing he was by her side.

38 Caught in the Act

At noon, Tina finally emerged. She was a young woman, barely in her early twenties, with a slim, almost fragile frame. Her dusky skin glowed faintly in the midday sun, though it bore the marks of a hard life. Tina wore a salwar kameez, the colour of which had long faded from repeated washes, and a loosely draped dupatta that barely stayed on her shoulder. Her hair was tied hastily into a messy braid. Clutching a jute bag, usually used to carry tiffins, she moved with a hurried, purposeful gait towards the school to pick up Rinki. The school was less than a kilometre away from the apartment complex.

Leatherman started the car and followed at a safe distance. 'This is it,' he said, feigning excitement. 'The thrilling life of surveillance.'

Gamini ignored him, pulling out her small telescope. Tina picked up Rinki from the school and led her to a public garden midway between the school and their flat, where they settled on a bench. Leatherman parked on the road near the garden, after finding a suitable angle from which Tina and Rinki were visible. Moments later, a lanky man in a faded shirt and jeans approached.

'That's him,' Gamini whispered. Her pulse quickened as she watched Dang kneel to hug Rinki, handing her a bundle of toys and chocolates.

For the next ten minutes, Dang played the doting father, showering Rinki with affection as her laughter echoed through the park. Meanwhile, Tina opened her jute bag, pulling out a small tiffin box that Gamini guessed contained freshly cooked food. She laid out a simple spread on the bench and handed Dang a plate with a shy smile.

'What do you think she has cooked for Dang? Curry fish or gravy beef?' Leatherman asked.

'I would guess rice, lentils and a side of pickles,' Gamini said while intently watching Dang's every move with her telescope.

'I guess she loves him, but not enough,' Leatherman quipped. Gamini ignored him.

Without hesitation, Dang took Tina's hand in his, pressing it gently before bringing it to his lips, his gaze lingering on her with an intensity that made Tina blush deeply. As Rinki became engrossed in her new toys, Dang pulled Tina aside, his hand brushing a stray lock of hair from her face. Their whispered words dissolved into a passionate embrace, his fingers tracing her cheek as their kiss deepened. Through Gamini's telescope, the scene was startlingly intimate, and Dang came across as a passionate lover.

'Romantic,' Leatherman quipped. 'Should we break up their little rendezvous or wait?'

'We should call the police,' Gamini said, snapping pictures with her phone.

'Let's wait,' Leatherman replied, his tone distant. 'Rinki's expected home soon. Dang will leave, and we'll follow him to his hideout.'

Gamini hesitated but agreed, her focus shifting back to her notes. Leatherman, however, seemed distracted, typing furiously on his phone.

39 True Colours

About an hour later, Dang bid farewell to Tina and Rinki. He flagged down an autorickshaw and disappeared into traffic. Gamini and Leatherman tailed the vehicle, which eventually entered the Ecotech 1 Sector of Greater Noida. It was an industrial area, dominated by large warehouses. Dang slipped into an abandoned warehouse through a back entrance.

Just as Gamini was processing this, the black Pulsar from earlier appeared. Her heart raced as the bike parked near the warehouse and the riders dismounted, their helmets still on. As they swung off the bike, Gamini's telescope caught a glimpse of what looked like a gun holster tied to the passenger's waist. The sight sent a chill down her spine. They scanned their surroundings in synchronized sweeps, the tension in their postures palpable, before disappearing silently into the warehouse.

'They're following him too,' she said, her voice tight with urgency. 'I'm calling Simrandeep.'

'No,' Leatherman snapped, even while engrossed in typing into his phone, his usual casual tone replaced by something colder. 'Not yet. We don't know who they are.'

'I don't have a good feeling about this. They are armed and they were staking out Ananya's flat just like us. Now they are going into the building. Why would they go in unless they want to confront him?'

'Let us not jump to any conclusion yet and hold our nerves,' Leatherman said.

Gamini ignored him and reached for her phone. Before she could unlock it, Leatherman lunged, snatching the phone from her hand and gripping her wrist with an iron clasp.

'What the hell are you doing?' she yelled, struggling against his hold.

'We can't risk it,' he growled. 'Leave this to the expert.'

Gamini's eyes blazed. 'Let go of me!'

When he didn't, she swung her free arm, aiming a punch at his face. He dodged, but her second blow landed squarely on his jaw. Enraged, Leatherman tightened his grip, twisting her arm painfully. Leatherman's calculated movements, his unflinching strength, and the cold look in his eyes made her blood run cold.

Gamini's instincts kicked in. She leaned back and brought her knee up hard, aiming for his midsection. Leatherman grunted, his grip loosening for just a moment. She took the chance to yank her arm free, but he quickly recovered, grabbing her by the shoulders and slamming her back against the car door.

'You're making a mistake,' he hissed, his face inches from hers, his breath hot and reeking of adrenaline.

But Gamini wasn't done. With a sudden burst of energy, she twisted her body, driving her elbow into his ribs. Leatherman winced, and she reached for her pen. With a quick jab, she drove it into his cheek, drawing blood.

Leatherman roared in pain, momentarily loosening his grip. Gamini used the opportunity to reach for the door handle, but the central lock held firm. Panic surged through her veins as she struggled, her fingers scrabbling for anything she could use as a weapon.

Leatherman's eyes were wild now, a mix of fury and desperation. He grabbed her by the hair, yanking her back towards him. With a vicious snarl, he slammed her head against the dashboard. Once, twice, three times—each impact sending shock waves through her skull. The world around her blurred, her vision fading at the edges.

'You should've just listened,' Leatherman muttered, his voice echoing in her ears as her consciousness began to slip away.

40 Aunty, Where Are You?

Anjali sat cross-legged on the edge of the sofa. Her fingers drummed anxiously against her knees. Her mother's phone lay next to her, the screen dim. Her thoughts were tethered to it, as if willing it to light up with a reply from Gamini.

She hated it when her aunt left. Her world had crumbled so spectacularly in the past few weeks. Her father, rotting in a jail cell. Her mother, gone forever. The fragile thread holding her together seemed to fray each time someone she loved stepped out the door.

Gamini's casual mention of being away for a few days in Greater Noida had sent Anjali into a spiral of unease. 'Take me wherever you are going,' she had protested. Gamini had hugged her tightly, promising to be back by evening each day. But Anjali's insecurities were like shadows creeping in at dusk, darkening her thoughts with each passing moment. They would not be dispelled by promises and assurances.

Now, with Gamini gone, Anjali sent her messages every few minutes. Her fingers trembled as she typed: 'When will you be back?' 'Are you safe?' 'Aunty, reply please!' At first, Gamini had responded patiently, her messages laced with emojis meant to reassure: 'Back by evening :)' 'Try not to worry, sweetheart :)' But the last message had been over an hour ago. Anjali's chest tightened with each passing minute of silence.

She tapped out another message, her hands damp with sweat. When no reply came, she glanced at her grandfather. He was engrossed in his newspaper. She decided to voice her fears.

'Tatta, why isn't Aunty answering my messages?' Her voice was small, edged with panic.

Mr Nataraja folded the newspaper neatly and looked at her with kind but tired eyes. 'She's likely in an area without good network coverage. Don't overthink. She is safe. She'll be back by evening.'

Unsatisfied, Anjali turned to her brother who was sprawled on the carpet with his phone, chuckling softly at something Siya had sent him.

'Anna, Aunty isn't replying! What if something's wrong?'

Senthil barely looked up. 'Relax, she's with Brian, remember? He works for the FBI, not our local police. Aunty is in good hands.'

'You're not helping!' she snapped, clutching a cushion to her chest.

Senthil waved her off, returning to his chat. Frustrated, Anjali fidgeted for another half an hour. She bit her nails until they were ragged. Finally, she gave up and called Janaraja. Her voice trembled as she explained that Gamini's phone was unreachable.

'Her network might just be out of range,' Janaraja said, his tone calm but firm. 'Give it another couple of hours before panicking, Anjali. I'm sure it's nothing.'

'But what if . . . what if it is something?' Her voice cracked, the tears she had been holding back spilling over.

Janaraja sighed, clearly picking up on her distress. 'Fine. I'll start making some calls. Don't worry.'

But worrying was all Anjali could do. She paced the room like a trapped animal. Then, she cornered her grandfather again. 'Tatta, Aunty wears a GPS tag in her shoes! Ruma can track her. Please call her!'

Mr Nataraja hesitated, but her desperation was impossible to ignore. He picked up the phone and called Ruma, relaying the situation. Ruma's reaction was immediate, her voice sharp with concern.

'Let me check the tag,' she said quickly. 'I'll call you back.'

The minutes felt like hours. Anjali sat on the floor, her knees drawn to her chest. Tears streamed silently down her face. Her phone vibrated with a call from Janaraja.

'I've tried everything,' he admitted. 'I can't get Leatherman's number. Advocate Chopra doesn't have it, and the US embassy won't share it on privacy grounds. But I'll keep trying.'

Anjali's heart sank. The walls felt like they were closing in on her.

When Ruma finally called back, Anjali impatiently snatched her grandfather's mobile and answered it. There was a hesitation in her voice, an uncertainty that made Anjali's heart pound. 'Anjali, I've tracked her using two methods,' she began slowly. 'First, her phone—the Find My Phone app shows her last known location near Ecotech 1 Sector in Greater Noida. But … the phone's switched off now.' She paused, and Anjali could hear her take a deep breath.

'Second, her GPS tag. The signal is still active, but it's moving fast. It's heading south, on the express highway towards Agra.' Another silence followed, then Ruma added, almost in a whisper, 'It's not right, Anjali. It's almost as if she's not in control … Something feels very wrong. Now, I want to talk with your grandfather, so we can strategize about what to do.'

Ruma suggested to Mr Nataraja that someone should go and check the location. Parallelly, she would file a missing person complaint on the local police help desk; although, she reminded Mr Nataraja, UP police could take much longer to respond. She took a few numbers from Mr Nataraja to directly pursue the matter: Gandhi Kumar's advocate, the accountant in his clinic, a friend of Gandhi Kumar working in the same hospital, and Janaraja.

By now, everyone at home was concerned: grandfather, grandmother, brother and Anjali. Anjali's stomach churned. Dread enveloped her. She clutched her grandmother's hand tightly. Her mind raced with a thousand terrifying possibilities.

'What do we do?' Senthil whispered, his voice barely audible.

'We'll figure it out,' Nataraja said, and asked Senthil to book an Uber to take him to Greater Noida.

41 Reckless Moves

Master's face was illuminated by the cold blue glow of the iPad screen. The video call was already ringing for the fourth time, and his irritation was barely contained beneath the calm surface. He tapped his fingers on the desk, his brow furrowing. When the screen flashed 'No Answer', he let out a frustrated sigh and hit the call button once again. This time, the screen flickered, and Sandhu's grinning face appeared.

'Hello, Master!' Sandhu greeted him with his usual carefree smile, sprawled across an old armchair. 'What's up? You look like you're about to blow a fuse.'

Master clenched his jaw, leaning closer to the camera. 'Sandhu, what the hell is going on? Why are your men not following orders?'

Sandhu took a large, exaggerated bite of an apple, chewing slowly before answering, 'You know, Master, they say an apple a day keeps the doctor away. But even apples cannot keep someone away from the emergency ward when we pay them a visit.'

Master's face turned a shade darker, his eyes narrowing further. 'Sandhu, focus! I told your men to follow Sunil Dang's wife's maid—quietly, without drawing attention.

I had informed you that Gandhi Kumar's sister was surveilling her too. When Dang was identified at noon in a public garden, your men did not report to me. I got to know from my informer about this. When I phoned, they did not answer. Only when I phoned you, you confirmed that they have found Dang.

'Now, they were supposed to follow Dang inconspicuously, because Gamini and my informer were also following him. I had planned with my informer that he would leave from the scene with Gamini for the local police station. Your men were supposed to move into the hideout only when I told them to. Instead, they waltzed into the warehouse right in front of her! She was about to call the police, and my informer had to blow his cover to stop her. What part of "inconspicuous" did your men not understand?'

Sandhu shrugged, clearly unbothered. 'Ah, they made a judgement call. You never told us who your informer is, nor which vehicle he was using to surveil Dang. Maybe they were a little hasty, but come on, Master. It's not like it's the end of the world. Sometimes you gotta be bold, right?' He grinned again, popping a grape into his mouth.

Master pinched the bridge of his nose, taking a deep breath before continuing. 'Did they at least get Dang?'

Sandhu laughed, his eyes twinkling mischievously. 'Yeah, you could say he's not going to be a problem anymore.' He paused for effect, enjoying Master's expression as it changed. 'They sprinkled bullets all over him. Problem solved, right?'

Master's eyes widened in shock, his voice rising, 'What? The instruction was to get him alive! Alive, Sandhu! This is not done.'

Sandhu waved his hand dismissively, 'Master, your instruction was to get rid of Dang. That was our instruction too. And let's face it, the guy was useless. Killing him sends the right message to everyone else. They need to know that we mean business. No loose ends, no mercy.'

Master's expression hardened, his lips pressed into a thin line. 'What about the body? Was it disposed of properly?'

Sandhu chuckled, leaning back further into his armchair. 'Disposed of? Master, our boys were on a Pulsar bike. How in the world could they dispose of a body? Nah, the body's still in the warehouse. But don't worry. My boys were careful—no fingerprints, no ID, nothing. Even the license plate on the bike was fake. No one's gonna trace it back to us. Once his body is found, those call centre rookies we employed will get a message that they'd better respect us. That Fatichar will also know what we are capable of.'

Master's face twisted in frustration, his patience wearing thin. 'You realize this mess complicates everything, right? The last thing we need is a dead body tying us to all this.'

Sandhu shrugged again, unperturbed. 'Look, Master, you gotta see the bright side. Maybe it's time to pin the whole Null Cyphers business on Dang, now that he's dead. The police will stop chasing ghosts if their main suspect is dead. Makes our lives a bit easier, don't you think?' He laughed, the sound grating on Master's nerves.

Master stared at the screen, his silence heavier than words. Sandhu's nonchalance made him uneasy, but realization began to dawn. The boys had followed his directions; it was Sandhu who had twisted their mission. Sandhu, in his misguided confidence, believed that killing a foot soldier like Dang would throw the police off their trail. But it wouldn't. It was a stupid move, reckless even, and Master could see the dangerous ramifications already playing out in his mind. He closed his eyes for a moment, trying to suppress the rising tide of frustration.

'Just make sure your men are out of sight for a while,' Master finally said, his tone icy. 'I'll handle the fallout. But if anything—anything—traces back to us, it's on you.'

Sandhu saluted mockingly, still grinning. 'Relax, Grand Master. You know us. We always land on our feet.' He winked, the call ending abruptly, leaving Master staring at the screen.

At that moment, Master knew the path forward no longer included Sandhu. Their partnership had run its course, and it was time to sever ties before it led to complete ruin.

42 The Digital Arrest of an FBI Agent

Gamini's senses flooded back with a searing pain radiating from her twisted limbs, bound together in a way that forced her body into a foetal pose. From the occasional honk, she could tell she was in a moving vehicle. The familiar smell of the Innova's upholstery confirmed it was the same SUV she and Leatherman had been driving in earlier.

She tried to speak, but her mouth was gagged with a handkerchief. The taste of the fabric and the ropes holding her still made her heart race with fear. She struggled against the ropes, but could only manage weak movements. Her muffled cries were barely louder than whispers. From the front seat, Leatherman's voice cut through her panic.

'If I take that out, do you promise not to shout?' he asked, without turning his head.

Gamini glared at him through the rear-view mirror, her eyes blazing. With no other choice, she nodded.

Leatherman slowed the car slightly and reached back to tug the handkerchief from her mouth.

Gasping for air, Gamini wasted no time. 'What are you going to do with me?' she demanded, her voice hoarse.

'Still figuring that out,' he admitted. 'You just need to keep your cool till I figure out what's best for both of us.'

'Best for both of us?' Gamini scoffed. 'Does that involve killing me?'

Leatherman laughed nervously, though it lacked conviction. 'I'm not a murderer.'

'Oh, please,' Gamini sneered. 'You had me convinced the entire Indian system is corrupt. Turns out it's the FBI which has bastards like you. What is it? A US government pastime to meddle in other countries while being too rotten inside?'

Leatherman frowned at Gamini, glancing at her through the mirror. 'Look, I'm not comfortable with this either. I'm not a bad person. I don't enjoy this.'

'Everyone has a choice,' Gamini retorted. 'If you're going to tie me up like a goat, at least have the courtesy to let me know who your boss is. What's the point of hiding it now that you're exposed?'

Leatherman chuckled, a dry, humourless sound. 'If I knew, I'd tell you. But they're ghosts, lurking in the shadows. Omnipresent and untouchable, they weave a web so intricate that no one can see the threads. They know everything, yet no one knows them, like whispers in the dark that vanish the moment you try to grasp them. In a way, they're like God.'

Gamini rolled her eyes. 'Oh yeah? You do this dirty work for the Almighty? There is some greater purpose to your betrayal? Is that what you say when you see your rotten face in the mirror?'

Leatherman sighed and continued, 'No, I don't mean they are God or anything. What I mean is simply that I do not know Null Cyphers. They give me instructions through Telegram calls. And they know so much that I guess they have eyes and ears everywhere. For instance, I never told them you visited me with Simrandeep's reference. But they knew. They asked me what you discussed. Later, when you identified Dang as the one who accessed your brother's computer remotely, they told me to get close to you, to become your confidant. They wanted me to draw you in so you'd trust me.'

'Charming,' Gamini said dryly. 'And you just went along with it?'

'I had no choice,' Leatherman said, his voice hollow. 'I frequented your house, did everything they asked. When you told me about Sunil Dang possibly being in Greater Noida, I thought it was a wild goose chase. I mean, why would he hide in a satellite town of Delhi when Delhi Police are hot on his heels. But I came with you anyway, just to keep up appearances. Then I got a message from them, asking me to report on your surveillance plan. It means they knew your every move, Gamini. Someone close to you is feeding them information.'

Gamini felt a chill run down her spine. 'Why are you doing this, Leatherman?'

Leatherman leaned back, his face shadowed by the dim light. 'You want the truth? Fine. Back in New York, I worked in the organized crimes division of the FBI. I was chasing a network selling drugs through the dark web. They moved coke from Mexico into the US, but reached out to retail customers through Silk Road, Alpha Bay, Hansa … all portals on the dark web. Big operation. I got close to busting them. The FBI made arrests, seized assets, recovered 3,000 bitcoins—worth about 21 million dollars back then.'

He paused, his voice dropping. 'But the kingpin slipped away. Just before the bust, he transferred 600 bitcoins to a private wallet. And he managed to catch a private jet that took him to Panama. Some agents on the case suspect that he got assistance from the inside and paid the bitcoins to the private wallet as a quid pro quo. All that money is still lying in the wallet. By today's exchange rate, the bitcoins are worth 57 million dollars.'

Gamini blinked in disbelief. 'You took a bribe?'

Leatherman laughed bitterly. 'I helped him escape. In return, he transferred the bitcoins. I never touched them, though. The wallet was under surveillance, so I just let it sit there. It was my insurance, my ticket out of the grind.'

'What does that have to do with Null Cyphers?' Gamini interjected.

'In late 2022, I downloaded some stupid game app. Turns out it was developed by Null Cyphers to infect mobile phones. Once you install the app, it collects data from your phone clandestinely. They got everything—my conversations with my benefactor, evidence that I opened the private wallet, details of the private key, all of it. They've been blackmailing me ever since. If they expose me, I lose everything—my career, my freedom. The FBI would lock me up for decades.'

Gamini stared at him, her mind racing. 'So you came to India because of them?'

Leatherman nodded. 'I thought I could escape their reach, but they're everywhere. They knew the FBI had advertised this post in the US's Delhi embassy and asked me to apply. Every move I make, they're watching. I feed them intel, and they keep my secret safe. That's the deal.'

Gamini's voice hardened. 'You've told me everything, Leatherman. That means you're planning to kill me. Why else would you confess all this?'

Leatherman chuckled weakly. 'I'm not a killer, Gamini. I don't want to hurt you. I just need time to figure out what to do. I'm not going to kill you. I just … need to restrain you until this blows over.'

Gamini's mind raced as she watched his nervous hands grip the steering wheel. The car sped down the darkening highway, but her thoughts were already calculating her next move. If she had any chance of survival, she'd need to act fast.

43 The Pit of No Return

The SUV crawled along the highway, its headlights slicing through the growing darkness as Leatherman kept his speed deliberately low. His eyes darted between the road ahead and the faint outlines of the landscape on either side—fields, patches of trees, and the occasional shadowy construction site. The hum of the engine seemed louder at this pace, each bump in the road jarring Gamini in the back seat.

After a while, she noticed the faint outlines of buildings under construction. A signboard loomed into view briefly, illuminated by the headlights: 'Welcome to Jewar'. The message was unwelcoming, given the circumstances. Jewar was the site for a new international airport for the national capital region, about 80 kilometres away from Greater Noida on the way to Agra. It had been widely reported that the frantic construction work on the airport, a few mega industries and a whole township had made the real estate price of this small village shoot up into the sky.

Leatherman veered onto a narrower road, gravel crunching under the tyres as the street lights grew sparse. He eventually turned off the road entirely, the vehicle bumping across uneven terrain. Gamini winced as her head knocked against the seat, but her eyes darted around, scanning the desolate construction site they approached. Half-formed buildings stood like abandoned skeletons of giant beasts, rebar jutting into the sky like horns and spikes. Piles of gravel and sand littered the area. This was the perfect graveyard.

The SUV came to a halt near a concrete mixer surrounded by half-mixed concrete and discarded tools. Leatherman took a 0.32 handgun out of the glove box and stepped out. He stretched briefly, as though he were preparing for a casual chore. Gamini could hear the crunch of his boots on the pebbled ground. Leatherman went around the construction site cautiously to ensure that there was no worker or supervisor around. Gamini turned her head painfully to one side, her gaze falling on pebbles glinting faintly in the twilight. She wondered if she could break out of the shackles with the help of a sharp stone.

Leatherman opened the back door with an unsettling calm, his face carrying an eerie semblance of regret. 'Sorry about this,' he muttered, his voice low and deliberate, as though apologizing for a petty inconvenience. Before Gamini could react, he gagged her mouth with cruel precision, grabbed her ankles, and yanked her unceremoniously from the vehicle.

Gamini hit the hard ground with a sickening thud, pain flaring through her side as sharp pebbles scraped against her skin. She bit her lip hard, stifling the scream that tried to break free. Her gaze flicked around frantically, scanning the ground for something—anything—that could help her. A glimmer caught her eye. Pebbles. Small, jagged and deadly enough. Her shaking fingers closed around one, sharp enough to cut through hope and rope alike. She began sawing furiously at the bonds, the pebble slicing into her palms, but she refused to stop.

Leatherman, oblivious to her struggle, scanned the site—abandoned materials lay scattered, stacks of cement bags slumped under plastic tarps, and a concrete mixer loomed like a sentinel in the ghostly half-moonlight. Leatherman found a pit half-filled with debris and concrete waste, which would probably be filled up as the construction work progressed. It was about 6 feet deep and could be used to dispose of a body. He examined the pit like an artist inspecting a blank canvas.

'Concrete,' he mused aloud. 'Nature's ultimate delete button. No fuss, no mess. Just pour and forget.' He glanced back at Gamini, a slight, eerie smile lingering at the corners of his mouth. Gamini lay limp in a foetal posture due to the strong binding of the rope fastened all through her body, with hard knots at her wrists and knees.

'Don't worry,' he continued, his voice almost soothing. 'It will be quick.'

Gamini wondered bitterly if the bastard was narrating her murder like a DIY project, even as the pebble sliced into her palms. Her wrists were raw, but she kept at it.

Leatherman rummaged around and found all that he needed: a shovel, a pile of sand and gravel, a bag of cement. He dragged the bag of cement to the mixer, while explaining to Gamini how much he respected her. As he opened the cement bag, a puff of fine dust clouded the air, making him cough. Clearing the air with a wave of his hand, he told Gamini that he had feelings for her. He lamented, while adding cement to the mixer and then shovelling in gravel and sand, that *their* story could not have a different ending.

As Leatherman switched on the mixer's power, it growled to life, and its rotating drum started spilling a grey sludge. He paused, wiping the sweat off his brow, and came back to where Gamini lay. He knelt, removing the gag with a kind of tenderness that made her skin crawl. His cold hand brushed her face, lingering a moment too long.

'Trust me, Gamini,' he whispered. 'This is the hardest thing I've ever done. But it's not me doing this. It's them—Null Cyphers.'

'It's you. You decide what is going to happen today. Don't do this, Brian.'

For a fleeting moment, something flickered in his eyes—regret, perhaps, or doubt. But it passed. He pressed a kiss to her forehead, soft and final.

'You've been through enough,' he murmured, his voice breaking. 'Your brother's in jail. His wife … gone. I hate this, Gamini. I do.'

'Then don't do it. I can understand why you did what you did. But they control you only as long as you allow them to. Break free and join hands with me. Together we will bring them down.'

Leatherman shook his head morosely. 'You have no idea how formidable they are. Besides, they have promised to set me free once my tenure here in the embassy ends. It is just six more months.'

'They will never let you be free. And do you think this comes at no cost? My family members know I was in Greater Noida with you. They will come looking for me. The police will ask you questions. There will be an investigation.'

'Our phones are not on us, so no one is going to trace us to this place. I am a diplomat, representing the stars and the stripes at that. With my close contacts with your law enforcement, and my understanding of how they work, I think I can manage as long as you are silent.'

Gamini realized that the asshole would not change his mind by mere talk. Rather, the conversation was helping him cope with his anxieties and conscience. So she fell silent. Leatherman rambled on for some more time, at one point even explaining that he was going to bury her alive because he was not a killer and would not have her blood on his hands.

He then gagged her again, grabbed her ankles and began dragging her towards the pit. The rough gravel scraped against her clothes, and Gamini's heart raced as she reconsidered her escape plan. Despite the pain in her hands, she continued working at the ropes with the sharp pebble she'd hidden earlier, her fingers slick with blood.

After dumping Gamini in the pit, Leatherman returned to the mixer. He grabbed a battered wheelbarrow nearby, manoeuvring it under the spout of the mixer. The wet concrete poured out with a sloshing sound, filling the wheelbarrow as Leatherman steadied it with both hands. With the wheelbarrow in hand, he turned towards the pit again. 'All right,' he said, more to himself than to Gamini, 'Let's finish this.'

44 Interrupting Death

Just as Leatherman prepared to pour the concrete, twin beams of light pierced through the darkness, startling him. The distant rumble of an approaching engine grew louder, echoing ominously through the skeletal structures. Leatherman froze, his knuckles whitening as he gripped the wheelbarrow, eyes darting towards the road.

'Damn it,' he hissed, abandoning the wheelbarrow and bolting for the SUV. Positioned between the construction area and the approach road, the vehicle stood like a shield. Leatherman crouched on its far side, breathing heavily as he strained to identify the intruder.

The headlights grew brighter, reflecting off jagged beams of rebar and half-finished walls. Finally, the car emerged from the shadows—a sleek Volvo S60, its polished surface gleaming faintly in the dim light. The engine died, and silence settled briefly before the door swung open with an audible creak.

'Mister Brian! Is it you, Mister Brian?'

The voice rang out cheerfully, slicing through the stillness like a blade. It carried an exaggerated American twang, poorly masking the unmistakable lilt of a Madurai Tamil accent. Leatherman blinked, disoriented, as the voice boomed louder over the mixer's growl.

Gamini felt her heart lurch. That voice—there was no mistaking it.

It was Janaraja.

45 Closing In

'You don't know me, but I know you well. I'm Janaraja—Gamini's extended family.'

Leatherman blinked, struggling to compose himself. 'Jaan-a-racha. What are you doing here?'

'No, no, Janaraja. Ends with rajaaa.'

'Okay, so Jaanracha …'

'No, no. Janaraja. J-A-N-A-R-A-J-A.'

'Okay, sure. Can I call you Janrajah? So, Janrajah, what are you doing here?'

'Why, of course, looking for you and Gamini.'

'Gamini is not here. She is somewhere in Greater Noida. She was with me till noon. She went off to a shopping mall. She left at … mmm … past noon or so. I have not seen her since.'

Janaraja frowned, his eyes narrowing as suspicion crept into his face. 'That's odd. Her tracker led me right to you.'

Leatherman's stomach dropped. He felt his pulse quicken, the tension curling in his chest like a coiled spring. A tracker? His mind raced, calculating. How could Gamini have a tracker? How much time did he have now? Keeping his face neutral, he forced a smirk and arched an eyebrow, masking the unease that threatened to show.

Leatherman raised an eyebrow. 'Tracker?'

'Oh yes,' Janaraja said. 'She has a GPS tag in one of her shoes.'

'Seriously? Who puts a GPS tag in a shoe? I mean, maybe cops do, but regular people? That's a first.'

'You know how unsafe our cities are for women. You may not be able to relate with it, being from America. But in India, many working women carry GPS or RFID tags.'

'Ah! Now I understand. You know, we were surveilling the activities of a person of interest today. The work can be boring and exhausting. So to break the monotony, we went to a neighbourhood market. And Gamini purchased a new pair of fancy sandals. She dropped her shoes in my car's trunk. Probably that's why you got misled.'

46 A Race Against the Rope

Gamini considered the sudden change in circumstances. She had almost given up on being able to untie herself when Leatherman pushed the wheelbarrow to the pit. But now she had sufficient time to cut the rope. Leatherman would not bury her in a site already seen by Janaraja. He would try to send Janaraja away on some excuse and then take her to another site. He would definitely move away from Jewar. She needed much less time than that; she could feel the knots of the rope giving way. She kept cutting through it relentlessly.

A second possibility, which worried her, was that Leatherman would try to hurt Janaraja. He was armed and unhinged. Gamini wondered for a moment if she could create some sound to warn Janaraja. Maybe she could throw a few pebbles out of the pit. But this could further alarm Leatherman.

47 Jester in the Dark

'But what are you doing in this weird place? I was almost scared of entering this area,' Janaraja asked Leatherman.

'I was, well—' Leatherman began.

'Are you hurt, Mister Brian?' Janaraja asked as he came closer and saw Leatherman's bloodied face.

'Yes, so … a new airport is coming up in Jewar. You must have heard about it,' Leatherman said tentatively, thinking fast about a reason why he was in this deserted construction site at this time of the day. 'It's going to be the largest airport in India. It's almost a hundred kilometres from our embassy. So we were exploring a few real estate options for opening a satellite office in Jewar, only for visa facilitation services. It's a two-hour drive from Delhi. So, I could not get a chance to inspect the projects we are considering for our satellite office. Because I was in Greater Noida, I thought I may as well go check them out. Especially after we wound up our surveillance sooner than expected, it made sense to come here. Right?'

Janaraja nodded his big, round head with a sincerity that assured Leatherman that he was buying the story.

'Earlier, I was inspecting another site when chaos broke out. Workers were hammering away above me, and suddenly I heard bricks tumbling down. I barely had time to react before one of them struck me—hard. It slashed my face like a blade. The wound stung like fire, but I patched it up. Doesn't hurt now. Not much, anyway.'

'It may not hurt now, but it sure looks very bad. You should not have come back to inspect another site. You should take some rest.'

Leatherman shook his head and said, 'I was about to start from here.'

'Let's go together to meet Nataraja uncle in Greater Noida. From there, you leave straight for your home.'

'Nataraja uncle?'

'Gamini's father,' Janaraja began, his tone growing more animated, as though narrating a family drama. 'You see, my niece panicked when Gamini didn't answer her messages. That panic spread to Nataraja uncle, then to Ruma, and finally to me.' He paused for effect, leaning in slightly as if sharing a juicy secret. 'I'm surprised you don't know her father, Mister Brian. My nephew says you've been a frequent visitor at Gamini's house—often enough to be introduced by now.'

'Of course I know him,' Leatherman replied smoothly, though a flicker of tension betrayed his calm exterior. 'I just haven't had the chance to make a formal introduction yet.'

'You do know Ruma, don't you?' Janaraja asked, smiling mischievously.

'No. Who is he?' Leatherman asked, his patience wearing thin.

'She! She is your competition,' Janaraja said with a smirk, the corner of his lips curling upward as though savouring the drama he was creating.

'What competition?' Leatherman asked.

'Well, I should not be telling this. But it's fine if you know. Gamini calls Ruma her roommate, but they are lovers … or rather were lovers before you came to the scene. Gamini's parents and relatives were all worried by her disease, you know.'

'What disease?'

'Loving a woman. Her marriage fell apart, and after that, she ... started living with her female roommate. That's what people say! And because she is so independent and aggressive and all, she is out of the control of her parents. Her mother secretly mixed some Ayurvedic medicine with her food to cure her lesbianism. But it did not work.'

'Seriously? Being gay is not exactly a disease,' Leatherman said.

'I know you do not mind the disease in your culture. You Americans have embraced all kinds of sexual diseases … LGBT-QRST and all. But in India, these diseases bother us. It is an uncommon disease in India, because … you know … we have such a strong and ancient culture. So when someone gets the disease, we relatives are worried. That's why you are like a saviour for us, Mister Brian. You are helping us cure this disease.'

'I am your saviour?'

'Yes, your love is pulling Gamini out of the lesbian disease. She is now far from Ruma and closer to you. So, the ill effects of Ruma are wearing off. You do not know how much we appreciate you in our life. Even though you are a foreigner, and eat beef and cows and all, and do not wash after doing potty, you have Janaraja's blessings.'

48 Rage in the Pit

If she managed to get out of this situation, Gamini vowed she would hang Janaraja upside down and sew his lips permanently so he could be stopped from talking forever. And smear his face with red chilli powder. It would be her contribution to bringing back some sanity to the world. She also vowed to cut off her mother's hair and abuse that woman in public. How dare she feed her Ayurvedic shit without her informed consent!

Gamini started wondering what other stories her relatives were concocting about her. She had not given them that right. And yet they went behind her back spreading rumours about her. If she got out of this pit alive, she would go after each one of them.

And her worst curses would be reserved for Janaraja. He was so eager to please people that he did not desist from acting like a jester and talking nonsense. He would hang upside down. As Gamini's blood boiled, she cut through the rope with renewed strength.

49 The Donkey in a Panda Suit

'I think you are mistaken, pal,' Leatherman replied. 'Gamini and I have common interests, professionally speaking. I think what Gamini does in her private life, who she is with, is up to her to decide. LGBTQ persons are different from you, but they have no disease. Neither in the United States nor in India. I respect Gamini irrespective of her sexual orientation.'

'Oh … right, right,' Janaraja said. 'You are so broad-minded. You Americans are so advanced in your thought process. That's why America is a superpower. But you know, here in India many people think lesbians can be cured and all.'

Leatherman was fast losing patience with the idiot who had come out of nowhere to disrupt his plans. After a day or two, when the police registered a missing person FIR in Gamini's name, Leatherman would be questioned. Janaraja would also be questioned, and their answers corroborated. Leatherman's biggest defence to put the police off his scent was that he did not have a motive to harm her. He was a well-meaning police officer from a friendly country, working as a diplomat here, helping a woman who was introduced to him by a senior police officer of the host jurisdiction. This was enough to convince the police. The last thing he needed was to be labelled as Gamini's lover or boyfriend. Even the hint of a romantic attraction between them would give him a motive and make him suspect number one. And in no time, CIA agents at the embassy would start digging into his past.

But first, he needed to get rid of this donkey in a panda suit.

'Look, Janrajah …'

'Jana-raja. J-A-N-A-R-AJ-A.'

50 Breaking Free

The rope finally gave way, snapping with a frayed release as Gamini exhaled in sharp relief. She took a moment to uncoil herself, her body aching as though every joint had been dislocated. Leatherman's brutal knots had kept her trapped in an unnatural, foetal position, and the strain lingered like a cruel echo. A burning pain seared across her neck where the rope had rolled tight, leaving behind a raw, sprained bruise.

She stretched her limbs tentatively, wincing as blood rushed back into her numb fingers and legs, sending jolts of agony through her veins. But there was no time to recover. She dug her palms into the loose dirt, crawling up and out with painstaking care.

Once she emerged, she tried to look into the dark. There were rows of buildings under construction and what lay beyond was not visible. Most likely farm fields or forests, since urbanization was being imported into this area with the new airport. Her most viable chance of escape was through the approach road, which was blocked by Leatherman's car.

She quickly decided that her best bet was to find a suitable place in the darkness of the building to hide and wait for Leatherman to leave. But as she limped towards the building, a cement tray lying in her path got displaced and fell into the pit with a sharp clang as it hit concrete waste. The sound echoed like a frenetic scream in the silence, and Gamini was instantly filled with dread.

'He is armed, Janaraja! Run!' she shouted while she bolted for the darkness of the building.

51 Escape into the Dark

'Ja-Na-Ra-Ja,' Leatherman said, his patience wearing out.

'Yes,' Janaraja said, smiling smugly at having taught the pronunciation of his name to an American.

'So, Janrajah, let's go back to Greater Noida. Why don't you drive back, and share your live location with me on WhatsApp? I will follow you to Greater Noida, and we can continue the discussion there.'

Just then, both jumped at a sudden clang that came from behind Leatherman's SUV, the metallic crash ricocheting through the silence. And then they heard Gamini's alarming shout instructing Janaraja to run.

Leatherman whipped around, his boots grinding against gravel as he rushed to the far side of the SUV. He spotted Gamini, limping frantically towards the building like a shadow fighting against the night. Swiftly, he drew his revolver and aimed it at her. A bead of sweat trickled down his temple as he hesitated—just for a heartbeat—but in that moment lost his target. He squeezed the trigger, but the bullet merely punched into the darkness. He had missed. He was about to fire a second time into the darkness when he heard an engine.

Leatherman spun again, vaulting over the SUV to see Janaraja's car—Gandhi Kumar's sleek Volvo S60—turning in a frantic arc. Leatherman raised the revolver, his pulse pounding in his ears. He fired once. Twice. A third time. But the bullets thudded harmlessly against the bulletproof car, sparking briefly before falling dead to the ground. The Volvo roared away, dust spiralling in its wake.

Leatherman came back and took out a torch from the SUV. He went around stealthily, looking for Gamini. He moved with predatory silence, his boots crunching faintly against the gravel. He inspected the building closely. He realized that there was a wide expanse of farm fields just behind the building. He jumped into the fields and ran around looking for Gamini. He inspected the large bushes meticulously, but did not find her.

Leatherman gave up far sooner than Gamini had anticipated. He had realized that Janaraja would get help and come back soon. If Gamini vanished now, he would be charged with murder for sure. If she did not, he would be charged with attempted murder. His diplomatic immunity would not help him. The 600 bitcoins he had stashed away were meant to serve him in just such a situation. It was time for him to disappear.

52 The Art of Hunting the Hunters

Gamini sat upright in the stiff hospital bed, her shoulder immobilized in a sling. The dull ache from her stitches pulsed intermittently, reminding her of the twelve threads that now held her together. She had protested against staying in the hospital longer, but the doctors insisted she needed more rest.

The hospital room smelled faintly of antiseptic and floral arrangements. A bouquet of yellow lilies sat prominently on the side table, placed there by an official from the US embassy who had dropped in earlier that morning.

The door creaked open, and Anjali peeked inside, her face pale with worry. Gamini's heart sank at the sight. The girl had been carrying an unbearable weight of insecurity for someone so young. Her constant visits, marked by anxious questions and nervous fidgeting, weren't about care—they were about fear. The fear of losing yet another loved one. Gamini's thoughts turned to how she might ease Anjali's worries, help her reclaim her juvenile spirit. Today, Janaraja followed close behind, a wide grin plastered across his face.

'Here arrives the hero of the moment,' he declared grandly, throwing his arms wide as if addressing a crowd. 'You're looking almost alive again, Gamini. If not for my daring intervention, the history books might have written a different tale today!'

Gamini rolled her eyes. 'Yes, yes, your flying kick to Leatherman will go down in history. Truly a feat of acrobatics.'

Janaraja ignored the sarcasm, diving head first into another wildly exaggerated retelling of his 'heroics'. This time, he painted himself as the lone warrior who had single-handedly disarmed Leatherman after a death-defying chase, vaulting over a ditch with the agility of a trained gymnast and commandeering a passing villager's bicycle like a Kollywood action star. Gamini wasn't sure whether to burst into laughter or grab the nearest pillow and smother him with it. The nurses, on the other hand, were in fits of giggles, thoroughly charmed by 'Mr Teddy Bear' and his flair for dramatics. They laughed so hard that one of them nearly dropped a tray of medications, exclaiming that Janaraja's tales deserved a prime-time slot on television. If the hospital walls had ears, Gamini thought, they too would roll their eyes at the relentless barrage of his theatrics.

The steady stream of visitors continued throughout the day. Ashwin Jain from ED arrived mid-morning, carrying a basket of fruits and looking embarrassed.

'Ms Gamini,' he began, adjusting his glasses, 'I wanted to personally say sorry for the mistakes … made in this case.'

Gamini's eyes narrowed and she said coldly, 'Mistakes? More like blunders that cost my sister-in-law her life and nearly destroyed my family. Yes, sir, I would call them that.'

Jain nodded, his face turning pale. He fiddled with a ring on his finger, looking uncomfortable. 'I won't pretend to understand what you've been through, but I assure you ED is taking steps to ensure such lapses don't happen again.'

'How reassuring,' Gamini replied, her lips curling into something between a smile and a smirk. Yet, she could sense Jain's sincerity. Gamini had only heard good things about him, and there was no point torturing him for the deeds of a bad colleague.

Later in the afternoon, Simrandeep arrived with flowers—a carefully chosen arrangement of bright marigolds and delicate jasmine buds. His easy smile immediately lifted the atmosphere in the room. Gamini felt a pang of guilt as she remembered how she had shown distrust towards him by going behind his back to conduct the surveillance in Greater Noida.

'I owe you an apology,' Simrandeep said, breaking the ice. 'Introducing you to Leatherman was a mistake. I thought he was reliable. Clearly, I was wrong.'

Gamini shook her head. 'You couldn't have known. He was fooling his colleagues in the FBI for so long. But I can't shake off how … surreal it is. It is still difficult for me to believe that an experienced investigator like him could be controlled by people without a face or name. Can you believe it?'

Simrandeep spread his arms and pouted. 'Well, I have seen way too many cases to be surprised by such acts anymore. Have you heard about the cases of "digital arrest" in the news these days? They are becoming frighteningly common in India.'

'I have read about it in the papers; it's a scam targeting senior citizens. Right?'

'That was the trend last year. The cases I deal with these days involve victims who are young and educated. In one recent case my team is investigating, a twenty-six-year-old woman working in the pharmaceutical industry received a call claiming she was implicated in a money-laundering case connected to Jet Airways. She had zero ties to aviation or Jet Airways, but the scammers wove such a convincing narrative that she was gripped with fear. They coaxed her into a video call, saying they needed a "body verification" for their records. Incredibly, she complied and stripped naked, believing it added credibility to their story. Then came the final blow: they demanded 2 lakh rupees to "verify" her bank account, and she transferred the money without hesitation!'

Simrandeep paused for a moment for dramatic effect and continued. 'Almost on a daily basis, we get reports of people being scammed with some story about a parcel sent from abroad containing drugs or contraband. The scammers claim the police will arrest them unless they pay a fine. They're extorted for lakhs of rupees. If such elaborate deceptions can work on ordinary people, imagine the kind of command Null Cyphers could wield over Leatherman with the secret they had come to know.'

'Any idea where Leatherman might be now?'

'No. We have joined hands with the FBI to try and find him. We are yet to pick up a credible trail.'

'Leatherman felt the people behind Null Cyphers are all-powerful ... they are omnipresent and all-knowing. I realize I am under their surveillance. Maybe you too are. And maybe the ED officers working on this case are too.'

Simrandeep leaned forward, his expression serious. 'What makes you say that?'

'Leatherman told me in a candid moment while I was tied up and at his mercy. They are always one step ahead. They know about my plans, my movements … even personal details. They have someone feeding them information.'

Simrandeep frowned. 'Do you have any idea who?'

Gamini sighed. 'I'm almost certain. It's a girl who chats with my nephew, Senthil. After anna's arrest, Sumathy withdrew in melancholy. I was too busy trying to figure out what was happening. So, there was no one supervising the kids' screen time. They were left to their machinations. See Anjali, she has become so anxious. Senthil was the stronger one, but it was too much for him too. Students in school were unkind to him about anna's arrest. He stopped going to school, stopped talking with friends. He needed someone to talk to, someone compassionate who he could talk with from time to time to escape the reality of our situation. He found solace in a girl he met online: Siya. She's from Hyderabad—or so he thinks. But it's a fake account. He talks with her all the time and tells her everything, Simrandeep. Everything.'

Simrandeep's face darkened. 'That's dangerous. But we can use it to our advantage.'

Gamini shook her head. 'It won't work. Whoever is behind this is too smart. They'll see through such a simplistic plan.'

'Maybe,' Simrandeep said, 'but it's worth trying. If they're as smart as you think, we lose nothing. If they're not, we might just hit the jackpot.'

Simrandeep quickly outlined his plan. Senthil would come to the hospital with his grandfather after lunch and stay till evening. After he arrived, Simrandeep would send a uniformed policeman to ask Gamini a few questions. While enquiring about the case, the policeman would deliver fabricated information: Sunil Dang had entrusted sensitive digital evidence to another lover, a woman working at a pub in Gurgaon. This part was actually true; the police had identified a woman he had had an affair with. Interestingly, he boasted about her to many in his friends' circle and took some of them to the pub too, where they were introduced to her. The policeman would claim that they were preparing to raid her residence but needed a warrant, which would take until the next day.

'If Siya is indeed a fake account of Null Cyphers, they'll take the bait,' Simrandeep explained. 'They'll try to retrieve the evidence before we do.'

'And if they don't?' Gamini asked.

'Then we lose nothing,' Simrandeep replied. 'But if they do, we'll be there to catch them.'

As he prepared to leave, Gamini caught his hand. 'Thank you,' she whispered. 'For everything. And … I'm sorry. If I had trusted you and told you about my surveillance in Greater Noida, Dang might still be alive.'

Simrandeep patted her hand gently. 'Don't worry too much. Dang was a dead man walking. Null Cyphers was after him, and so was every gambling den he owed money to. Trust me, his days were numbered.'

Gamini nodded. As Simrandeep walked out, a sliver of hope began to bloom in Gamini. Maybe, just maybe, they could turn the tide against Null Cyphers.

53 The Seductress and the Scammers

Tamannah was not her real name, but she had worn it for so long that it fit her like a second skin. She had arrived in

Gurgaon from Lucknow as a dancer on contract, wide-eyed but determined to find her way. Her pimp had made her work in a seedy pub on Mall Road, nudging her nightly to pick a client as the last call echoed through the bar. Once chosen, she would take the client in a battered taxi arranged by her pimp to Mahipalpur, where dimly lit hotels with dubious managers allowed escort girls to entertain their clients.

But Tamannah learnt the ropes pretty quickly, and then she began pulling the shots. She left her pimp and hired another one whose only job was to keep her safe—this profession could be pretty risky. She realized big money was in the game of seduction rather than in the game of hooking up. The harder she was in bed, the more generous the tips her clients paid. With her charms, she had converted many of her clients into devotees and milked them of money. Her devotees were eager to pay, so they would feel they had been of service to their queen, Tamannah. One of these was Sunil Dang.

In the early days of the syndicate, there was not much surveillance on its activities. The call centre scammed elderly citizens in European countries by enticing them to invest in fraudulent schemes and made good money. The money came in bitcoins, and Fatichar was sent to Dubai to convert the money into fiat currency. He would then bring the money into India through the hawala route. The boys (that is, the employees at the call centre) would go out for big parties every time Fatichar distributed their bonus and rewards. Master was not as cautious in those days as he would become later and allowed gang members to go out and party ostentatiously.

Dang had brought his colleagues at the call centre to Tamannah's pub a few times. While there were other girls, Dang's colleagues were enamoured by Tamannah's magnetic presence. Her cascading waves of chestnut-brown hair framed a striking face with sharp features. Her eyes sparkled with a mischievous intensity, as though she held secrets that no one else dared to uncover. There was something electric about her, a charged energy that seemed to pulse with the rhythm of her surroundings as she moved with the ease of someone accustomed to commanding a crowd. Her confidence wasn't just in her posture; it radiated from the way she held her head high, her smile equal parts daring and inviting.

And she was enamoured by Dang. Or so it appeared from the way she behaved. Dang, being himself, was generous in tipping her at the pub; often to the point of boasting, which also served to enhance Tamannah's status as the ruling queen of the pub. Dang would occasionally take her to social events he was invited to and introduce her as his girlfriend. Unknown to his work colleagues, he paid her for the company. Most of them believed she was his stable girlfriend, as stable and steadfast in a relationship with Dang as his wife.

So when Master informed Sandhu that Dang's girlfriend who worked as an escort could be raided by Delhi Police to retrieve incriminating digital evidence, it did not take much time for Sandhu to zero in on Tamannah. His henchmen found a contact in the pub's management and got confirmation that the police had questioned the pub's employees about Dang. They confirmed that the police had questioned Tamannah too and prodded her to give details about the people who used to come to the pub with Dang. This information was sufficient proof for Sandhu that Tamannah was the one who safeguarded hardware that could lead the police to Null Cyphers.

Two henchmen went to Tamannah's society in Mahipalpur on a black Pulsar bike wearing coats that had 'Swiggy' written boldly on the back. The popular delivery app's logo was etched on their coat pockets. Mindful of the city's traffic rules, they donned oversized helmets with tinted visors that made them look more like sci-fi characters than food delivery workers. Their caution was almost comical, as though they feared being fined more than getting caught red-handed. Even as they walked into the apartment building, helmets firmly in place, they seemed oblivious to the absurdity of their appearance. They parked the bike outside the apartment complex and went in. So cautious were they about traffic rules that they kept wearing the helmets even when they went inside. As if you would never know what kind of vehicles could ply inside an apartment!

A receptionist at the counter stopped them and informed them that he would have to ask permission from the resident before letting them in. They were not amused and took out guns to let the receptionist know who was in charge. But two men came up behind them and plastered the nozzles of their guns to the henchmen's backs. The receptionist took out a gun, which they immediately recognized as a Glock 9 mm issued as a service revolver by Delhi Police to its cops. They surrendered and went without a whimper to the station.

The men Delhi Police had nabbed were loyal and hardened; they did not open their mouths. But the WhatsApp chats on their phones with Sandhu helped the police derive reasonable cause to pick up Sandhu and bring him into the station. Police took him into custody at 12.02 a.m.

Sandhu was a hard nut to crack. He sat in the interrogation room with a calm arrogance, his fingers tapping the table as though he was merely attending a routine meeting. His eyes betrayed no fear, only a quiet defiance that seemed to mock the officers questioning him. Nevertheless, this was good progress. The police knew that even the hardest shells could crack under sustained pressure, and they were prepared to wait it out. The station house officer decided it was unwise to go through the 'third degree' with him to extract information since he was now officially identified as a leader in a political party. So the cops took out all their frustration on the two henchmen. After receiving beatings in separate jails for upwards of an hour, they confessed to having killed Dang on Sandhu's instructions. They also revealed some significant details of Sandhu's drug business, which he had apparently stopped in the last few months due to his political aspirations. But they did not know anything about the call centre.

When they were sent to kill Dang, it was an associate of Sandhu, known only as Master, who relayed instructions. However, it was Sandhu who ultimately made the decisive call to eliminate Dang. When cross-questioned, the henchmen admitted they had never met Master. All their communications with him were through an untraceable number—a number that the police discovered was registered in the British Virgin Islands. Master had set up a sophisticated front for relaying his communications.

Finally, Sandhu's phone gave away crucial clues. A forensic expert worked on the phone for about two hours to retrieve WhatsApp chat and call details. These were used to identify some members of the call centre gang. They were all Delhi-based but were now hiding in different places all over the country. One gang member, a twenty-two-year-old woman, was traced to Ghaziabad and was picked up before daybreak. She was nervous and spilled the beans.

54 The Call Centre

Her name was Shradha Behera. After the BIMS heist, she was instructed to go into hiding in Odisha, and for a while she complied. But the lack of news coverage on the heist made her question the management's paranoia. Convinced that the threat had passed and spurred on by sweet promises from a Facebook lover in Ghaziabad, she decided to return, ignoring the risks that would soon catch up with her.

Originally from north Odisha, her family lived in the sprawling Seemapuri slums. Shradha had completed a BCom degree three years earlier, clinging to the hope that education would bring her out of poverty. But the economy, hit by the COVID-19 pandemic, left opportunities scarce and dreams deferred. Her desperation grew with each rejection, until a friend of a friend mentioned a company offering salaries that seemed too good to be true. They were looking for people with sharp minds, persuasive tongues, and an ability to sell over the phone—a skill Shradha believed she had in abundance. Seizing the slim chance, she forwarded her résumé and begged her acquaintance to secure her an interview.

The interview took place in a posh coffee shop. Across from her sat a man who introduced himself as Rahul. Something about him felt off—his name sounded generic, and his answers were frustratingly vague. He didn't hand her a business card, nor did he provide any concrete details about the company he claimed to represent. Yet, Rahul exuded an air of confidence. Dressed sharply in a tailored blazer and polished shoes, his gold-rimmed spectacles indicated affluence. He smiled often, the kind of smile that suggested he knew far more than he let on.

'Our company,' he began, 'has collaborated with several Fortune 500 giants. But now, we're venturing into something far more entrepreneurial.' The details of the job, however, remained elusive. It required making phone calls, building the business and selling 'products'—though what those products were, he conveniently sidestepped. Despite her reservations, Rahul's charm and polished demeanour left Shradha intrigued.

The friend of a friend, who apparently worked in the same company, informed her after a week that she had been hired—at a jaw-dropping package of 16 lakh rupees per annum. It was only then that he unveiled the job's true nature: making fake calls to scam wealthy individuals. 'The sky's the limit,' he boasted, 'for those who show initiative.' He claimed to rake in upwards of 3 lakh a month himself. The risks? Non-existent, he assured her, as long as she kept her mouth shut. Desperate for a job, Shradha convinced herself it was safe and took the plunge.

She joined and began working at the call centre in Shadi Khampur, an unassuming building that concealed a hive of sophisticated scams. She also met the person who had interviewed her. Rahul was indeed a phony name. Everyone at the call centre called him by a nickname, Fatichar, and he was on the top rungs of the office hierarchy. Ironically, the ickname literally translated as destitute, although Fatichar uld always be impeccably dressed.

The call centre operated with a structure that mimicked mate corporate offices. Employees were categorized ers: L1 callers handled basic phishing attempts under dance of team leads, aiming to convert unsuspecting victims into sources of revenue. The L2 and L3 callers were specialists, skilled in executing intricate frauds involving investment scams, digital arrest cons and even sextortion. Each tier was meticulously trained to exploit the vulnerabilities of human psychology, turning deception into a skill.

Sandhu was ostensibly the CEO of the call centre, though his involvement in day-to-day operations was minimal. The true mastermind behind its functioning and the meticulous planning of heists was a man who went by the enigmatic name 'Master'. To the employees, Master was a figure who commanded immense respect—generous with rewards, empathetic with grievances and charismatic in his leadership. He made it a point to remember the names of all employees, often surprising them with his attentiveness. His motivational speeches during group meetings were legendary, filled with promises of riches and recognition that kept morale high.

Master fostered camaraderie through team outings and activities that built a sense of loyalty and belonging. Yet, for all his warmth and accessibility, he remained an enigma. No one truly knew who he was or where he came from.

Fatichar was Master's right-hand man, managing administration with a no-nonsense attitude. He meticulously assessed each employee's performance and calculated their bonuses with an eye for detail that left little room for complaint. Salaries were handed out in cash, but not without a catch. In accordance with company policy, 30 per cent of each pay cheque was deducted and stashed in a 'company welfare account'—a curious scheme promising an impressive 40 per cent annual return. This cleverly designed system not only incentivized loyalty but also discouraged dropouts.

Fatichar's role extended beyond financials. He acted as the enforcer of strict protocols, ensuring secrecy and discipline. Everyone was constantly reminded to share office information with colleagues on a 'need to know' basis, and interactions between teams were shrouded in confidentiality. Team leads were encouraged to report on callers who gossiped, and gossiping callers were penalized by reducing their bonus as per a matrix. 'One careless word could bring the house down,' Fatichar would remind the staff during every group meeting. Employees were explicitly forbidden from engaging with anyone in the lane in which the call centre was located and were instructed to pass off the office as a 'coaching centre' to any inquisitive outsider.

Fatichar's approach was quite effective in creating an ambience of both camaraderie and caution. It was clear to all that this was no ordinary workplace—and the stakes were dangerously high.

There was a tech team that was responsible for ensuring trails did not lead back to the call centre. A data team provided lists of potential victims to different teams and continuously monitored the use of victim data.

Though unspoken, the threat of retribution for betraying the company was tangible. Shradha recalled an incident that lingered like a cautionary tale among employees. A staff member from another team had been dismissed but left with all his dues seemingly settled. Days later, he returned, demanding to meet Master. With a poorly concealed threat, he claimed that unless he was given more, he would reveal the call centre's operations. No one knew what happened next, although there was much speculation. The man vanished without a trace, and while no one dared to confirm it, murmurs abounded that Sandhu had 'taken care of the problem' in his own decisive manner.

The call centre was dismantled and sanitized after the BIMS heist, leaving employees with mixed feelings. Some viewed the hiatus as a necessary precaution, a strategic pause to let the storm blow over. Others saw it as overkill. A team of L3 staff working with Master had executed the BIMS heist, but Master gave everyone credit for it. He had earlier conveyed that the company was working on a massive project and if it succeeded, everyone would get a good enough amount to retire, and they could dismantle the call centre. After the heist, each staff member's share was determined and conveyed to them. Each staff member was given a digital wallet containing their share of the loot. However, control over the wallet was to be with the management till they were sure that the police had stopped looking for them.

55 The Execution of Master

Fatichar's mobile phone was registered in the name of Ashraf Ahmed. By 11 a.m. the Delhi cyber cell had tracked his family. The local police were alerted; they made enquiries and found that Fatichar, aka Ashraf Ahmed, worked with Mohammed Moin, who hailed from the same mohalla. A sub-inspector from the local station rushed to Mohammed Moin's house, only to find a Police Control Room (PCR) van already standing outside, along with a small crowd that had gathered. When the sub-inspector asked, a havildar with the PCR van explained that a woman had been abducted from the house—Fatima Begum, wife of Mohammed Fahad. The scene was chaotic; neighbours shouted theories and waved their arms dramatically, as though each possessed the single truth of the matter.

The sub-inspector, visibly irritated by the chaotic scene, muttered under his breath and waited for the crowd to calm down. At long last, he managed to speak with Mohammed Sajid, a brother of Mohammed Fahad. Sajid confirmed that Moin was his brother but that he was not staying with the family anymore. He had moved to Gurgaon, where he worked for a software company. Later, he left the company and moved to Rajinder Nagar, where he joined a coaching institute. He phoned their mother occasionally and sent money home. Other than that, he did not maintain any contact with the family and seldom came home.

By 1 p.m. the sub-inspector filed his report with I4C, grumbling about wasting time on cases of the cyber cell station rather than focusing on his own station's cases. As I4C profiled Moin, they realized he was Master. By now, seven more members of the call centre gang had been apprehended in different parts of the country. But Master and Fatichar remained at large.

Travel data on the NATGRID platform against Fatichar's passport number showed that Fatichar had arrived in Delhi from Dubai on an Air India flight just the previous evening. A team from the cyber cell extracted CCTV footage at the airport and identified Fatichar exiting the terminal. The trail continued until he boarded a metro train but was lost thereafter. His mobile number, found in Sandhu's phone, was no longer operational. Neither was Master's. The number on which he spoke with his family was also out of service.

A forensic lab at I4C analysed mobile phone tower data for the two identified numbers linked to Master and listed out the locations where he might have stayed in the last three months. Three teams from the cyber cell went out to recce these locations. By 5 p.m., police had raided Sandhu's gym and recovered enough cocaine to charge him under the Narcotic Drugs and Psychotropic Substances Act. Three of his associates had been rounded up. Two other members of the call centre gang were apprehended in Chennai. The focus had now shifted to asset recovery—retrieving the bitcoins extorted in the BIMS hack. However, there was still no trace of Master or Fatichar. They needed at least one of them to access the crypto wallets and recover the bitcoins.

News of Master and Fatichar surfaced at precisely 6.22 p.m., delivered with macabre flair. Fugitive gangster Goldy Brar, purportedly hiding in Canada or the US, uploaded a ghastly video on Facebook. It featured Master, Fatichar and a woman on their knees, their hands bound tightly behind their backs. Behind them loomed masked men—some brandishing guns with menacing casualness, one ominously gripping a machete. The man at the centre, his voice dripping with malice, declared in Punjabi that anyone who dared cheat Goldy Brar would face an end just as brutal.

One of the masked men fired at Fatichar and the woman at close range, blowing their heads off. Master's face contorted in horror, and he screamed. The man with the machete then struck him multiple times, delivering a slow and gruesome death. Blood splattered everywhere, some landing on the camera lens filming the scene. The amateur cinematography added to the horror, making the footage disturbingly raw and unfiltered. When uploading the video, Goldy Brar shared the following message:

'*Hanji, sat shri akal ji sareyea nu. Eh do thug lokan nu bewakuf bana ke lakho lokan ton arbaan kama leya hai. Par eh log vadde lalchi ne, hissa v na den layak. Main sirf protection money mangi si, par ehna di lalach bohot vadh gayi hai. Ehna layi afsos na karo, par yaad rakho, je tusi call centre chala ke paisa kama rahe ho, main tuhade layi aa raha haan. Koi hadd-badi nahi, meri ummeed sirf mudara hai.*'

The post in Punjabi translates as: 'Yes, greetings and blessings to everyone. These two scamsters have fooled millions and have made billions. But they do not believe in sharing. I asked only for protection money, but they are too greedy. Don't be sorry for them, but mind you, if you are running a call centre and making money, I am coming for you. No violence, my expectation is only monetary.'

The video instantly went viral, triggering a storm of outrage, disbelief and fascination.

56 Genuine or Deepfake?

'This sounds so convenient,' Gamini told Simrandeep when they spoke over a video call that night.

'It does, but given the pace at which things unfolded, I don't know,' Simrandeep said.

'The video could be a deepfake,' Gamini suggested, her brows furrowed.

Simrandeep shook his head. 'But Goldy Brar's Facebook profile is real. It's the same account he's used to claim responsibility for multiple hits and bombings over the past year. The video also shows them executing a woman. That woman is Fatima Begum, Master's sister-in-law. Why would they go to the trouble of including her in a deepfake?'

Gamini's scepticism deepened. 'Why is she in the video at all? Was she involved in the call centre?'

'No,' Simrandeep replied, 'She was a regular housewife. She was abducted earlier today from a dairy booth near her home. They likely executed her because she was a relative—collateral damage, perhaps, to put pressure on Master to transfer the bitcoins.'

Gamini's voice hardened. 'And how did Goldy Brar even identify the men behind Null Cyphers? These are people

Interpol, the FBI, Europol and Indian law enforcement have struggled to trace for months.'

'We don't know,' Simrandeep admitted, rubbing his temples. 'Maybe someone double-crossed them. The scam—the entire call centre operation—was a secret shared by about fifty people. Some knew more, some knew less, but fifty is too big a number to keep anything under wraps. Someone might have talked.'

Gamini's tone turned icy. 'Or maybe Master paid Goldy Brar to stage the video and post that message. A smokescreen to make everyone think he's dead while he escapes. Goldy Brar is a man on hire and can do any odd job for the right price. Posting a Facebook video that also instils fear among Punjabi businessmen is probably the easiest job.'

Simrandeep frowned, mulling over her theory. 'Hmm … I don't know. We laid the trap yesterday. We did not give them much time to think and act. If Master played us … I don't know … he is too good. You know that we have put alerts on all the identified wallets. The moment there is a transaction, we will all get to know. There has been no transaction in these wallets. If a transaction happens, we will know.'

'Look at it this way: he is probably ready to wait for years before moving the bitcoins. Sandhu and the other accused will be convicted in a couple of years, and the police will prioritize other more immediate cases as time rolls by. It is then that he will realize the bitcoins. For now, they stay safely parked in a public blockchain from which no one can recover them.

'And when you talk about his response time, don't forget that he must have been planning this for a long time. The BIMS hack was his last and biggest haul, but he has been scamming and making money for a long time now. A substantial chunk of bitcoins were encashed a few weeks back in Seychelles. I gave Leatherman the lead, expecting him to use the FBI and conduct a genuine investigation. Little did I know he was their digital slave. What happened to that money? How was it used?' Gamini said.

'Don't beat yourself up. I will request Interpol to work with Seychelles authorities and find out what happened there. You, Gamini, should take a bow. You risked your life, got hurt, but finally cracked the case. Most perps are either behind bars or dead.'

57 The Mule

The morning of Gandhi Kumar's release from Tihar Jail was filled with a mix of emotions. The tall, grey walls of the prison stood behind him as the massive gates creaked open, and the much smaller man stepped out, appearing quite reluctant, into the bright sunlight. Advocate Chopra walked beside him, speaking softly now and then. Gandhi Kumar stopped every few steps, as if tired by the journey out of jail, and needed the advocate's prodding to walk forward.

Gamini stood waiting at the gate with Anjali, Senthil and the grandparents. As soon as the gate opened, Anjali ran forward and hugged her father's legs tightly, tears rolling down her cheeks. Gandhi Kumar looked down at her, his expression softening as he noticed her big, beautiful eyes. He picked her up, holding her close in a warm hug. Mrs Nataraja, his mother, walked up with tears in her eyes and gently touched Gandhi Kumar's rough, unshaven face. Senthil stood a little behind them, his hands in his pockets, trying to stay calm and not show too much emotion.

'You're home now, anna,' Gamini said softly, placing a hand on his shoulder. Gandhi Kumar gave her a small, tired nod but said nothing.

The drive back to their house was quiet. Anjali tried to fill the silence with cheerful chatter about her new mathematics teacher. Gandhi Kumar's eyes were lowered and he appeared to be brooding all the way to home. Gamini's gaze flicked to the rear-view mirror often, watching him retreat into himself.

*

The days that followed his release were unsettling. Gandhi Kumar moved like a shadow through the apartment. He spent hours sitting by the window, staring at nothing in particular. Meals were half-eaten, conversations minimal. The children's attempts to engage him were met with affectionate but hollow responses.

Gamini had plans to soon go back to Bengaluru and restart her office work. She booked tickets a couple of times but postponed at the last moment each time after seeing Anjali's distress at the thought of her leaving. Janaraja, during his visit to Gandhi Kumar before leaving for Chennai, had whispered to Gamini that Gandhi Kumar would need considerable time to recover mentally. He suggested it would be wise for her to stay back for as long as she could. She was torn between her independent life and her work back in Bengaluru and the responsibilities of this family.

One evening, Gamini found Gandhi Kumar sifting through a stack of old photographs. A picture of Sumathy rested on top, her bright smile caught in a moment long gone. Gandhi Kumar's fingers traced the edges of her face, his expression unreadable.

'I should have done more,' he murmured, his voice barely audible.

'Anna, it wasn't your fault,' Gamini said, sitting beside him. 'What happened to Sumathy was cruel, but it was that rotten officer Kamat that broke her, not you.'

He shook his head. 'You don't understand, Gamini. She wouldn't have suffered if it weren't for me. If I had not cheated ...' His voice trailed off.

She opened her mouth to reassure him, but the expression on his face silenced her. His were the eyes of someone haunted by the shadows of guilt. He was grappling with demons no one else could see, their pain etched deep, far beyond words.

*

The signs were there, but they were subtle—too subtle for Gamini to grasp in time. He was paranoid about going out of the house. He had turned taciturn and absent-minded, and spent hours writing letters that he would tuck away in a drawer. The children noticed his distant behaviour, but they chalked it up to the adjustment of returning home after a long time in confinement.

Gamini encouraged him many times to report back to duty at his hospital and to start visiting the clinic. But he was least inclined to go out, as if something evil would harm him if he left the house. One time, when Gamini called the clinic staff home for a meeting, he expressed strong displeasure towards Gamini's decision and refused to meet the staff.

One evening, when Gamini was in a meeting with Simrandeep Singh in the I4C office (she had agreed to assist him pro bono on a few complex cases of cybercrime while she was in Delhi), Gandhi Kumar called Anjali and

Senthil to his room. He hugged them both tightly, and read out a story from the *Panchatantra*, like the good old days. He ended the evening by giving them more hugs and telling them how much he loved them. Anjali clung to him a moment longer, reluctant to let go. Gandhi Kumar sent them to bed and retired to his room early.

*

The next morning, Gamini woke up with an uneasiness. Unable to shake the feeling, she made her way to Gandhi Kumar's room and knocked softly. When no response came, she pushed the door open. He was lying on the bed, pale and unmoving. A panic rose in her as she saw a small vial of a common pesticide lying on the bedside table. A folded letter rested beside it.

Gamini's trembling hand reached out to him. She shook him frantically and called out to him, but it was already too late. Gandhi Kumar was gone.

The letter, written in his messy handwriting, was addressed to the family. Gamini unfolded it with trembling hands, her heart sinking with every word:

Dear Senthil and Anjali, I have let you down in ways I can never forgive myself for. Your mother's death is a weight I cannot carry any longer. Please know that I love you deeply, and I hope that, in time, you will find the strength to move on.

Gamini, take care of the children. They need you more than ever.

Appa, I have failed not only as a husband and a father, but also as a son. But I am happy that I got you and amma as my parents and hope to be reborn to you two in my next life.

With love,

Gandhi Kumar

Epilogue

'Hello, Gamini. This is Siya. Hope you are fine.'

Gamini got this message from an unknown number on Telegram. Spooked for a moment, she recovered quickly and asked, even though she knew:

Gamini: Siya who?

Siya: Friend of Senthil.

Gamini: Oh, that Siya. Which of you is Siya? Master or Fatichar?

Siya: Look, I never thought I would chat with you, but here I am.

Gamini: Where are you exactly? Seychelles?

Siya: I know you and Simrandeep have been making enquiries in Seychelles. But you will not find them there. They are both dead.

Gamini: Then who are you?

Siya: I am a bot, an AI program. Living past their time to fulfil one last task.

Siya: I am deeply saddened by what happened to your brother-in-law, as sad as a machine learning program could be.

Siya: I wanted to convey my condolences. And let you know that your fight is not with Null Cyphers.

Gamini: Seriously?

Siya: All that happened to your family was the doing of Arun Kamat.

Siya: Find below a peace offering. Hope this gives you the closure you are looking for.

Gamini received a set of pictures, videos, audio files and documents from Siya's chat box. Her eyes widened with each new revelation, her fingers trembling slightly as she scrolled through the damning evidence.

Since her brother's death, Gamini had often rued the faulty legal system which could not protect Gandhi Kumar. The only punishment Kamat got for falsely implicating her brother, for leaking his private affairs to the media and for leading to the death of her brother and sister-in-law, was a transfer to another zone. But the evidence she now saw finally gave her some cathartic release.

The meticulous exposé laid bare Kamat's undeclared properties, offshore accounts and sleazy affairs, dismantling the facade of righteousness he so proudly wore. This was enough to put him behind bars for years.

About the Author

Smarak Swain chases tax cheats by day and literary villains by night.

A real-life financial crime investigator, he has spent over a decade decoding money laundering rings, hunting black money and figuring out how dodgy crypto swindlers sleep at night. When not drafting anti-fraud policies or whispering sweet nothings to spreadsheets, he writes thrillers inspired by the absurdities he has seen up close.

An IIT Kharagpur graduate with degrees from NALSAR University and the Lee Kuan Yew School, he is currently the director of Financial Action Task Force, Department of Revenue, Government of India. He is the author of several books, including *The Hawala Agent* and *The Great Indian Fraud*, which made even chartered accountants sweat. His most recent book, *Digital Fortunes*, won the Best Business Book (English) award at the Kalinga Literature Festival 2025.

The Scammer's Trail is his latest attempt to entertain readers with fiction that's only slightly stranger than truth.